PARTNERS

PARTNERS

DAVID CRAY

An Otto Penzler Book

CARROLL & GRAF PUBLISHERS
NEW YORK

PARTNERS

An Otto Penzler Book
Carroll & Graf Publishers
An Imprint of Avalon Publishing Group Inc.
245 West 17th Street
New York, NY 10011

First Carroll & Graf edition 2004

Library of Congress Cataloging-in-Publication Data is available.

ISBN: 0-7867-1292-9

Printed in the United States of America
Interior design by Paul Paddock
Distributed by Publishers Group West

PARTNERS

ONE

WHEN A LOADED EIGHTEEN-WHEELER BACKFIRES on the street outside Finito's window he comes instantly awake. His fingers curl into a fist and he jerks into a sitting position, mouth open, breathing hard. His eyes search the room, jumping from point to point, the cobwebs in the corners, the broken plaster on the ceiling, the peeling paint on the walls, the dirty mattress. Only when he is certain the shadows conceal no enemies does he falls back and close his eyes.

Finito is one day removed from the Otus Bantam Correctional Center on Rikers Island where he served ninety days for breaking into a car. Just a few years earlier, this misdemeanor, criminal mischief in the fourth degree, would have resulted in a sentence of probation, or even conditional release. But now, at age twenty-seven, Finito's yellow sheet runs to four pages. Now he can no longer be sentenced to drug treatment centers, or returned to school, or made to perform community service. He is an opportunistic thief; he will take whatever he can, whenever he can. The cops, the prosecutors, and the judges all know it. Even his Legal Aid lawyers know it. Even Jorge "Finito" Rakowski knows it.

• • •

Finito would like nothing more than a few additional hours of sleep. But after ninety days of rising at five-thirty to the sound of a buzzer loud enough to vibrate the cot he slept on, sleep is out of the question. He rubs his eyes, then lets his arms fall to his sides.

"Shit," he tells the world. "Shit, shit, shit."

Even now—his face unshaven, his body unshowered, his hair not only disheveled but the victim of a Rikers Island haircut—Finito is a strikingly handsome man. Rugged about the jaw and brow with a sharply triangular nose, his sensual mouth invites intimacy. His hair is sandy brown and wavy, a bequest from the Polish father he never knew, as are his penetrating green eyes.

Finito's full lips and square chin, on the other hand, might have been lifted from a photo of his mother, if any such existed. Finito has never seen a picture of his mother and would have no interest in receiving one. In fact, on those rare occasions when he thinks of her at all, he invariably follows her appearance in his consciousness with the word *puta*.

Admit it or not, Finito owes a debt to Iris Alvedo, the woman who bore him. It was at her knee, and the knee of her mother, and the knees of their many paying guests that he learned the Spanish of the New York City streets. This skill has served him well over the years. It has allowed him to move through New York's many Latino neighborhoods without being challenged by turf-conscious adolescents, and to find allies within the Latino population while incarcerated, allies who became co-conspirators on the street.

On the other side, his father's entirely physical legacy also figures in Finito's survival strategy. With his light hair and green eyes, if properly dressed, he attracts little attention in Manhattan below Ninety-sixth Street, the land of the rich white people. The land of opportunity.

July sunlight pours through a white sheet covering the room's only window to fall directly across Finito's body. Already sweating, he is now fully awake, his eyes wide open. Still, he doesn't move, not right away. Instead, he watches a small cockroach trace a zigzag course toward a much larger cockroach on the ceiling. The larger cockroach is stationary, even its antennae unmoving, and it appears to be asleep or dead.

The small cockroach comes to within inches of the larger, then stops, its own antennae moving with the speed and precision of an African drummer. After several seconds, it turns abruptly and speeds away.

Most people, in Finito's place, would pass some fleeting judgment, maybe on the struggle for survival or the good sense of the little cockroach. But not Finito Rakowski, a man without a past to which he returns or a future he is willing to contemplate. The show is over. The little cockroach has survived.

Finito rises to his feet and stalks into the bathroom, stepping across the bodies of two junkies sprawled on narrow mattresses in the hallway. He is in a shooting gallery, an apartment where, for the contents of a single bag of dope, one can inject oneself with heroin and nod off in relative safety. The apartment belongs to the building's super, Batuka Morales, and his junkie girlfriend, Lisa.

Finito hasn't traveled from Queens Plaza, where a Department of Corrections bus disgorged him at five o'clock on the prior morning, all the way to the Bronx neighborhood of Hunts Point just to use heroin. If that was all he'd wanted, there was a shooting gallery in the Queensbridge Houses a mere three blocks from the Plaza. No, Finito has voyaged to heavily industrialized Hunts Point because (according to a fellow crimey at Rikers) Batuka Morales specialized in warehouse burglaries and might be looking for a helper.

Unfortunately, when Finito sounded him out, Batuka had shaken his head decisively. Things were too good at the moment, he'd explained. He had his free apartment and his salary and enough customers to keep him high on most nights. Warehouse jobs took a long time to plan and sometimes fell apart at the last minute, so it just wasn't worth the trouble. Now, if the right job somehow fell into his lap, he wouldn't hesitate. He hadn't lost his nerve. He was as macho as ever. But nothing like that was going on now. Sorry.

That leaves Jorge Rakowski, as he stares into the mirror over the sink, with seven dollars in one-dollar bills and thirty-seven cents in coins. It leaves him with no place to lay his head until his cousin, Rosaria Montes, comes back from Puerto Rico. Rosaria is the only member of the family who will put up with him. Most likely that's because she's a degenerate junkie and when he comes to see her, he usually comes with a gift.

The facts on the table are simple enough, even to Finito, who has spent most of his life avoiding painful truths. He must get to work, pronto. If he doesn't, or if his work is unproductive, he will sleep on the streets.

Of course, Finito has slept on the streets many times in the past, beginning when he was still a child. But he senses, very dimly, that he is fast approaching a crossroads. If he doesn't climb out of this hole, the streets will claim him. He will find himself drinking cheap wine in vacant lots, shaking a cup downtown, becoming dirtier and more alien by the day.

Angry now, Finito dresses, then walks into Batuka's room without knocking. Batuka's junkie girlfriend lies naked on the sheet, but Finito doesn't give her a second glance.

"Batuka, *mira*. I got to go, man. Gimme the keys."

"*Ay, mamao*, you know what time it is?"

Finito extends his hand. "It ain't my fault you put up locks that gotta be opened from the inside with a key."

Unwilling to surrender the keys to his apartment, Batuka rises to his feet. He glances down at Lisa who snores softly, then prods her with the big toe of his right foot. "Hey, *chingada,* cover yourself." When she responds by rolling onto her back without opening her eyes, he shrugs and walks away.

Less than two miles across and barely a mile long, Hunts Point is a heavily industrialized peninsula jutting out into the East River. Isolated from neighboring Bronx communities by the Bruckner Expressway, the Oak Point Freight Yard and the Bronx River, there was always the likelihood that its small residential neighborhood would be neglected by the politicians who control city services. That likelihood was made nearly inevitable by the community's economic anchor, the Hunts Point Terminal Market.

Most of New York's produce—more than eighty percent—and nearly half of New York's meat, pass through Hunts Point. Overwhelmingly, the carrots and pork chops arrive in refrigerated semi-trailers driven by men who haven't seen their wives in weeks. Lonely men. Men far from home with nobody looking over their shoulders.

What could be more natural than a supply reaching out to a captive market, a market amounting to a million truck drivers each year? What could be more inevitable?

Hunts Point has been a major stroll for as long as anyone can remember. Generations of pimps and prostitutes have responded to its opportunities, bringing with them drugs and drug dealers.

"You want a date, sugar?"

The Point is up and running when Finito steps out onto Seneca Avenue at seven-thirty in the morning. A steady breeze rolls in from the East River, and the early-morning air is cool and wet. Above, the sky is flat, a sheet of tin nailed to the rooftops, while Seneca Avenue lies in shadow, the sun that awakened Finito having yet to clear the tenements to the east.

The breeze is redolent of the Point's unique blend of fragrances.

Gasoline and diesel exhaust permeate an atmosphere already burdened with high levels of summer ozone. Fainter, the stench of rotting garbage issues from a half-dozen massive transfer stations where city trash is prepared for transport to states far and wide. Fainter still, the odor of human feces drifts from the Hunts Point Sewage Treatment Plant fronting the East River.

Finito breathes these odors, takes them through his nostrils deep into his lungs. His eyes swivel back and forth, noting a stream of pedestrians on both sidewalks. They are walking to work, one of the benefits of living in the Point, with its twenty thousand jobs. Finito descends to the sidewalk and instantly becomes one of their number.

As he walks, Finito is supremely aware of his environment. He looks into every car window, into doorways, at the handbags of women, the wallets of men. He doesn't see possibility here, given the number of pedestrians, and his glances are mere reflex, but he glances nonetheless. If opportunity should knock, he will be ready. At all times he knows who is in front of him and who behind.

Ideally, Finito would like to work the Hunts Point Market, which commands the majority of the point's industrial acres. But the market is heavily defended by fences, videocameras, and a small army of rent-a-cops. Penetrating these defenses is simply beyond him, and he is forced to settle for a less attractive option, the smaller businesses located outside the market. There are dozens of warehouses in the Point, including meat and vegetable wholesalers unable to find space inside. Each of these is a potential target.

Finito turns onto Bryant Avenue, directly into a sun bloated by haze and smog. On his left, a tall corrugated fence surrounds a lot. The fence is covered with graffiti, mostly gang tags, and the posts that support its panels are joined by razor wire.

Two blocks farther east, he comes upon C&R Auto Parts. C&R

is housed in a windowless brick building, a perfect cube, its smooth sides broken only by narrow doorways and a small truck bay. Finito approaches to within six feet of a man standing on the truck bay's platform. The man wears a brown workman's uniform with the name José stitched above the pocket of his shirt.

"*Busco trabajo.*" Finito tells the man that he is looking for work.

"*Ves a Gus, en la oficina.*"

"*¿Pero,*" Finito persists, "*algún trabajo?*"

A sigh. "*Ves a Gus, en la oficina.*"

"*Gracias.*"

By the time Finito turns away in search of Gus, he has identified a stack of antilock brake computers on a skid. The skid is close enough to the edge of the loading dock for him to lift a few computers without climbing up onto the platform. These computers, he knows, are worth several hundred dollars each and can be quickly unloaded at retail parts stores on the other side of Bruckner Boulevard. He cannot get at the computers now, not with José watching, but unless his fortunes radically improve, he'll make another pass when he finishes with Gus.

Finito circles the block until he finds a narrow door on the northern side of the building. To the right of the doorknob, a small sign declares: OFFICE/Ring Bell. Finito gives the button above the sign a quick push, then is surprised when he is immediately buzzed inside.

TWO

CLOSING THE DOOR behind him, Finito looks around as if trying to get his bearings. He is in a small room with a row of windows cut into the wall to his left, and a door with a tiny window directly ahead. The windows look out on row after row of steel shelving piled with auto parts. Although it's just after eight o'clock, there are men at work, pushing supermarket carts, climbing ladders, filling orders. A forklift carries a skid loaded with boxes toward the shadows at the far end of the building where a block of fluorescent lights has gone out.

To Finito's right, four battered desks and a dozen file cabinets crowd the room. Three of the desks are unoccupied. At the fourth, a woman sits before a computer, her shoulder bag hanging from the back of her chair. The bag is open, a gray leather wallet exposed.

"Can I help ya?"

Finito does not immediately reply, nor does he look into the woman's eyes. Instead, he stares down at the surface of her desk while observing her in his peripheral vision. He notes her brassy red hair, two near-perfect circles of eyeliner, crimson lipstick extending an inch beyond her lips in a vain attempt to make them appear more full. She is white, perhaps forty years old, and wears no wedding ring.

When he finally raises his head, Finito puts into play a

second-language skill acquired in childhood. Finito passed his fifth, sixth and most of his seventh year as the foster child of Judy and Mark Tannenbaum, both of whom taught English in the public schools. Finito's mastery of the spoken language had been a stated goal from the beginning.

It was a goal the Tannenbaums came very close to achieving, though they were less successful in their efforts to restrain Finito when he was out of their sight. In his first year at P.S. 132, Georgie (as they insisted on calling him) was suspended six times for fighting, stealing, or both.

"My name is Filipo Velez," Finito announces without a trace of a Spanish accent, "and I'm looking for work. José told me to ask for Gus."

He notes a flicker of interest in the woman's dark brown eyes, a certain gleam which he welcomes. When those same eyes survey his body, he tightens a set of pecs sculpted by many hours in a Rikers Island weight room.

"What could ya do, Mr. Velez?"

"I can drive a forklift." Finito cocks his head to one side and smiles. "Somebody told me I should see Gus."

Finito is hoping the woman will go in search of Gus, whereupon he will seize her wallet and be gone. Instead, the warehouse door opens to admit a large, middle-aged man. A cigar hangs from the corner of his mouth, and he rolls it over his fleshy lips when he speaks. "Yeah? Whadda ya want?"

"I'm looking for Gus."

"So, I'm Gus. Whadda ya want?"

"Work. I thought maybe you could use someone?"

Gus looks Finito up and down, pausing to note the T-shirt and wrinkled jeans, the battered Nikes, the day-old beard, the lopsided haircut. When he speaks, his tone is dismissive. "We're doin' fine the way we are. See ya later." Then without looking at her, he addresses the woman still seated at her desk.

"Hey, Gladys, I thought I told you not to let anybody in here ya didn't know."

Gladys replies without missing a beat, "If you weren't so cheap, you'd fix the goddamned intercom and I wouldn't have to go to the door. I got a herniated disc, if ya remember. I oughta be on workmen's compensation."

Finito gives it up two hours later, at ten-thirty. The temperature is now ninety-one degrees and the sun is high enough to roast the streets and sidewalks. Finito is soaked with sweat, his T-shirt and jeans glued to his body. Sweat drips from his hair onto his shoulders and back.

He walks along Edgewater Road, toward the subway station at Southern Boulevard and East 167th Street. His immediate priority is relief from the heat, and the only relief he can afford is an air-conditioned subway car.

A block ahead, near Garrison Avenue, he spies a black prostitute wearing a chartreuse miniskirt and a blue halter. The prostitute walks back and forth, calling out to the passing cars and trucks. Her halter is soaked with sweat and her small unfettered breasts are virtually exposed. When she notices Finito, she turns to face him, placing her hand on her hips.

Finito drops to one knee and fiddles with his shoelaces. Directly ahead of him, Edgewater Road leads up to Bruckner Boulevard. To his right, a narrow lot fronts the Bronx River. The lot's northern boundary is marked by a grassy hill broken by a narrow tunnel just wide enough to shelter a single railroad track. Perhaps fifty feet long, the tunnel's interior is deeply shadowed.

There are residential buildings seventy-five yards away, on the far side of Edgewater, many with open windows. He observes silhouettes in several of these windows, but they are too distant to trouble him. Nor is he worried about the sparse traffic headed north toward Bruckner Boulevard. Finito is looking for other prostitutes or for a pimp. When he discovers neither, he rises and continues his walk, careful to keep his gait casual, his expression neutral. Finito has been without a woman for ninety-one days.

"Yo," the prostitute calls when Finito is within fifty feet, "come over here, man."

"Tengo prisa."

"Damn, man, speak English."

"I said, I'm in a hurry. I got no time for *chingadas* today."

"Don't be that way. Everybody got time for a little lovin'. My name's Darlene, sugar. What's yours?"

"Alberto."

Up close, Darlene is gaunt, her collarbones nearly as prominent as her breasts, and the pupils of her black eyes are shrunken to pinheads. Above plucked brows, an irregular reddish bruise dominates the tan skin of her forehead.

Finito absorbs these facts and draws certain conclusions. It's almost eleven o'clock in the morning and the truckers have done their duty, coming and going. For the next four hours, the Point will be quiet. That's why there are no other whores on the street. They're all at home, feeding the various monkeys that cling to their backs. Darlene is out here because she's being punished. Maybe she didn't earn last night. Maybe she snorted her earnings instead of passing them on to her pimp. Maybe she just shot her mouth off once too often. The why of it doesn't really matter. What matters is that she's standing right in front of him. All alone.

"You look like you need yourself a woman." Darlene's smile reveals a gold upper canine on the left side of her mouth.

"Yeah, but I'm late for somethin'."

"I can make it fast, baby." She delivers her pitch with practiced ease. "And I can make it sooooooo good. Fact of the matter, when I get finished, y'all are just gonna have to go kill yourself, 'cause there ain't gonna be nothin' left to look forward to."

The beads of sweat in her corn-rowed hair look, to Finito, like maggots. He starts to turn away. "I don't got no car. Where we gonna go?"

"In the tunnel. Nobody gonna bother us in there."

"There's like a train goes through tha' shit." Finito shakes his head. "I don't want to get caught with my pants down."

"Where you been, man? Ain't no train come through that tunnel in twenty years."

Though his expression remains dubious, Finito asks, "How much?"

"That depends on—"

"I want you to suck my *bicho*."

"Thirty dollars, baby, and cheap at the price."

"Twenty."

Finito, of course, has just seven dollars and thirty-seven cents to his name. But he has never let that stop him before. Finito will take sex from this woman the way he takes anything else, the sole constraint being lack of opportunity. Like his barrio accent, the bargaining is meant only to reassure.

"Honey, I'm too good. I just don't cut no special deals."

"Twenty-five." Finito spreads his palms. "*Mira*, it's all I got."

"Okay, but you gotta use a rubber."

Finito trails behind Darlene on the way into the tunnel. Just as well because already his face is changing, his face and his attitude. If she were to note his expression now, she would more than likely hightail it back to whatever rat hole she calls home.

"You can pay me, honey."

"I don't got twenty-five dollars," Finito replies, shaking his head. "I don't even got ten dollars."

When Darlene's right hand drops to the waistband of her

miniskirt, Finito punches her in the side of the face. He puts his full weight into the blow and she flies over backward, a long switchblade knife dropping from her hand to clatter on the steel track.

Finito kicks the knife away, then unzips his fly. He does not expect further resistance. Darlene is a woman of the streets and will bow to the underlying principle upon which street life is based: Might makes right. Thus he is initially astounded, then enraged when Darlene struggles to a sitting position and tosses a handful of gravel in his face. That rage is multiplied many times over when she begins to scream. Almost of their own volition, Finito's hands reach out to encircle her throat.

The first thing he needs to do is shut Darlene up. He must quiet her in order to ensure his personal safety. Still, despite the fact that Darlene is instantly silenced, he continues to press his thumbs into the hollow of her throat. He does not stop when she is loses consciousness. He does not stop when she begins to convulse. He does not stop until she is dead.

Finito puts off all consideration of his actions until he thoroughly searches Darlene, eventually discovering a ten-dollar bill in the toe of her shoe. He slides the bill into his pocket before rising to his feet. Everything, he thinks, has changed.

Instinctively, Finito attempts to repress a swelling uneasiness. The bitch deserved what she got, he tells himself. The bitch asked for it. The bitch is better off dead. If I had it to do over, I'd do it again and again and again and again.

But reality continues to intrude. Everything has changed. There's no getting away from it. And not just the murder, not just that he is a now a murderer. The change he senses is much more fundamental. More fundamental and intimately tied to the erection contained by his ratty jeans.

Finito looks down at his victim and discovers that her eyes are wide open and she is looking directly at him. He knows, of course, that it's time to put some distance between his sorry ass and Darlene's corpse. But he does not move, not right away. Instead, he continues to stare at Darlene for a moment, then takes three steps, to where some considerate citizen has left a bag filled with household garbage. Finito hefts the bag, carries it back to his victim, finally drops it onto her face.

Three months later, in mid-October, Finito kills for the second time. There are a number of similarities between this and his first kill. Both murders are of street prostitutes, both occur during an off-hour on a well-established stroll, both are unplanned. In addition, both stem from a sudden onset of rage, and both, in Finito's judgment, are entirely justified. Darlene should not have fought back. Maria Estevez should not have called him a *maricón* bastard.

But there are differences as well. This time Finito has more than one hundred dollars in his pocket and can pay for his sex, as he has many times in the past. This time he follows Maria Estevez into the back of a rubble-strewn lot near the border of Brooklyn and Queens, then strikes her before requesting her services pro bono. This time, his victim does not resist. Instead, she falls to her knees and half-whispers, "Don't hurt me," whereupon he becomes instantly erect.

It is only after the sexual act is completed that he finds an excuse to kill. He is turning to leave when Maria, perhaps thinking her ordeal is over, hurls the epithet that triggers his attack. Fifteen seconds later she is unconscious. A minute later she is dead.

As before, Finito stares down at his victim. As before, he thinks, everything has changed. As before, he delays his escape long enough to conceal his victim's face.

Nine hours later, Finito is again lying on a mattress in a small bedroom, only now he has a companion, a woman named Janice Hunt. Both Finito and Janice are naked, and both drift in a gentle, heroin-induced nod. To their right, a scattering of syringes and cotton balls surround a candle on a small table.

The apartment belongs to Janice. Finito is her guest, a relationship that will last as long as he continues to supplement her moderately severe addiction. This arrangement seems to him perfectly natural. If the first law of the street is might makes right, the second is nothing for nothing. Unless presented with physical force, no player gives it away.

As Finito drifts, his thoughts turn to the day just past, and to the future. Not in any systematic way, of course. He is far too stoned for that. But the fact that he considers past and future at all is significant. It means he has turned a corner. He no longer wonders if he will kill again, or asks how it could have happened in the first place. The point, now, is not to get caught. Though Finito is unaware of the exact penalty for serial homicide, he is certain that should he be arrested, he will spend the rest of his life in the sort of hellhole he has thus far successfully avoided. And that's only if the state doesn't kill him.

A cluster of thoughts rise to command his stoned consciousness. I've made a lot of mistakes, he tells himself. I fucked up royally. I've been a chump.

Pulling women off the streets in broad daylight? Killing women in semipublic places? Leaving DNA evidence? Leaving shoeprints and fingerprints? How stupid could you be?

Finito knows that most of the crimes he commits are unplanned, that they are crimes of opportunity. True, he brings a number of skills to the table, but he's been busted enough times to accept the limitations of those skills. And to understand that if he wants to get away with the crime of murder, as opposed to criminal mischief in the fourth degree, he has to plan ahead. He has to be slicker, smarter, more premeditated, more disciplined. He has to evolve.

Satisfied for the moment, Finito places his hand on Janice's thigh. "Hey," he says, "you wanna fuck?"

THREE

Tuesday, December 25, 3:45 P.M. Christmas Day.

"DAMN," DETECTIVE BELINDA MOORE announced to her partner, Frederick "Pudge" Pedersson, "I broke a nail. Pull over, lemme fix it before it tears off."

Belinda fumbled through her purse, removing tiny bottles of nail polish remover and clear nail polish. Her partner, meanwhile, did not so much as glance in her direction. He didn't slow down, either.

"C'mon, Pudge, I paid forty-five bucks for this manicure and it's only two days old. I gotta fix it."

As this was not the first time Belinda had used this particular appeal, she was unsurprised when it fell on deaf ears. "Bad enough," she muttered, "I gotta wear my nails short. I don't have to wear 'em raggedy. Last time I looked, raggedy didn't appear in the dress code."

They were driving north on Broadway, approaching Eighty-sixth Street on Manhattan's Upper West Side. Though the Caprice's interior was toasty, it was bone-numbing cold out on the street. The temperature had dropped nearly twelve degrees since they'd begun their shift and was now approaching single digits.

"Pudge, you listenin' to me?"

Pedersson finally broke his silence, though he didn't slow down. "We been through this before," he said. "I'm not gonna repeat myself like an idiot."

For Pedersson, the issue was simple. If his partner stunk up the car with nail polish remover, he'd be wheezing until the end of their shift. Therefore, his allergy to Belinda's nail polish remover trumped her forty-five-dollar manicure. Case closed.

"You're in a bad mood, right?" Moore asked. "Because you and me, we're the only detectives working on Christmas at the two-five. Just like last year."

When her partner maintained his silence, Belinda took matters into her own hands by unscrewing the top of the nail polish remover. It was a bluff, as the nail would have to be filed before removing the old polish and she couldn't do it while the car was bouncing over New York City's potholes. But she figured Pudge wouldn't know that and she was right. He pulled the Caprice into a convenient bus stop, got out and stalked off in the direction of a McDonald's at midblock without saying a word.

It was Belinda who finally broke the ice. She knew she couldn't outsulk her partner. Pudge Pedersson was the king of the sulkers. Inspired by every indignity suffered in the course of an indignity-saturated life, Pudge could (and did) sulk for days at a time.

"So," Belinda said, "whatta ya hear from the widow?"

Pudge Pedersson flashed a grin expressing equal measures of triumph and glee, then lit a cigarette. In fact, he'd been waiting for his partner to raise the subject ever since they'd come on duty. "You're not gonna believe this," he said as Belinda sniffed once before rolling down her window. "We finally dumped Arthur."

The widow in question was Annie MacDougald. The Arthur in question was her husband, dead and cremated a year before. Pudge had been courting Annie almost from the day her widowhood began. Thus far she'd responded to his attentions by inviting him to the occasional home-cooked dinner, and by allowing him him to sit next to her at the First Calvinist Church of Staten Island. Annie, it seemed, was not only determined to observe a very traditional period of mourning, she'd somehow elevated Arthur to near-sainthood on the day he took his last breath, despite his general neglect and his many infidelities.

Arthur's ashes were a case in point. Though it was Annie's stated intention to scatter them to the elements, they'd been sitting dead-center on her mantel for the past year. Worse yet, Annie had placed a photo of her dearly departed in front of the urn so that Arthur stared down accusingly whenever Pudge had a sudden impulse to place his arm around his love's shoulders.

Nevertheless, as patience was his singular virtue (and obstinance his conspicuous flaw), Pudge was undaunted. Annie MacDougald was the woman he'd been searching for since his own wife deserted him a decade earlier. Eventually she would succumb to his many kindnesses.

"It came outta the blue," Pudge explained. "Like, one day the ashes connected Annie to his life force and the next she needed to reestablish her own karma by dumping them in the ocean."

Belinda shook her head in wonder. Pudge Pedersson, the Calvinist cop. Annie MacDougald, the New Age Calvinist. It never ceased to amaze her.

"Naturally," Pudge continued, "I offered to assist her in any way possible. I said—"

A city bus pulled alongside the Caprice and Belinda quickly raised the window. Her partner's cigarette fumes were infinitely preferable to the truly foul stench of a bus's exhaust.

The front door of the bus flew open with a hiss and an elderly woman emerged to stand abreast of the Caprice. As the car had prevented the bus from reaching the curb and she walked with the aid of a cane, the woman was understandably annoyed. She stared at Pudge through the window until he finally acknowledged her presence, then blasted him with the worst reproof in her arsenal.

"Jesus was born today, ya know."

But the woman's timing was off and the roar of the departing bus drowned out her words. Pudge could do no more than shrug, a gesture that served to further infuriate her. With considerable effort, she raised her cane above her head, then banged it once on the car's roof before hobbling away.

"So," Belinda said, ignoring the assault, "when did Annie make the big decision?"

"Yesterday, Christmas Eve. See, it was all very symbolic. According to Annie's horoscope, the cosmos was in the right place for a big change and she had to stage her rebirth then and there. The moment was fated, she told me, and why couldn't I see that?"

"But you did see it, right?"

"I was ready to pour the ashes down the nearest storm drain."

"Now, why do I think Arthur's departure required a bit more ceremony?"

"Because you know Annie. First thing, she says we gotta drive out to Coney Island because that's the place Arthur loved best." Pudge drew a cross over his heart. "Swear to God, Belinda, I wanted to tell her that Arthur loved Coney Island because that's where Karen Cereno lived. But . . ."

Belinda watched her partner intently. Pudge Pedersson's nickname derived, not from the extra twenty pounds loosely attached to his gut, but to his chubby cheeks. Baby-faced to a fault, his eyes were small, his nose short and broad, his mouth little more than an irregular pink line midway between his nostrils and his cleft chin. Mostly, he looked harmless, and sometimes hurt, but those looks were deceiving. Pudge Pedersson was a gigantic man. Standing 6-4 and weighing upward of 250 pounds, he was the strongest cop in the two-five and the most formidable when provoked by disrespectful miscreants.

"Of course," Belinda prompted, "you accepted your marching orders as written."

Though Pudge blushed, he acknowledged his perpetual subservience with a sharp nod. "The deal was that we drive to Coney Island, walk out on a jetty, cast the ashes into the sea. Tell me, Belinda, what do you remember about yesterday?"

"Christmas Eve? Putting up the tree, opening the presents at midnight—"

"I mean the weather."

Belinda thought it over for a moment. "I don't remember anything special about the weather."

"You remember the wind?"

"Ah, I see where this is going."

"It was nearly as windy yesterday as it is today. Only yesterday the wind was blowing out of the northeast."

"And that's no good for scattering ashes in Coney Island?"

"Partner, the minute I step onto the beach, I know that bad things are gonna happen. First, the wind's blowing right in my face and it's blowin' hard. Second, the tide's up and the waves are spraying over the top of the jetty. Those jetties, they're just piled rocks. Maybe the rocks are laid so the surface is kind of flat, but trust me, it's not like walkin' down the street. Now Annie, she doesn't seem to notice. She stops me on the beach and tells me how lucky she's been to have me for a friend, how much I've meant to her. She says that without me, she might not have made it through the year. Meanwhile, she's gotta shout over the wind to be heard."

Pudge took a last pull on his cigarette, then rolled down the window and tossed the butt out onto Broadway. "What am I gonna do?" he asked. "Am I gonna tell her, let's wait for a better day? Let's wait till the tide turns? She's already taken the cover off the urn, and she's pulling out the plastic bag inside. If I don't go with her, she's goin' alone."

"And you couldn't let that happen."

"Could you?" Pudge continued on before his partner could express her indifference to Annie MacDougald's karmic follies.

"Anyway, off we go, Annie in the lead. I'm behind her, tryin' to steady her while tryin' to keep my own balance. Before we get ten feet out, my pants are soaked from the spray. It's worse for Annie because she's wearing this dress Arthur always loved, which barely comes to her knees and which the wind is blowin' up around her hips. She holds on for maybe another ten feet, then she turns and hands me the bag. 'Would you do this for me?' she says."

Pudge turned to look down at his partner. "So, I take the bag, naturally, and I squat down at the edge of the jetty and dump a little bit of Arthur into the ocean. Just to see what happens."

"Which was?"

"Which was this gray ash blew straight back onto my legs and stuck there. Which was also what happened when I duck-walked to the other side of the jetty. In fact, no matter where I poured Arthur, he blew back onto my pants and my shoes. When I finally stood up, it was like my legs were coated with concrete. *Frozen* concrete. I could barely bend my knees. As for Annie, I think she musta had salt water in her eyes, because she gave me this big hug and said, 'He's gone now. He's gone for good.' "

"And what did you say?"

"I said, 'I don't know, Annie. I kinda think Arthur's gonna be stickin' around for a while.' "

The radio suspended beneath the dashboard crackled into life before their laughter died away.

Pedersson? Moore? Where are you?

Belinda picked up the mike. This was not gonna be good. The voice belonged to Sergeant Mike Levine who was supervising the only detectives working on Christmas Day. As Levine was an observant Jew, he was more than happy to trade Christmas and Easter for Rosh Hashanah and Passover.

"Moore," she said.

Moore, you're supposed to be on channel five. I've been tryin' to get you for twenty minutes.

Now what? Explain that channel six had been reserved to the precinct's detectives for the past two years, that channel five was choked with the cross-chatter of the sector cars? Or that Levine might have called on Belinda's cell phone? One thing certain, if she annoyed Sergeant Levine, he would complain to her supervisor, Lieutenant Malden, who already hated her.

Fortunately, Levine interpreted her silence as evidence of contrition and got down to business.

We got a DOA at 637 West 112th Street, apartment 3E, which appears to be a homicide. Sergeant Cho is on scene. Stay in touch. 10-4.

Pudge glanced at his partner as he shifted the Caprice into gear. Belinda Moore liked to describe herself as a strong black woman, and for the most part she lived up to her advertising. Case in point: for the last two years she and her partner had been taking abuse from their immediate superior, and Belinda hadn't folded yet. If she felt sorry for herself, she never showed it. Her gaze was frank and unafraid, the set of her full mouth firm and determined. She lived, she'd declared often enough, not for the job, but for her family. Between herself and her husband, Ralph, their yearly income exceeded six figures. They vacationed in Bermuda and lived in a four-bedroom house. Their children went to parochial school and would go on to college, not on the government's Pell grant, but on the Moore family's own dime. For a woman who'd grown up in a family that lived from paycheck to paycheck, this was no small accomplishment.

That didn't mean, as she was quick to explain, that she didn't take pride in her work. Belinda was a good cop who'd proven herself, at least in Pudge Pedersson's eyes, again and again. Hence she had no apologies to make to anybody. And as for Lieutenant Jerry Malden . . . well, black people had been putting up with white people's bullshit for a long time. From what she could see, they'd be putting up with it for a long time to come.

It was a good argument, describing, as it did, a stance Pudge Pedersson could only wish to emulate. And Pudge would have been the first to acknowledge his admiration and his envy. Nevertheless, Belinda did have one little vulnerability, one tiny crack in that polished armor.

Though she'd never spoken the words aloud, over the two years they'd been partners, Pudge had come to realize that dead people made Belinda Moore very nervous. She didn't like to look at them, didn't like to be around them. Hence, when they finally got to 637 West 112th Street, Pudge would be left to check out the body while Belinda examined the crime scene, interviewed a relative or neighbor, consulted the first uniforms to arrive.

That was okay with Pudge. Because sooner or later he would discover some item of interest to which his partner's attention just had to be drawn.

Belinda, you better come have a look at this.

"Hey, Belinda," Pudge Pedersson called to his partner, "you better come have a look at this."

Though unsurprised, Belinda frowned. There were times when her partner reverted to the nasty little boy he'd undoubtedly been. The kind of kid—like her brother, Ray—who'd put a handful of earthworms under your pillow, roll on the floor laughing when you found them and screamed. It pissed Belinda off, but there was nothing she could do except gather her resolve before looking directly at the victim she'd barely glanced at upon arriving.

According to the contents of her wallet, now scattered across a thick carpet fronting the couch in the living room, Jennifer Denning was thirty-seven years old and worked in the accounting department at Columbia University. She had four credit cards, belonged to the New York Public Library, held a charter membership at Gold's Gym, was a sustaining donor to the Metropolitan Museum of Art and the Public Broadcasting System. Her dentist was named Lillian Lieberman, her internist Preston McNamee, her gynecologist Kiran Chawla.

Belinda had examined these cards without touching them, crawling from one to another, until her attention finally settled on a blue card spotted with pale red hearts. The card announced Jennifer's willingness to donate her organs should she suddenly expire. That wasn't going to happen, of course. Jennifer's organs had a hot date with an assistant medical examiner who would measure, weigh, and section them. After which they would only be of value to the criminal justice system. Such as it was.

The soles of her shoes extending to within six feet of the front door, Jennifer Denning was lying on her back in a small foyer. Though the buttons of her coat had been torn off and her skirt yanked up, her sweater and bra were still in place. Above a thin gold necklace, four distinct lines of bruising traced the curve of her throat and neck, finally disappearing into her matted blond hair. The lines converged at her throat, where the skin was punctured in two places. The cuts were thick and the surrounding tissue was tucked inside the wound. They'd been made, or so Belinda concluded, by her assailant's thumbs.

Denning's body was in full rigor, arms and legs raised slightly, as if she were still trying to run away, or to fight back. The effect was pure illusion, as the dish towel covering her face made abundantly clear. The yellow towel had been carefully centered, then molded to the victim's features, to her brow, eyes, nose and chin. It could only have been placed after she'd stopped moving.

"What's up?" Belinda asked as she approached the body.

"See that towel? That towel was put there after she was dead. I mean, look at the blood, how it's smeared."

In fact, the back of the victim's skull was lying in a small pool of blood which had been smeared from side to side, probably in the course of a struggle.

"So," Pedersson continued when his partner remained silent, "if the towel was put across the victim's face when she was alive, like a blindfold, it'd be off-center."

"That's it, Sherlock? That's what you called me for?"

Pudge's narrow lips compressed into near-invisibility. "As a matter of fact, it wasn't. Check this out, on her leg."

With no viable option, Belinda tracked an invisible line from her partner's finger to a point on the inside of Jennifer's right thigh, midway between groin and knee. The flesh here was purple on the underside, where her blood had settled, bone-white above. Straddling the divide, a small, colorless stain reflected the overhead light. The stain was dry and slick.

"Semen?"

"Wrong."

Belinda ignored her partner's grin, having thoroughly anticipated its appearance. She knew better than to argue with him on matters of evidence. Pudge took courses at John Jay College of Criminal Justice, courses like Advanced Investigative Techniques, Analytical Toxicology, Interviews and Interrogations. All in the vain hope that his abilities would be finally recognized, that he'd be promoted to detective second grade, win Detective of the Month honors, be transferred to a more prestigious division. Fat chance.

"So, you gonna tell me, Pudge, or do I have to keep guessing?"

"What that stain's gonna turn out to be, when it's examined under laboratory conditions, is lubricant from a condom, maybe mixed with vaginal secretions."

"You sure?"

"Sure enough to risk my next paycheck."

Belinda wasn't tempted to accept the bet. Instead, she took a moment to place the information into context. "There's something I want to show you," she finally said. "Come with me."

Belinda led her partner into the dining area of a large, L-shaped room, to a long sideboard placed against the wall on the far side of the dining room table. Like the table, the sideboard had been polished until it gleamed.

As she approached, Belinda traced a zigzag path around and between a dozen Christmas cards littering the floor. The cards had been swept away by Jennifer's assailant when he'd systematically removed the sideboard's drawers and dumped their contents onto the dining room table. It was also in the course of this search, or so she assumed, that he'd leaned down onto the top of the sideboard, leaving five near-perfect ovals in an otherwise smooth layer of polish.

Belinda pointed to these ovals and asked, "Tell me what you don't see."

Pudge bent close, nodding as he did so. "What I don't see are ridges and whorls. Our boy used gloves."

"That wouldn't mean much, it being winter and all, but if he also brought a condom along . . . guess I'd have to say the man was prepared." Belinda swept her arm in in a broad arc covering the dining and living rooms. Both rooms had been systematically searched. Every drawer had been dumped, every cushion pulled. The books from a gray Formica wall unit lay in a heap against the wall separating the bed and living rooms.

"The bedroom and bathroom," Belinda told her partner, "they're clean as a whistle. Far as I can tell, the perp never went inside either one."

Pedersson jammed his hands into his pockets. He let his eyes sweep back and forth across the crime scene for a moment, until they finally settled on Jennifer Denning. Unlike his partner, Pudge Pedersson yearned for those rare homicide investigations assigned to the team of Pedersson and Moore. It was here that he felt most alive, most at home. It was here that he felt most inspired, a soldier in the army of the Lord facing off against an ancient, implacable enemy.

The only child of a Calvinist minister, Pudge had grown up in a world without a neutral zone. There was good and there was evil. Pick the wrong side and you burned in hell for eternity. This was the message coming from both sides of the family, Pudge's mother being even more committed to the struggle than his father. Pudge's earliest memories were of the prayer meetings and Bible study sessions she held in their Staten Island home.

"He blitzed her," Pudge finally said. "He waited until she unlocked the door, then took her down so fast, she cracked her head on the floor." Pedersson jerked his chin at a set of keys lying a few feet from the body. "She didn't have time to unbutton her coat."

Pudge looked over at his partner, challenging her to challenge his theory. When she didn't, he announced, "I'm gonna take a look around the neighborhood, let the witness sit for a while."

The witness Pedersson referred to was Rosemary Paulino who lived with her husband and two children on the seventh floor. According to Sergeant Leonard Cho, who'd briefly interviewed the woman, Jennifer Denning had been invited to Christmas dinner at the Paulinos. When she didn't show, Rosemary had gone to Jennifer's apartment where she'd first rung the bell, then banged on the door, then taken the next logical step. She'd tried the doorknob, found the door unlocked, finally pushed it open to discover her closest friend lying dead in the foyer.

Rosemary was back upstairs now, recovering from the shock. The way the uniforms told it, they'd found her near the elevators when they rolled up, vomiting into the compactor chute.

FOUR

Sergeant Leonard Cho poked his head into the apartment before the door closed on Pudge Pedersson's back. Cho was tall and very slight, with skin so pale his features might have been carved from alabaster. "The medical examiner's gonna be on scene in twenty minutes," he told Belinda Moore.

"And CSU?"

"The Crime Scene Unit's hung up on a multiple in Queens, a family dispute. They won't be coming by any time soon."

That was fine with Belinda, who intended to personally document the scene before CSU swarmed over it. To that end, she pulled a sketchpad, a pencil, a tape measure and a Polaroid camera from the evidence kit she and Pudge carried with them in a small suitcase.

Belinda did not resent the job at hand, to sketch and photograph the crime scene, though her efforts would be duplicated, in many respects, by CSU. Nor did she resent her partner, who was off somewhere doing his creative thing. She understood that their aims were different and nothing was going to change that. Pudge Pedersson wanted to be a hero. He wanted to be admired, respected, even loved by his peers. Not so Belinda Moore.

Cover your ass. That was the piece of advice given to Belinda on her first day by a ten-year veteran with the improbable name of Betty Crocker. It was advice Belinda Moore took to heart early on. She was, she reasoned, a black woman in a white man's world, a black woman who'd never, not for a single moment, not in her wildest fantasies, hoped to become one of the boys.

Though her partner thought Belinda's mistrust of her peers to be not only self-fulfilling prophecy but a grave impediment to career advancement, Pudge had no quibble with her evaluation of Lieutenant Jerry Malden. When it came to Lieutenant Malden, their immediate supervisor, they were in complete agreement.

There are bad things (as every cop knows) that can happen to you in life. Unavoidable things, afflictions undeserved. Just ask Jennifer Denning. Jerry Malden was one of those bad things. The other detectives on the squad, like most of the white cops Belinda had worked with over the years, were good old boys. To be sure, when they were among themselves, the n-word dropped easily from their lips. But they weren't generally mean-spirited or spiteful. They greeted you when you came through the door and worked with you effectively when your partner was on vacation. Belinda could live with them.

Not so Jerry Malden. Malden had the eyes of an Alabama cracker, blue eyes that ran back to some dead-violent childhood nightmare. On the rare occasions when he deigned to meet Belinda's studiously neutral gaze, those eyes burned with equal measures of hate and contempt.

Pudge had witnessed the exchange so often, he now attempted to shield his partner by drawing Malden's attention to himself. Whereupon Malden's hatred vanished, leaving only his contempt. Malden had once offered to find Pudge Pedersson a new partner, and Pudge had politely blown him off.

Belinda first outlined the dining and living rooms, then positioned Jennifer Denning's body in the sketch, drawing circles to indicate the woman's various injuries and the stain on her thigh. That done, she began to measure the L-shaped room.

The task was purely mechanical and Belinda worked over the facts at hand as she proceeded. First and foremost, there was evidence of haste all around her and she quickly noted three examples. Jennifer Denning had been killed immediately. Her sweater and bra had not been removed, though the assault had been sexually motivated. The search of her apartment appeared to have been hastily conducted and was definitely incomplete.

The point here was not the haste, but the fact that there'd been no real need for haste. Jennifer was in full rigor mortis, right to the tips of her toes, which meant she'd been killed eight to twelve hours earlier. As her dinner appointment with Rosemary Paulino was still many hours away, her killer might have lingered as long as he liked if he'd known her schedule.

Belinda's eye was drawn to the pile of books in the living room. Most of them were lying open and Belinda assumed they'd been shaken out in search of cash before being tossed away. Citizens commonly stashed money in books, and every drugged-out crimey in the city knew it. Even drugged-out crimeys from New Jersey knew it.

Using Jennifer Denning's abdomen as a vanishing point, Belinda measured the distance out to the various piles of evidence, then photographed the crime scene before turning to the minutiae. She knew she had to be careful here. As she could not catalog every item in these piles, she was subject to being second-guessed if she omitted anything of importance. Practically speaking, that meant every item had to be examined in the hope it would lead back to Jennifer's killer. In the hope he'd left some piece of himself behind.

She began at the end of the living room farthest from the body and slowly worked her way to the dining room table, discovering only the bits and pieces of Jennifer Denning's life along the way. This was a trail Belinda followed reluctantly.

Pudge Pedersson's belief that his partner avoided dead bodies was true. It just didn't go far enough. Victims, for Belinda, began as strangers, as pure objects. Putting flesh on their bones (just as mother nature was stripping it off) was part of her job. If she was diligent, these objects would eventually become fully human, in many ways as intimate as her closest friends, who all just happened to be (except for Pudge, of course) members of her family.

Belinda Moore didn't care for this aspect of the dead body business either.

By the time he let himself into the stairwell outside Jennifer Denning's apartment, Pudge Pedersson had drawn a single, tentative conclusion. Noting the evidence of haste, he, like his partner, had pronounced the search of Denning's apartment the work of a man operating well outside his comfort zone. A man who feared being caught in the act when he had, if not all the time in the world, at least the next six to eight hours. A stranger.

Nevertheless, Pedersson was taking this stroll in a effort to reduce the likelihood that Jennifer Denning was killed by a stranger. He didn't fear the challenge presented by stranger homicides, always the most difficult to clear. It was just that he knew he had forty-eight hours (at most) to make an arrest before the case was shipped off to Manhattan North Homicide. That wouldn't be possible if Jennifer Denning was murdered by someone unknown to her.

As he descended the stairs, Pedersson reminded himself that not everybody who knew Jennifer Denning also knew her schedule for Christmas Day. She might have been killed by a neighbor, an ex-husband, even a spurned suitor. Until you started digging into a victim's life, it was better not to draw conclusions.

Pedersson held on to this thought until he reached the basement and discovered, a few feet from the door leading outside, an irregular sooty patch on the floor. There were a number of shoe impressions, both within the patch and leading away from it. They would have to be photographed and Pedersson hesitated long enough to jot down a note reminding himself to alert his partner when he next saw her. Then he stepped through the doorway into the open space behind the building.

Roughly thirty feet deep and running the width of the building, the space was lit by a pair of floodlights mounted on a chain-link fence separating the lot where Pudge stood from the lot to the north. The fence was at least ten feet high and topped with coils of razor wire. To Pedersson's left, another wire-topped fence, mounted above a stone retaining wall, separated Jennifer Denning's building from the building to the west, an eight-story apartment house. Between Broadway and Riverside Drive, 112th Street slopes down toward Riverside, and the individual lots are terraced in back. These terraces, from where Pudge stood, appeared to be a series of steps cut into the hillside.

The fences, the razor wire, the floodlights—they were all necessary precautions in an upper-middle-class neighborhood bordered on three sides by poverty. Pedersson knew this. But he also knew that the landlord might have taken his precautions a bit further (and made Pedersson's life a bit easier) by covering the back door with a videocamera. He hadn't, though Pudge had noted a videocamera above the main entrance fronting 112th Street when he first arrived.

Beginning from the southern end of the building, Pedersson traced the course of the razor wire to the northern end. He took his time about it, until he was certain the coils had neither been spread nor flattened. That left him with a narrow alley separating Denning's building from the building to the east. He walked over to this alley and stared at the far end, where six concrete steps led to the sidewalk. At the head of the steps, a wrought iron gate barred the way. The gate was set into a frame, also of wrought iron, that rose to a height of ten feet. Like the fences in the back, the frame was topped with undisturbed razor wire.

About to turn away, Pudge's eye was drawn to the far edge of sidewalk, next to the curb, where the building's trash had been piled. The bags of garbage were not the sort used routinely by homeowners. In buildings as large as Jennifer Denning's, trash is tossed into chutes located on every floor. The chutes feed down into the basement where the trash is compacted, then wrapped in heavy plastic before porters ferry it to the street, usually the day before pickup.

"Help you with something?"

Startled, Pedersson turned to find a man standing in the doorway. The man was tall and well built, maybe thirty years old. He held a short-handled shovel in his right hand.

"Police," Pedersson said, flashing his shield and ID. "Detective Pedersson. And you're . . ."

"Frank Mariello. I'm the super."

"Ah, the super. Well, I need to speak to you, Frank. Let's go inside."

Pudge walked an unprotesting Frank Mariello across the basement to the stairwell, his sole intention to establish control of the interview. He would lead. Frank would follow. Besides, it was a lot warmer inside.

"This morning," Pudge asked, "between six and noon, were you in the building?"

"I live here. I already told ya that." Mariello was wearing a clean white shirt with the sleeves rolled up to the elbows and a pair of pants that could only have been the bottom half of his best blue suit. He was a slender man with a deeply lined face, a narrow mustache, and the sinewy forearms of someone who made his way by manual labor.

"So you're saying you were in the building between six and twelve."

"Yeah."

"Were you working?"

"C'mon, it's Christmas."

"So you didn't do any work today? No regular duties, no emergencies?"

"I did get one call, to 5E, the Weissmans. Had a clogged sink."

"What time was that?"

"Around one o'clock."

"I see." Pedersson took a spiral pad and a fountain pen from his jacket pocket and began to write. After a few words, he stopped and looked back up at Frank Mariello. "You have keys to the apartments?" he asked.

Pudge knew, even as he posed the question, that landlords have the right to access a tenant's apartment whether the tenant is at home or away. The only question was whether Frank would lie to him.

"I keep 'em in a locked box. Nobody can get to 'em."

"Except you."

"Hey . . ."

"See, the thing is, we got a murder on our hands and we can't figure out how the murderer got into the building."

"How do you know she didn't let him in herself?"

Pedersson shrugged. "That's most likely the way we'll go," he said, "once we're certain that every entry point to the building was secure at the time of the murder. Tell me, who took out the trash?"

Mariello seemed to shrink, to literally curl into himself. He'd forgotten, or so Pudge assumed, all about the trash. Either that or he figured the dopey-looking detective who stood before him was too stupid to notice.

"I took it out," Mariello admitted. "Tomorrow's pickup day and they come early."

"Exactly when did you take the trash out? And don't lie to me, Frank. Don't treat me like I'm an asshole. I'm very sensitive, and I get upset when people treat me like an asshole."

"Around eight o'clock this morning."

"By yourself?"

"Yeah. My porter had the day off. But it was no big deal. I used a hand truck."

"How many trips back and forth?"

"Christmas, you get a lotta trash. I'd say around ten or twelve."

"Did you tie the gate back, or did you unlock it every trip?"

For the first time, Mariello broke eye contact. He turned slightly to the left and looked down at the floor, his Christmas, at the moment, anything but merry. "The boss finds out," he said, "I'm gonna lose my job."

"Jennifer Denning lost her life."

"Because of me?"

"Maybe." Pedersson took off his watch cap and jammed it into his pocket before continuing. "Did you leave the gate open, Frank? Did you get distracted, maybe go to the kitchen for a cup of coffee? If you did, if that's what happened, tell me now, and I won't have to ask your wife. You have a wife, right? And kids?"

"Yeah."

"Well, I don't want to disturb them any more than you want them disturbed. As for your boss . . . I work for the City of New York, not your boss, whoever he is. If it turns out the open gate played no part in the crime, it'll never come out. But you gotta tell me the truth here. You just gotta."

Mariello took only a few seconds before acknowledging the wisdom underlying both the offering of peace and the heartfelt admonition. "I got a phone call," he said.

"What time?"

"Around eight-thirty. I was gone like twenty minutes, a half hour at most."

"And during this time the gate and the back door were open? You had both tied back?"

Mariello raised his chin, his nostrils pinching together as though assaulted by the odor of something he'd rather not deal with. "Look, that phone call, I hadda take it. I'm into the shy-locks big-time. They crook their little finger, I come runnin'."

"So you couldn't take a minute to lock the back door?"

Mariello shook his head. "You wanna hold on to your thumbs, you don't make these people wait. Especially when you spent this week's vig on presents for your kids."

FIVE

WHEN PUDGE PEDERSSON RETURNED to the crime scene a few minutes later, he found Belinda Moore sitting at the dining room table. She'd cleared a small space amid the rubble and was examining an address book, pausing occasionally to add a particular name to a list she was compiling in a small pad. An assistant medical examiner, a Nigerian pathologist named Hamani Babangida, was in the apartment, squatting beside the body. His two assistants were out in the hall, passing the time of day with several uniformed officers.

At some point, Babangida had turned Jennifer Denning onto her side. He was exploring the wound to the back of her head when Pedersson knelt beside him.

"What's it look like, doc?" Closely examining a victim's injuries is standard procedure for detectives at the scene of a homicide. As Belinda was present when Babangida arrived, it was a task she might have accomplished before Pudge's return.

"The injury appears to be a severe laceration with a consequent displaced fracture resulting from a fall." Babangida's English was tinged as much by his Oxford education as his Nigerian origins.

"*One* laceration? *One* fracture?"

"Thus far."

"Was it enough to kill her?"

Babangida smiled, his teeth startlingly white against his dark skin. "The deceased's larynx and trachea were crushed, and she exhibits prominent pecteciae on her cheeks and eyelids. The probability that manual strangulation was the cause of her death is extremely high. Nevertheless, we intend to conduct the autopsy mandated by New York State law."

That was confirmation enough for Pudge, who rose and joined his partner at the dining room table. As he now imagined the sequence of events, the attack on Jennifer Denning was a random event. An intruder made the best of an opportunity, the open gate and back door, to prowl through the building in search of gain. He happened upon Jennifer Denning as she entered her apartment and assaulted her without warning. The assault was vicious and unrelenting. It carried her down onto the parquet floor, where she cracked her head against the hardwood; it continued until she was dead. All the rest—the sexual assault, the towel, the search—had come later.

"The towel was wet," Belinda said without looking up. "When he put it over her face."

"How do you know that?"

"The spa."

Pedersson grunted. He absolutely hated allusions, especially when he had no idea what was being alluded to. Nevertheless, he took the next step. "Spa?"

"You remember."

"I don't, Belinda."

"My vacation? On Paradise Island? Which I just came back from two weeks ago and told you all about?"

"Ah." Now he understood the purpose of the conversation. Belinda's husband, Ralph, was a unionized airline mechanic, his rate of remuneration so inflated he might have been paid by the minute instead of the hour. That's why the Moores vacationed on Paradise Island while Pudge Pedersson drove up to Connecticut in an eight-year-old Taurus.

"You remember, I told you I went to the hotel spa? That I had a facial?"

"Oh, right," Pudge said, though he had no memory of the conversation.

"First thing they did was put a warm towel on my face to open my pores. I remember the towel was wet and the beautician molded it to my features, that it went on like a second skin." She gestured to Jennifer Denning's body. "You look, you'll find water spots on the floor. From where the towel dripped."

Pudge did look and did find a few colorless stains that might have been made by dripping water. Impressed, he turned back to his partner. "I braced the super a few minutes ago," he announced. "The gate to the alley and the back door were open and unguarded for at least twenty minutes, starting around eight-thirty this morning."

"They have a surveillance camera back there?"

"Nope."

Dr. Babangida interrupted the conversation when he instructed his assistants to remove Jennifer Denning's body. Though Pudge watched the process while Belinda averted her eyes, neither spoke as Denning's frozen limbs were forcibly arranged to fit the contours of a body bag. A moment later, she was gone.

"What'd the perp come for?" Belinda asked. She was staring at the door as if afraid the body would be returned to the scene of the crime. "Did he come to steal or to kill?"

"What I think," Pudge said, "is he would've settled for either. But that's not the point, Belinda. The point is how he got out. The way I read it, the gate was relocked by the time our boy finished his business."

"Well, if he went out through the front, he was caught on video." Belinda stripped off her gloves and dumped them in her bag. "You know, when he strangled her, he must've gotten blood on his gloves. And when she hit the floor, he most likely got some of the spatter on his pants or his coat. It's not gonna help us find him, but it does show that he makes mistakes." Belinda rose. "Whatta ya say we get a canvass going, then interview the witness?"

"Rosemary Paulino?"

"That's the one."

Ten minutes later, after briefing Sergeant Cho whose uniformed officers would visit each of the twenty-five apartments in the building, Belinda Moore knocked on Rosemary Paulino's door. The focus of their investigation had now shifted to the victim.

The door was opened by a middle-aged man who introduced himself as Rosemary's husband, Dominick. Moon-faced, Dominick's pronounced five o'clock shadow disappeared into a forest of tightly curled hair revealed by the open collar of a white shirt.

"We need to speak with you and your wife, Mr. Paulino," Belinda Moore explained. "I know this is a bad time, but we'll be as brief as possible."

As Belinda, followed by her hulking partner, had already stepped into the apartment, there was little Dominick could do except lead them into a living room dominated by a Christmas tree set before the window. Rosemary Paulino sat on the couch, her eyes shot with red veins and noticeably swollen. A trash basket, filled to the brim with tissues, rested beside her feet.

From somewhere in the back of the apartment, the squeals of overexcited children filtered into the living room. Though Belinda found the contrast between the kids' excitement and Rosemary's grief somewhat disconcerting, she took a seat in an armchair to Rosemary's left while Dominick dropped down next to his wife. By agreement, Belinda would conduct the interview.

She began by apologizing for the intrusion, then asking Rose-mary to describe the chain of events that led her to the Denning apartment. Belinda wasn't particularly interested in the answers because Jennifer Denning had been murdered long before Rosemary Paulino showed up. She asked the question because she wanted to ease Rosemary into the interview.

The only important bit of information revealed by Rosemary's response was that she'd phoned Jennifer around nine o'clock in the morning and gotten no answer. At the time, she'd assumed that Jennifer was taking the brisk walk she took every morning before breakfast.

"I keep thinking," Rosemary said, "that if I'd just gone down there, I could have—"

"She could have gotten herself killed is what she could have done." Dominick Paulino put his arm around his wife's shoulder. Clearly, he'd decided to protect her from the big bad cops.

"Tell me about Jennifer," Belinda asked. "What did she do? What was she like?"

"Meek," Dominick said. "That's what she was like. And what she did was work."

"Dom, please," Rosemary protested. She turned to look at Belinda for the first time. "Jennifer and I, we were best friends from high school. We talked almost every day."

"For hours," Dominick added.

Though Belinda racked her brain, she couldn't devise a reason to separate the Paulinos that passed the sniff test. "Mrs. Paulino," she finally said, "I went through Jennifer's address book and wrote down some names." In fact, Belinda had noted every male name, of which there were a grand total of eight, including two of Jennifer's three doctors. "If you could identify these individuals, it would be very helpful."

"Sure."

"Kevin McDermitt."

"Her former boyfriend."

"Former?"

Predictably, Dominick Paulino had his say. "Kev dumped her a year ago," he declared. "Traded her in for a new model."

"Were they still in contact with each other?"

"I don't think so," Rosemary replied. "He moved out to Seattle right after they split up."

"With his new girlfriend," Dominick added.

The rest of the interview went no easier and was no more productive. The few men in Jennifer Denning's life included her stepfather who lived in Phoenix, a man named Roger Cohen with whom she'd had all of three dates, an analyst she'd visited briefly after the Kevin McDermitt affair, and her immediate superior at Columbia University.

And no, Jennifer wasn't having an affair with her boss. And Jennifer Denning did not patronize after-hours clubs or singles bars, or publish personal ads on the Internet, or frequent chat rooms. And she got along well with her neighbors and her coworkers.

"We came here, to New York," Rosemary explained, "right after graduating from Ohio State. It was the big adventure, our chance to escape from Cleveland. You know, if we can make it here, we can make it anywhere. But Jennifer, she fell in love with the city. Even during the worst of it, when you were afraid to step out onto the street, when all you talked about was moving to the suburbs, she loved this town."

Rosemary began to cry, the tears quickly spilling onto her cheeks. Impatiently, she snatched a tissue from the box on her lap, then looked briefly at her husband. Belinda noted an element of challenge in that glance, as if Rosemary were daring him to deny the claim. A moment later, a young girl, perhaps four or five years old, dashed into the living room. The girl skidded to a halt at the sight of Pudge Pedersson and Belinda Moore. She looked from one to the other, then to her mother, then burst into tears.

• • •

At eight forty-five the following morning Belinda took a white mug from her desk at the Twenty-fifth Precinct and made her way across the squad room, past Detective Samuel Day who held a telephone receiver to his ear. Day was Lieutenant Malden's favorite, a nice enough guy who nevertheless maintained a polite distance from the two detectives perpetually in his rabbi's doghouse. "Hey," he said as Belinda passed his desk, "what's up?"

"Cops and robbers," Belinda said as she continued over to a coffeemaker set atop a green filing cabinet. "Crime and punishment." She filled her mug, then glanced at Pudge who was watching her every move with undisguised envy.

The root cause of this envy, Belinda knew, was the widow MacDougald's cat, Sleepy, who lived up to her name, snoozing for sixteen hours a day on the same living room furniture the hyperallergic Pudge Pedersson used when he visited.

"Red eyes and a runny nose," Pudge had more than once commented, "do not a sexy lover make."

True enough, Belinda had told herself when Pudge first broached the subject, but the brown suit, blue shirt, green tie and scuffed cordovan wingtips don't help, either.

In any event, the remedy for Pudge's allergy, prescribed by the widow after careful consultation with her herbalist, required that Pudge substitute a tea composed of bitter orange, Chinese kudzu and giant arrow leaf for the eight cups of coffee he normally drank in the course of a day. As Pudge desperately wanted to conquer his allergy (and knew which way Annie would go if forced to choose between Sleepy and himself), he'd been holding to a steady, miserable course for the past month.

Belinda sipped at her coffee, then added a dollop of nondairy creamer, recalling her Jamaican grandmother, Reba, in whose care she'd been given while her parents went out to work. Reba had regularly dosed her charge with Woodward's Original Gripe Water and Zion Blood Root Elixir. Belinda shuddered at the memory, then reminded herself to pick up a half-gallon of ice cream on the way home.

Lieutenant Jerry Malden was in his diffident mode when he summoned Pedersson and Moore into his office two hours later. He was leaning back in his swivel chair with his feet up on the desk, perusing a book designed to prepare him for the captain's exam which he'd twice failed.

"Let's hear it," he said without looking up.

As Pudge began a carefully structured description of the crime scene and the evidence thus far uncovered, Belinda felt her sympathy index slowly rise. The poor jerk. All that enthusiasm was going to be thrown right back in his face and he knew it. He knew it, but he couldn't help himself.

Pudge loved his job; that was his problem. Two problems, actually, because the man not only loved the job, he was good at it. If he'd been a plodder, content to go along to get along (like Bobbie Conditto who occupied the desk next to him), Pudge would have settled into his lowly status long before. He would have a found a comfortable, if not entirely palatable, spot near the bottom of the ladder. Instead, Pudge read a new beginning into every investigation, a chance to redeem himself when he hadn't done anything wrong in the first place.

For Belinda, on the other hand, settling in was not a problem, not even when Lieutenant Malden launched into diatribes against affirmative action in her presence. Not even when he began sentences with "those people," sentences that inevitably included the words "reverse racism." Not even when he paused in mid-diatribe to glance in her direction, his inner smirk more than apparent.

Bottom line, for Belinda Moore as she waited for her partner to conclude his remarks, she knew how to fight and Pudge Pedersson didn't.

"We've got the tape from the surveillance camera at the

victim's dwelling in hand," Pudge declared after thoroughly exploring the reasons behind his and Belinda's conclusions, "and we should get the tapes from other cameras up and down the block by early afternoon. They won't be all that hard to review. The canvass turned up several neighbors who heard a loud thud between eight and nine o'clock, and one who swears she looked at the digital clock on her cable box and it read eight forty-seven. That makes the time frame pretty narrow, so I'd say if the other landlords cooperate, we could have a pretty good picture of the doer sometime tonight."

When the coup de grâce was pronounced, when the too-predictable hammer dropped, Belinda Moore was not only unfazed, she was pleased. The less time spent in Malden's company, the better she liked it. Not so Pudge Pedersson, who seemed to diminish, moment by moment, under the onslaught.

"Frederick," Malden said, pronouncing each syllable distinctly, "what you're saying, it's all bullshit. Look at the overkill, the punctured throat. Somebody with a grudge murdered the Denning woman, somebody who hated her guts."

"Or somebody who hated women in general."

"A serial killer?" Malden rapped his knuckles against his forehead, once, then again. "Frederick, you gotta get control of that imagination. You wanna know why the bedrooms weren't searched? How 'bout the perp was looking for something in particular and found it? How 'bout the scene was staged for our benefit? Say in the hope we'd go searching for a serial killer." Malden paused long enough to draw a breath before continuing in the same vein. "That bit with the towel, it's straight out of Hollywood. And that condom, it doesn't prove a damn thing, even if you're right about that stain, which remains to be seen. Every unmarried guy in New York has a condom in his wallet. Half the married ones, too. In case you haven't noticed, this is a very promiscuous town."

Malden's full mouth had a pronounced downward turn at the corners, rendering his expression habitually sour, as if he was just waiting for the next subordinate to ruin his morning. Even with favorites like Samuel Day, Malden's tone of voice ranged, unpredictably, between mistrustful and caustic. He was now at the caustic end of that range.

"You want me to believe," he continued, his slightly protruding eyes still fixed on the ceiling, "that some junkie or some pipehead just happened to walk out of darkest Harlem on Christmas Day looking for somebody to kill. You want me to believe he just happened to pass through this open gate, which just happened to be unguarded for all of twenty minutes, then happened to encounter the victim when she happened to be opening the door. Is that right? Is that what you want me to believe?"

"But that's exactly how street thieves operate," Pedersson foolishly protested. "They're like jackals or coyotes. They just keep going until the right opportunity presents itself. Our doer might have been in search of a victim for weeks."

"Coyotes? Jackals? Next thing, you'll have the bastard howling at the moon."

Malden's basic problem, Belinda had decided long before, was that he wasn't very good at what he did. The first job of a supervisor is production, which can be measured simply by comparing the clearance rate of one squad with that of other, similar squads. By that standard, Malden was a loser, a man who'd risen to a position he couldn't handle. As a sergeant, he might have been able to put the fear of God into his charges, but detectives spent most of their time unsupervised. If they didn't like their lieutenant, if they didn't want to cooperate, to keep their shoulders to the wheel, there was only one thing Jerry Malden could do about it. He could (and did) farm out challenging cases at the earliest opportunity.

"It doesn't matter anyway," Malden finally declared, "because

I'm passing the case over to Homicide this afternoon. That means I'll need you to put the paperwork on my desk by eleven, after which you take a ride out to scenic Pike County, Pennsylvania. They got a woman in the local lockup, Evienne Rai. Rai's wanted in the County of New York for the crime of grand larceny in the third degree. I'm sending you and your partner because I want a woman cop along for the drive. That way there shouldn't be any claims of sexual harassment."

SIX

Monday, February 4, 7:00 A.M.

THE PAST FIVE MONTHS have been good to Finito Rakowski, and not only does he know it, he takes full credit. His life has changed for the better because he changed his basic approach to his life. A prime example lies on the bed next to him. Abigail Stoph is not a miserable junkie willing to give herself up, orifice by orifice, like Janice Hunt. She's a thoroughly respectable, a thirty-five-year-old nurse with a master's degree who thinks she's found the love of her life.

Years before, at nineteen, a hustler at the Queens House of Detention had taken Finito under his wing. Between his good looks and his mastery of the language, Patty Grogan had explained, Finito could hustle his way to a steady income, a place to live and a decent wardrobe in no time at all.

"There are thousands of desperately lonely women in New York," Grogan told his cellie, "and lonely men, too, if you wanna swing that way."

As Finito very much wanted the life Grogan described, he launched himself into an experiment that produced middling results. Finito did learn to consistently identify, then attract the vulnerable, the first task being the more difficult and crucial. But he lacked patience for the end game, the final gambit, a character trait essential to the long con. Inevitably, after a week, two at most, he snatched any small item of value and all the cash in the house, then headed off to chill out in one of the city's many barrios.

But everything has changed now. Finito is much stronger. He is the master of his fate. If he needs a secure base from which to operate, he will make one for himself.

Encouraging Abby's belief in his essential worthiness is Finito's most immediate aim at seven o'clock in the morning when Abby first begins to stir, when she rolls toward him and throws a heavy thigh over his hip. He reminds himself of this goal even as a wave of physical revulsion floods his body.

The truth is that Finito Rakowski—now Georgie Aguilar—despises Abigail Stoph. He despises her because she is thirty pounds overweight. He despises her because neither she, nor the Greenwich Village apartment she owns, are truly clean. He despises her because she wept upon discovering a dying pigeon in Washington Square Park. He despises her because her back hurts and she gets headaches and she rejects many different foods. He despises her because her many doctors can find no cause for her many ailments.

But most of all, Finito Rakowski despises Abigail Stoph because she is his victim. He thinks Abby should see past the tissue-thin fabric of lies he's offered. He thinks that she would see right through them if she weren't so weak. He thinks Abby wants to be scammed, to be eventually betrayed, because if it weren't for hustlers like Finito Rakowski, she wouldn't have anyone.

And then there's the fact of her intense sexual desire for a man eight years her junior, a man of the streets, a macho man. Abby's lust for his toned body and sensual mouth is readily apparent to Finito. As he understands it, his task, at this stage of the game, is to alternately arouse, then satisfy that lust. All the while pretending that he, inspired by Abigail Stoph's sensuality, is the aggressor.

For all his despising, Finito never thinks about deserting his new girlfriend. Over the past months, especially since Jennifer Denning, he's been reviewing bits and pieces of his life with an eye to the future. This experience is new to Finito. In the past, his attention was always focused on the world around him. He had needs, like anybody else, but he never questioned those needs. They were just there. But things are different now that he knows he'll continue to kill women until he's caught. In that sense, he now has a future he's willing to contemplate.

Finito rolls on top of Abigail Stoph and buries his lips in her throat. He has no trouble achieving and maintaining a full erection. He simply allows his thoughts to drift to the look in Jennifer Denning's blue eyes when he came out of the stairwell. The instinct to preserve life, to fight or flee, an instinct with which Finito is intimately familiar, was entirely absent. In its place he found resignation, as if Jennifer Denning had been expecting Finito Rakowski for all of her life. That resignation had inspired a degree of sexual arousal that bordered on ecstasy.

"*Mí corazón,*" he whispers into Abigail's left ear. When she squirms beneath him in response, he quickly adds, "I'm crazy about you, *muy loco,*" before settling down to await her orgasm.

"Are you working today, Georgie?"

"Yeah." Finito fills Abby's cup with coffee, then fills his own. "But I don't have to be in before ten. After work, I'll be going to my *Tía* Suzanna's."

Patty Grogan had been very specific. Some part of the game must be designed to let you occasionally escape. Otherwise, you'd go crazy.

Check it out, he'd explained, *these are women who get rejected ninety-nine percent of the time. That's because they're so completely obnoxious even their own families can't stand 'em. Take this to the bank, Finito, you hang with those bitches 24/7, you'll go fucking nuts.*

Finito's entirely fictional Aunt Suzanna not only gives him an excuse to spend days away from Abby, it contributes to the sympathetic biography created for her benefit.

The Georgie Aguilar known to Abigail Stoph came up on the mean streets of the South Bronx. Yes, he was in trouble as a youngster. Yes, he once kept bad company, the worst. Yes, he used drugs. But he's straightened up and now wishes only to fly right. In fact, that's the main reason he came downtown, to avoid the temptations of the barrio.

To be forever free of the South Bronx is Georgie Aguilar's most fervent wish. And perhaps, with Abby's help, he will someday achieve that worthy goal. But for now he still has a pair of ties to the old neighborhood. First, his job as drug counselor at a rehab center on the Grand Concourse. Second, the woman who saved his life, his *Tía* Suzanna.

After Georgie's parents were gone—his mother to her grave, his father to God knows where—his aunt had taken him in, had sheltered him until he was old enough to survive on his own. She couldn't make him a good boy. Far from it. But she did embody a moment-to-moment strength he was later to consciously adopt in his efforts to escape the fate assigned to him at birth.

The irony is that, as he has grown stronger, his *Tía* Suzanna has grown weaker, until now she is a sick, elderly Latina surviving from day to day in a Mott Haven housing project. In fact, if not for her family, who take turns nursing her, she would have been institutionalized long before. That's why, it being Georgie Aguilar's turn, he will spend the next few days in his aunt's apartment.

"I'm gonna miss you baby," Abby says. For a moment, she stares at him through misting eyes. Then she digs into her pancakes.

• • •

As Finito emerges onto Hudson Street, he reveals another element of the transformation he's undergone since encountering Darlene seven months before. He does not think about getting stoned, although he's been drug-free (except for the odd bottle of beer) for the past two weeks.

Above him, the winter sun is just high enough to flood the west side of Hudson Street with angled light, the sky just blue enough to allow the illusion of warmth. Finito stands in the sun for a moment, eyes closed against the glare, then realizes that he enjoys fucking with Abigail Stoph's head. He likes pushing her buttons, watching her eyes light up with love when he caresses her throat, with lust when his hand moves farther down. If a pair of dice were as predictable as Abby, he'd be a billionaire.

As he starts off down the street, Finito's thoughts jump to his lucky escape, not from the consequences of his recent actions but from the consequences of his entire life. Like Georgie Aguilar, Finito has sidestepped his fate. He will not die a piss bum in a rubble-strewn lot, his legs swollen black and covered with ulcers, his eyes crusted with mucus. No, at worst, Finito will die on a gurney in a sterile execution chamber, a well-known (and by some well-respected) murderer.

Finito looks good now. He's clean-shaven, his hair recently cut, his slacks recently pressed. His Overland sheepskin jacket (purchased like the rest of his wardrobe from a fence on the Lower East Side) clings to his shoulders and chest as if designed for his torso. Thus he attracts no undue attention in the upscale, very white neighborhood of Greenwich Village. When he stops for coffee and a *Daily News* at a neighborhood deli, except for an encouraging glance from a reasonably attractive brunette, nobody even notices him.

For all his undeniable gains, Finito Rakowski's life is not without its difficulties. True, he now has a secure base and a spiffed-up appearance; he has erected a facade that allows him to pass for human. The problem is that he has yet to accumulate the cash to maintain the facade.

Not good, because at this stage of the game he is expected to pay his own way, to split the cost of meals, movies, and groceries, to live up to Abby's ideal. Not good, because Abigail Stoph has a liking for restaurants that charge eight dollars for a salad, cab rides up to Central Park, gorgeous B&B's in Connecticut. And then there's the cell phone. With no credit and no work history, Finito must purchase minutes in advance, a continuing expense made all the worse by Abby's frequent calls whenever they are apart for more than a few hours. With cell phones, you pay for all calls, incoming and outgoing.

The intersection of Eighth Avenue and Fourteenth Street marks the Manhattan terminus of the L line, and the train Finito enters sits idly in the station, awaiting its scheduled time of departure. Finito unfolds the *Daily News*, turning to the headlines on the second page, and begins to read.

The words come to him slowly for two reasons. First, he is nearly illiterate, having left school, in spirit if not in fact, halfway through the fourth grade at P.S. 238. Second, his only goal is to erect a facade for Abby's benefit. Otherwise, he could give less of a shit about the mayor's latest battle with the comptroller, or the tax reform bill currently being debated in the Senate, or the war on terrorism.

When the L train begins to move, so does Finito. He walks into the next car, positions himself near the center door, scans the passengers on both sides. Finding little of interest, he moves on. He rides all the way out to Rockaway Parkway, in Brooklyn, then back into Manhattan. At no time does he display or feel any impatience. Nor is he surprised when opportunity knocks.

He is sitting in the rear car as the train approaches the Third Avenue station. A young woman, white and well dressed, leaves her seat and walks to the door. She carries a Stone Mountain shoulder bag carelessly draped over her left shoulder.

Born of pure reflex, a series of calculations rush into Finito's consciousness. The single exit at Third Avenue on the L line is at the far end of the platform. Riders who use the L regularly know this and tend to gather in the first few cars. Hence, the woman, when she exits, will likely find herself far from the aid of any bystander with heroic intentions.

His escape will be no problem, either. The L runs every ten minutes and there's only two blocks of tunnel between the Third and First Avenue stations, a bare quarter mile. As an adolescent, Finito and his buddies spent many hours exploring subway tunnels. It was a test of personal courage, a rite of passage they dutifully marked with cans of semimetallic spray paint.

Finito does not strike until the doors close behind him and the train begins to move out. Then he takes one quick step before driving his fist into the woman's back just below her shoulder blade. The blow drives her to her knees, taking her breath away. With practiced ease, Finito grabs the strap of her bag at shoulder level and yanks it down past her elbow and over her wrist. Seconds later, he is inside the tunnel, moving fast despite the uneven surface, despite the active third rail just a few feet away.

There are lights every fifty feet in the tunnel, placed at shoulder level and focused down toward the tracks. Finito pauses beneath one of these to rummage through the bag. Inside, he discovers three items of interest: a tightly packed roll of bills held in place by a rubber band, a small-caliber automatic pistol and a plastic bag containing numerous smaller bags of powder cocaine.

Finito looks up at the blackened ceiling and moans with

pleasure. He's been going out every day for months, searching for that big score, and now he's found it. Now he can spend the hours away from Abby doing what he was meant to do.

Look out, all you bitches, he thinks. The boogeyman's comin' out of the closet.

Almost contemptuously, he flings the coke away. Under New York's tough sentencing guidelines, the coke would earn him a ten-year prison sentence if he got caught with it. He is about to do the same with the little gun when his hand stops in midair. Punching a woman and snatching her purse would probably result in his spending a year on Rikers Island. Robbing her with a pistol, on the other hand, given his priors, would earn him seven to ten upstate. Finito knows this, but he also knows that times have changed.

For a while, after killing Jennifer Denning, Finito had enjoyed a deep and satisfying calm that bordered on true peace. That calm had begun to wear down ten days later. Within three weeks it was gone altogether as he became more and more obsessed with how much the experience could be improved if he made a single alteration to the old game plan. If he kept his next victim alive until he was truly done with her.

Finito Rakowski drops the little automatic into one pocket of his coat, the roll of bills into the other. Fate, he decides as he climbs up onto the First Avenue platform two minutes later, has been very, very good to him. Not so for his victims-to-be, of course, to whom he will now be able to devote all his free time, but that's neither here nor there. What matters, what truly matters is . . .

What truly matters, Finito tells himself as passes through the turnstile and heads up the stairs toward the street, is getting the fuck out of here. To that end, he steps into the road at the intersection of First Avenue and Fourteenth Street, then lifts his hand above his head. As though awaiting his signal, a yellow cab pulls alongside.

SEVEN

ALTHOUGH FINITO HAD eagerly anticipated the evening's pleasures, he now finds himself thoroughly disappointed by Rosaria Montes and by the tablet of Dilaudid he swallowed an hour before. It is not Rosaria's fault. She is everything he expected, is in fact lying naked beside him. The Dilaudid has also done its work and he is thoroughly stoned. Still, neither act nor substance relieves an itch that simply must be scratched.

When Finito abruptly stands and begins to dress, Rosaria comes to a sitting position. "*Mira*, Finito, wha's up whi'chu tonight? You jumpin' around like you got a flea up your ass."

"I have to leave now. I'm sorry."

Rosaria waves a limp wrist as she mimics Finito. "I have to leave now. I'm so, so sorry. Tell me, Finito, you goin' *blanquito* on me? You tired of bein' a spic? Cause you are soundin' more and more like those Tannenbaums who gave your ass back to the state."

Finito zips his pants and buckles his belt. Far from upset by Rosaria's accusations, he has to fight an urge to tell her everything. He and Rosaria have ties stretching far enough into the past for her to know how he got his street name. Back when he was still a toddler, on those rare occasions when his mother brought him over, Rosaria's stepfather instructed his family to guard the food at all times. Because if you turned your back, even for a minute, whatever you'd put out was gone. It was *finito*. The boy was that hungry.

Finito reaches down into his pocket and fishes out a square of aluminum foil. He unwraps the foil to reveal two OxyContin tablets. When he hands them to Rosaria, her attitude brightens.

"Gracias, hombre," she says, her smile wide enough to reveal a missing incisor. *"Mira,* you know I'm a crazy broad, right, *una bollo loca*. What could I do?"

His mind on other things, Finito leaves Rosaria's apartment without answering the question.

When Finito emerges onto Avenue C and 7th Street, the temperature is in the midforties, twenty degrees too warm for New York in February, and saturated with moisture. As usual, he has no plan. All his life he has been tugged along by his needs, and tonight is no exception. But this time his need is not a few bucks so he can buy a flop, or cop some dope, or get laid. Finito's already decided that he wants extra time with his next victim. No more hit and run. But how to do it without taking unacceptable risks?

Problem-solving has never been one of Finito's strong points and he's definitely uncomfortable with the process. Nevertheless, he persists. He admits that he made mistakes with Jennifer Denning, as he had with his first two victims. When Denning opened the door to her apartment, he'd listened from the stairwell for her to greet somebody; when she hadn't, he'd been reasonably sure there was no one else home. But that didn't mean somebody couldn't have come along while he was inside, say a boyfriend with a bad attitude. Sure, he'd played the odds by getting his ass out of there half an hour later. But that tactic is now as dead as Jennifer Denning. Half an hour will no longer get him what he wants.

Finito's high is just past its peak when he reaches Times Square. As on his first visit to Forty-second Street nearly two decades before, he is instantly drawn into the explosion of light and color. He feels as if the colors are running inside him, pulling him along, as if the colors are moving.

Though it is past midnight, the Square is still active. Tourists meander along, necks swiveling, cameras clicking, perhaps drawn by the unusually warm temperature. Dozens of police officers, on foot and on horseback, are also in attendance. Their mission is to protect the tourists, and they are always on the lookout for street predators like Finito Rakowski. Nevertheless, when he saunters by a pair of beat cops, a man and a woman, they give him no more than a passing glance.

Finito passes the next hour in a bar, the Oriole on Broadway, chatting up a woman named Maureen Owens. In her midthirties, Maureen toils in the Overseas Division of New York Life Insurance. Her job, as she is quick to assert, takes her all over the world. She has voyaged on business to every continent except Antarctica.

"And if penguins bought insurance policies," she informs her drinking companion, George Espinosa, "I'd have been sent to Antarctica, too."

Except for a few trips to New Jersey, Finito has been outside of New York City only once in his life. For two years, he lived in the town of Dannemora, near the Canadian border, a guest of the state. He does not, of course, mention this experience to Maureen Owens. With a tested IQ of 117, Finito is far from stupid. He needs to invent an acceptable life, one Maureen will admire, and he know it. That's why he tells her that he works for the Human Resources Administration, supervising a unit dedicated to making the last months of indigent AIDS patients as free from suffering as possible.

"Housing," he explains, "it's mostly about housing. A roof over your head that's made of something more solid than cardboard."

Maureen is on her fourth glass of Chardonnay when she

announces, with just a hint of defiance, that she is a practicing Catholic and believes in angels. This statement allows Finito to segue neatly into a riff he's worked many times before. This riff is designed to make his Puerto Rican identity an asset instead of a liability.

His grandmother, he tells Maureen, is a *lyolocha*, a priestess in the religion of Santeria.

"She serves the goddess Oshun," he declares, "who rules over the waters of the world."

Here, Finito pauses to search for a tell, for some indicator of Maureen's reaction. He does not have to wait long. Her smile and the sudden light in her blue eyes convey a message easily deciphered: Wow, wait'll my friends hear about this!

Finito goes on to describe Oshun's altar—the statue clothed in a flowing silk gown of red and yellow surrounded by peacock feathers, a water-filled chalice, mirrors, fans, seashells and gourds. The details flow easily because Finito's grandmother was, in fact, a *lyolocha* serving the goddess Oshun. Every word he speaks is the truth. His only lies are lies of omission.

He doesn't, for instance, describe the struggles of the chickens whose throats his beloved grandmother cut to get Oshun's attention. Nor does Finito mention the *botánicas* his grandmother sold to barren women seeking fertility, or that these *botánicas* were created, in the main, from plants gathered almost randomly in Van Cortlandt Park, then dried in the oven.

Finito has been in the Oriole for less than an hour when Maureen gets to the point. Though her smile is firmly in place, there's a little flutter to her voice that raises the hair on the back of Finito's head. As he understands it, the question is an open invitation to spend the night together.

"Where do you live?" she asks.

"I live with a roommate," he responds with a sigh. "The apartment's tiny. One bedroom. And my roommate's a complete jerk. I'm looking to move out as soon as I find a place. How about you?"

"I live alone." Maureen giggles. "Thank God."

And that's it. Maureen lives alone and she will escort him to her apartment. They will not be interrupted, not at this hour, nor will he risk his freedom getting to her. He can now depart the Oriole with two pieces of the puzzle in hand.

As for Maureen, she will live to spend another inebriated evening perched on an Upper West Side bar stool. The Oriole is a singles joint patronized by thirtysomething professionals. Too young and too attractive for this crowd, Finito was evaluated by every female within seconds of entering. Should something unpleasant happen to Maureen (should she, for instance, be raped and murdered), they will be sure to remember him.

It is almost one-thirty by the time Finito settles his tab and walks back out onto Broadway. The air is cooler now, and the wind has picked up even as pedestrian traffic has diminished. Finito decides to hike up to Eighty-first Street and Central Park West. If he discovers nothing of interest along the way, he will call it a night and take the subway back to Rosaria's apartment.

Finito is on Seventy-eighth Street between Amsterdam and Columbus Avenues, a block from the Museum of Natural History, when fortune smiles. Thoroughly prepared to take advantage, he has both evaded a surveillance camera on the south side of the street and is sure there are no more cameras on the short block. No cameras, no pedestrians, and no faces in the windows. Thus, when a yellow cab pulls to a stop before an apartment building fifteen yards from where he stands, he is free to give it his full attention.

After a bit of a struggle, a woman emerges from the taxi and stumbles across the sidewalk toward the door of the building. She has not taken more than a few steps before a surge of adrenaline pours into Finito's bloodstream. For just a moment, as the hormone reaches his brain, his nostrils flare and he freezes in place as though awaiting a command. Then the world around him snaps into sharp focus, the wintering ginkos on either side of the block, a line of bowfront town houses, the elongated shadows cast by a pair of fire escapes, the rusting carcass of a stripped bicycle chained to the base of a No Parking sign. He sees every detail, every shadow, all at once. He misses nothing.

Then he is in motion, crossing Seventy-eighth Street, pulling a set of keys from his pocket, rehearsing a bright reassuring smile. As he comes up behind the woman, he jingles the keys softly to attract her attention. This tactic proves effective, as it has in the past when his only interest was money. The woman turns in alarm, then is noticeably relieved to find a handsome, decently dressed white man (a fellow tenant, obviously) with his keys in his hand. Returning his smile, she politely holds the door open.

"Getting colder out there," Finito says.

"Freezing," the woman responds. She stands with her hands jammed into the pockets of a down overcoat that covers her from neck to ankles. Though her dark hair is somewhat disheveled, and her upper lip bears a streak of lipstick that somehow missed her lower lip altogether, she is quite attractive. Her skin is clear, her hazel eyes, even dulled by alcohol, quick and mischievous.

Inside the elevator, Finito pushes the button for the twelfth and highest floor. Like his gambit with the house keys, this gesture, revealing his destination before she reveals her own, is meant to reassure. The risk is that she lives on the twelfth floor and knows her neighbors well enough to recognize him as an interloper. In that case, she will live.

The woman's right index finger trembles briefly as she takes aim, then stabs the button for the fourth floor.

"Got it on the first try," she announces. "I must be havin' a good night."

• • •

When the elevator stops on the fourth floor and the woman opens the outer door, Finito says, "Take care." When that same door closes, he pushes the button for the fourth floor, holding the elevator in place. By this time, his flesh is on fire, as if the erection pressing against his trousers somehow occupies every cell in his body. Nevertheless, salvation for this woman is still possible. She might realize that the motor controlling the elevator has not started up and turn back to check before she opens her door. Or she might wander off down the hallway, past the point where Finito, looking out through a small pane of glass, can see her. Or a neighbor might emerge even at this late hour, toting a bag of garbage destined for the compactor room in the basement.

But none of these things happens. Though her apartment is directly opposite the elevator, she's far too involved with the task of inserting the correct key into each of the two locks on her door to listen for any motor. And when she finally gets the door open, she doesn't call out to anybody inside. Instead, she fumbles for a light switch, then trips as she crosses her own threshold, dropping to one knee.

At this point, even before Finito's left hand clamps down over her mouth, before he jams the barrel of the .32 against her scalp, before he carries her into the apartment, before he eases the door closed with his right foot, her fate is sealed.

EIGHT

"I GOT A PROBLEM," Pudge Pedersson admitted over lunch at the Crete Coffee Shop on Amsterdam Avenue.

"That why you been mopin' all morning?" Belinda's own mood bordered on joyous. The hot rumor was that Lieutenant Jerry Malden was being transferred to the Detective Bureau's Statistics Division, where he would pass the remainder of his career chasing numbers. Bye-bye, scumbag.

Good news for Pudge, too, or it should have been. Though Malden would undoubtedly make his opinion of Pudge's detecting skills known to his replacement, there was now at least the chance that Pudge might someday pull himself out of the basement, maybe even climb that staircase to the stars.

"It's Annie." Pudge kept his eyes riveted to the faux marble swirls on the Formica tabletop. "She wants to come to my apartment. You know, to see how I live."

"When?"

"Like, tonight."

To her credit, Belinda not only kept a straight face, but managed to force a trace of compassion into her expression. A tiny trace. Belinda had been inside Pudge's Bay Ridge apartment

69

once. On the top floor of a two-family house, the place was a nightmare of neglect, every part of every room. In the kitchen, peeling paint hung from the ceiling like stalactites from the roof of a cave.

"Pudge, when did you find out about this?"

"Last week."

"And what did you do?"

"I was gonna clean up, but we drew overtime. . . ."

"That was yesterday. What about the day before, and the day before that?" Belinda raised her hand to forestall a response. She was imagining the widow MacDougald entering that apartment. One look and she'd have to know the Pudge was strictly high maintenance. You took him for a mate, you'd be propping him up for the rest of your life. But there were women who liked that, who wanted to be the solid core at the base of a man's obsessions. And there was a good chance the widow was one of them. If not, or so Belinda reasoned, she would have dumped Pudge a long time ago.

"Okay," Belinda said with a shrug, "you didn't clean up. So what?"

"Whatta ya mean, 'So what?' "

"Here's the way it works, Pudge. If Annie still wants any part of you after bearing witness to your living conditions, she'll try to reform you. And what you'll do, if you have any brains, is *pretend* to reform. After that, it'll most likely be okay."

Pudge shook his head. "I can't let Annie see my place the way it is."

"Well, that's easy enough. Just call at four o'clock, tell her you made an arrest and you're gonna be tied up well into the night."

Pedersson's gaze was now frank. He'd already thought the matter out. "I don't wanna start lyin' to her, Belinda. I see that with cops all the time. Lying to their wives and their girlfriends. I don't wanna go down that road. No, I think what I'm gonna do is stop by that linen store on Broadway."

"Why?"

"To buy some new sheets and pillowcases, maybe a comforter."

"Are you crazy?"

"Hey . . ."

"You think she's coming over to sleep with you?"

"No."

"Then why are you cleaning up the bedroom? And what's Annie gonna think when you proudly display the new sheets? No, you wanna clean one room, make it all sparkly bright for your lady love. I got just the room."

"And what room would that be?"

"The bathroom."

Driven by absolute biological necessity, Belinda had used Pudge Pedersson's bathroom on her one visit to his apartment. As she'd closed the door behind her, her first thought was, *Disease lives here.* And when she finally worked up the courage to sit down, the cracked toilet seat had grabbed her butt with the ferocity of a Carolina crab fighting for its very life.

Pudge thought it over for a minute. "What am I saying?" he asked. "What's the message?"

"That you care about the things that are important to Annie. That you're thinking about her and not about yourself. Besides, you don't have time to clean up the rest of the house. The way you set it up, you only have time for one room."

"And you definitely feel I should do the bathroom?"

"I do."

Pudge Pedersson drew a long breath. "What do I need?" he finally asked, his normally robust tones reduced to a near-whisper as he took a notebook and a pen from his coat pocket. "Give me a list."

"For starters, a new toilet seat, the soft kind, with a nice furry cover for the lid."

By the time they finished lunch, the list included scouring powder, tile cleaner, mildew remover, a mop and bucket, six rolls of paper towels, a can of Drāno, a scrub brush, and a gallon of bleach. A plan had emerged, as well, part one of which required Pudge to sign out for the afternoon.

They were driving back to the house when list and plan were rendered irrelevant by two NYPD cruisers. The units were running fast, one behind the other, with their lights on, though without sirens. They came up on Pudge and Belinda as the partners waited for the light to change at West Eighty-second Street and Columbus Avenue. The first unit hesitated at the intersection just long enough to bring the eastbound traffic to a halt, then buzzed through. The second pulled to a stop next to Pudge who quickly rolled down his window.

"Sarge," Pudge said, "what's up?"

"A DOA," Sergeant Cho replied, "on Seventy-eighth Street. The first uniforms are sayin' it's a homicide, without doubt. I was gonna call in for detectives, but as long as I got you . . ." Message delivered, Cho signaled to his driver who quickly pulled away.

Pudge flipped on a pair of red lights concealed behind the unmarked Impala's grille. "Ya know," he explained to his partner, "with Annie, if she doesn't come over tonight, it could be six months before the signs are right again."

"Before the stars line up?"

"Something like that."

"And six months before you have to worry about reforming."

Pedersson flashed his sneaky-toddler smile. "Something like that, too," he admitted.

Elly Monette was lying on the carpet when Pudge Pedersson forced his oversized hands into a pair of latex gloves, then walked into the living room of her apartment. She appeared to be in her twenties, though establishing her age was made more difficult by the silvery duct tape that covered her face and scalp, leaving only her nostrils exposed. The duct tape had been tightly wrapped, the strips carefully placed across her features and over the top of her head. That her killer had intended more than to merely blindfold and gag her was obvious at a glance.

Jennifer Denning's image rose into Pudge's mind, the jump more reflexive than considered. Not Denning features, but the tracing of her features revealed by the towel placed over her face.

In no hurry, Pudge filed the image away for later reference, then dropped to his right knee and rolled Elly Monette onto her side. Pudge was looking for an obvious cause of death, but there were no holes in the woman's still-buttoned overcoat, nor was her throat bruised or her neck broken. The only evidence of violence was to her hands, which were taped at the wrists behind her back. At some point, she'd clenched her fingers so tightly that her nails had torn into her palms. Her fingertips were smeared with blood, and there was clear evidence of human tissue beneath several broken nails.

As he returned the victim to her original position, Pedersson finally noted a second injury, a small circular abrasion just behind Monette's right ear. He looked at it for a moment before deciding that it could only have come from the barrel of a gun pressed into her scalp with great force, then twisted sharply.

You caught her as she came in the door, Pedersson told himself, and put a gun to her head. You taped her mouth first, then her wrists, then . . .

Pudge fell to both knees and leaned forward to examine the strip of tape covering Monette's eyes. It had been placed above the strips covering the bridge of her nose and her brow. That meant it had been placed last.

"Hey, partner, you need to talk to this guy."

The voice, Belinda's, shocked Pudge into realizing that he

was on both knees, bending far forward, with his big ass waving in the air. Swiftly, his grace belying his bulk, he rose to his feet, becoming aware, as if for the first time, of the havoc wreaked on Elly Monette's apartment. Every cushion on the couch had been slashed. A set of French circus posters had been lifted from the wall and cut to ribbons. The photos from a pair of family albums had been removed, torn into small fragments and scattered.

"This is Alex Kepevitch," Belinda continued, indicating a short muscular man wearing the navy-blue uniform of a Fire Department paramedic. "Alex thinks he knows the cause of death."

Pudge sighed. "Which is exactly what?"

"Hey," she said, in an effort to make amends, "if you already know . . ."

But Pudge Pedersson did not know. That was the whole point, as his droopy expression made abundantly clear.

"Here," Alex Kepevitch said, "I show you." Kepevitch's face was a study in pastels, from his pinkish skin, to his cornflower blue eyes, to his white-blond hair. Smiling, he dropped to his knees and leaned forward to place his nose a few millimeters from Monette's taped mouth. "Smell here," he said. "You will see."

With no option, Pudge did as he was told. The result was all too painfully clear. From a few inches away, the acrid stench was sharp enough to make his eyes water. Elly Monette had aspirated her own vomit. She'd drowned.

Now all that destruction made sense. Her killer wanted to keep Monette alive. When she thwarted him by dying inconveniently, he got even by destroying her apartment. Perfectly reasonable if you were medically, if not legally, insane.

"Okay, Alex, thanks for the help. We'll take it from here." Belinda waited for the paramedic to leave the apartment, then asked Pudge, "You think he's right?" She, herself, was not about to put her face that close to the victim's.

"Yeah." Pudge regained his feet and led his partner on a quick tour of the small apartment. There was something bothering him, an element that had yet to capture his attention.

"Have you seen these?" Belinda asked.

Every soft item in the bedroom where they stood had been slashed—the mattress, sheets and blankets, the shades of the lamps on the night tables, the curtains on the windows. A feather pillow was pinned to the mattress by a long carving knife. Belinda, however, was not referring to any element of the destruction wrought by Monette's killer. She was pointing to several pairs of handcuffs and a pair of shackles nestled inside a shoe box, the lid of which she held between two gloved fingers.

Pudge took a close look. "Keys and all," he said. "But it's not what we're looking at here. This isn't bondage gone bad."

Belinda nodded agreement. "If we'd found her nude, or even seminude, I'd say it was possible. But the victim still had her coat on. And the way her face was covered? I don't care how deep you were into S&M, nobody would submit to that, not voluntarily."

"Amen to that." Pudge waited for Belinda to replace the paraphernalia, then said, "Let's go in the living room. There's something you need to see." He led his partner back to Elly Monette's body where he dropped to one knee and brushed her hair away from the side of her face. "You see this abrasion?" He pointed to the circular wound behind the victim's ear.

"That made by a gun?"

"Yup, small-caliber. And it was ground into her scalp. That's how he controlled her long enough to gag her and bind her wrists." Pudge's eyes widened as he shifted into higher gear. "The way I see it, when Monette died before he got his jollies, the perp went crazy. He got that knife and started cutting away, and he didn't stop until he finished with the bedroom. So—"

"So, why didn't he use the knife on Monette?" Belinda asked. "That the question?"

"Do you always interrupt people? Or is it just me?"

Belinda ignored both queries. "It's the blood, Pudge. He might've been pissed off, but he wasn't gonna contaminate himself with blood. You see those statues?" Belinda gestured to a small collection of porcelain figures set behind the glass doors of a wall unit. "They're German, Meissen. That means they cost a ton of money, which means they meant a lot to the victim. Now if the perp was so mad that he yanked photos out of an album, one at a time, just so he could tear them up, why didn't he destroy that porcelain?"

"Because he couldn't do it without making noise. Because at every minute, he was limiting his exposure to risk." When Belinda smiled in agreement, Pudge continued. "Monette's in full rigor. That means she died somewhere between midnight and five o'clock this morning. Given the early hour, he must've figured he could take his time without fear of being interrupted by a chance visitor. That's why there's no evidence of haste, only of anger. But if he made any noise, if he smashed her things, threw her possessions against the wall, there was always the possibility a nosy neighbor, maybe an insomniac, would overhear and call the cops."

Pudge rose to his feet before continuing. "I'm gonna take a walk," he said, "have a look around, sneak a smoke. You wanna handle the neighbor who called 911?"

"Isabel Cruz? Sure, I'll take her. I'll get a canvass going, too."

Pudge took several steps before turning back to his partner. "He's escalating, Belinda. He wasn't satisfied with Denning. She went too fast. He wants to play with them now. And he's getting better, don't forget. He had tons of street smarts to begin with, and he's still getting better."

"Then you're sure Monette and Denning are connected?"

"I already called Lieutenant Malden."

"And what did he say?"

"He said he was gonna hedge his bets."

"By doing exactly what?"

"By calling it in to his masters at One Police Plaza."

"Ah, the bosses. That's all we need."

NINE

PERHAPS BECAUSE THEY SPEND so much time in public, most New Yorkers habitually guard their privacy. Isabel Cruz was no exception. Although she and Elly Monette had shared an elevator dozens of times, they'd never broached any topic more intimate than the weather. Isabel could, therefore, shed no light on her neighbor's personal habits, or on her neighbor's friends, or on her enemies. As for Isabel's discovery of the crime scene, the event was entirely accidental. In fact, Isabel had nothing to do with it. It was her three-year-old son, Tomas, who was ultimately responsible.

The way Cruz explained it, she was behind her desk at Kellogg Management when her son's nanny called to say she was ill and could not pick up Tomas at his day care center two hours hence. With no options (her husband was away on business), Isabel had postponed her afternoon appointments and gone to fetch her son.

"Me and my husband both work," she explained, "so Tommy has issues. One of the things he does—not every day, just once in a while—is knock on neighbors' doors. I know it's annoying, but its basically harmless and nobody gets too upset. Only the door he picked out this time was slightly ajar, so when he knocked, it came open. I went to close it right away, of course, and I saw the apartment was torn to pieces. That's when I called 911."

"But you didn't actually enter the apartment?"

Cruz shook her head decisively. "I didn't have any desire to see what was in there. And I didn't want Tommy to see, either."

Belinda was negotiating with Sergeant Cho in the hope of borrowing a few of his uniforms to canvass the building when the elevator opened to disgorge Pudge Pedersson and a broad-shouldered woman, perhaps twenty-five years old. The woman wore a patchwork leather coat, knee-high boots and a blue scarf that hung to her waist. Her short, heavily moussed hair was dyed a shade of electric red that had no counterpart in nature. In her left ear, she sported a crescent of tiny gold studs tipped with even tinier colored stones.

Without hesitation, Belinda broke off her conversation when Pudge signaled her to join him. Whoever she was, the woman was clearly important to the investigation. In that light, Pudge's decision to include his partner in the interview was flattering, if not actually gallant. Pudge would know that, of course, but still . . .

"We met in the lobby," he explained before making a quick introduction. "Detective Moore, this is Tracy Fariello, a friend of Ms. Monette's. They were supposed to have lunch together. Now, Ms. Fariello, would you tell my partner what you told me downstairs?"

Tracy Fariello had a small face, the face of a gamin, with sharply slanted eyes and a markedly upturned nose. Though Pudge must have told her that Elly Monette was dead, her expression betrayed not a hint of grief. Instead, her lips were compressed and her eyes blazed with anger.

"The bastard killed her," she half-shouted. "How many times do I have to tell you?"

"Not that part," Pudge interrupted. "About where you and Ms. Monette were last night, when you left, like that." Pudge was more than happy to be the focus of Fariello's anger. Given that the interview had to be conducted in a public space, an unrestrained display of grief would have been extremely inconvenient.

"There's nothing to tell. We left Club Venez, on Fifteenth Street, a little after one. Elly was pretty far gone by that time, so I put her in a cab. Then I walked back to my apartment on Twenty-seventh Street." Fariello jammed her hands into her pockets, her shoulders rising as she turned to face Belinda. Despite the anger, the look in her brown eyes was pleading. "The bastard was waiting for her," she insisted. "He always said he'd get her, and now he's done it."

Belinda ignored the comment. "Did Elly Monette go to Club Venez often?" she asked.

"Yeah, pretty often. It was, like, her place."

"But you go there, too?" Belinda rushed on before Fariello could misinterpret the question. "The reason I'm asking is because it's possible that someone who saw her at the club followed her home. We have to consider that possibility, so if you'd just take a minute to think about it . . ."

Fariello complied, which pleased Belinda, who'd been anticipating some resistance. "It was Monday," she finally said, "so the club was quiet. Elly danced a couple of times with guys I never saw before, but nobody really hit on her. There were regulars, too, only . . . only they wouldn't have any reason to hurt her. Mostly, they're guys we already went out with."

"You didn't see anyone leave while you waited for the cab?"

"Nope, I . . . hang on a minute. Now I remember, I watched the cab drive up Third Avenue. I watched it for at least a block. There was other traffic, but I don't remember any cars pulling out of any parking spaces. No, what I remember is there was nobody else around and I was gettin' nervous about walkin' home alone. That time of night, I always have a can of Mace in my pocket, which I keep my hand around, but still . . ." She stopped long enough to refocus, then stared into Belinda's eyes.

"Nobody followed Elly home last night. She was killed by Eddie Schwann."

Tracy Fariello's argument was convincing. It was Schwann who'd introduced Elly to the joys of submission and the paraphernalia of bondage. It was Schwann who'd broken her nose and her right arm when Elly grew bored with the game. It was Schwann who'd spent three months on Rikers Island for this assault. It was Schwann who'd called Elly, day and night, upon his release. It was Schwann who'd declared, in Tracy Fariello's presence, that he'd make Elly Monette pay for what she'd done to him.

"See, I don't have any objection to a little fun and games," Fariello concluded. "As long as everybody plays by the rules. In bondage, the way it's supposed to be, the slave holds all the cards. That's because the master isn't allowed to use force. The slave comes to the master of her—or *his*—own free will."

"But that's not the way Eddie Schwann saw it?"

"Listen, detective, to what I'm telling you. Eddie Schwann is a bully with a good pickup line. Threats and violence are part of his everyday life. They're his thing, what he does. They're who he fucking *is*."

That was enough for Pudge Pedersson. Eddie Schwann was now a suspect. They would have to pick him up, put him through his paces, and they would have to visit Club Venez as well, talk to the regulars and the bartender. One way or another it was going to be a long night, for which he was infinitely grateful.

Pudge excused himself, moved a few feet away, and took out his cell phone. A moment later, when the widow Annie Mac-Dougald answered, he declared, his voice dropping a full octave, "Annie, I'm not gonna be able to make it tonight. I'm workin' a homicide."

The crime scene was still humming when the two bosses,

accompanied by Lieutenant Jerry Malden, arrived at four o'clock. A half-dozen CSU cops (shadowed, much to their annoyance, by Belinda Moore and her Polaroid camera) were scouring the inside of the apartment. Beside Elly Monette's body, an equally annoyed pathologist fielded questions from Pudge Pedersson.

The two bosses worked out of the chief of detectives' office at One Police Plaza. They were present, as all understood, to protect the interests of the job and not the interests of the victims, much less those of Belinda Moore and Pudge Pedersson. The big boss was Inspector Frank Carter. A large man, Carter towered over the little boss, Captain Meyer Wideman.

Carter in the lead, the bosses walked directly to Monette's body, whereupon Detective Pedersson moved off without being asked. The bosses were silent, even respectful, as they absorbed the obvious.

"Detective Pedersson," Inspector Carter said when he'd seen enough, "if you can spare the time, we'd like to speak with you and your partner."

Pudge watched the two bosses leave the apartment, then looked at Belinda who raised her brows inquisitively.

"We're summoned," Pudge told her.

By necessity, the interview was conducted in the only private space available, Inspector Carter's department-issue Mercury Grand Marquis. Captain Wideman was behind the wheel when they began, Belinda Moore alongside him. Pudge Pedersson sat behind his partner, with Inspector Carter to his left. As both Carter and Pudge were very large men, their shoulders were touching, even with Pudge squeezed against the door.

Initially, all four of the participants stared forward, those in back at the heads of those in front, those in front at the rapidly accumulating snow on the windshield.

"Make the case, Detective Pedersson, for these murders being related." Carter was tall and wiry, a dark-skinned black man with an oval face and a long nose. A thin mustache tracked the corners of his full mouth. His black eyes were small and deeply recessed, his gaze merciless. "I'm familiar with the Denning file," he added.

Pudge was not put off by Carter's glare. He knew what was expected and he was determined to produce. The main thing, from his point of view, was that Jerry Malden had been left to cool his heels, most likely because the bosses didn't value his opinion.

So this was Pudge's chance, his opportunity, another shot at redemption. True, he'd been here before, only to slide back down the ladder. But there was an element to the Calvinist doctrine of predestination that had been drummed into him by his various Sunday school teachers. You can't know your fate in advance. You have to live it first.

He began with a quick description of the Monette crime scene, then responded directly to his superior's command. "The two killings have a number of things in common," he said, ticking the items off on his fingers. "Both victims were women, both lived alone, both had their faces covered, both were attacked as they entered their apartment, both had their apartments trashed. Covering the faces was the most important of these. The perp didn't need to place that towel on Jennifer Denning's face in order to commit the crimes of rape and murder. And while you could say that gagging Elly Monette was necessary, the perp went much further. He was signing his work."

"Why would he do that?"

Pudge shrugged. "Why do some burglars raid their vic's refrigerators or urinate on the bed? A true professional would take care of business and get out. Just last week, me and my partner interrogated a mope who got caught in somebody else's apartment. He was wearing his vic's lingerie and we used that to tie him to a dozen priors. Now he's lookin' at eight years upstate."

Carter raised a hand, bringing Pudge to an abrupt halt. "And the disparities, detective? If you don't mind."

Commanded to make the argument against his own beliefs,

Pudge decided to make it fully. In large part, he was motivated by loyalty to the job. The bosses, he knew, were here to answer a simple question. Which would be worse, from the job's point of view? To link the murders, assemble a task force and inform the press, only to have the homicides prove to be unrelated? Or not to link the murders when a serial killer was loose in New York, then have the press find out a month or two down the line?

The victims, Pudge explained, lived very different lives and had been attacked at different times, Denning about nine o'clock in the morning, when the city was up and running, Monette in the wee hours, when the city was quiet. The attacks and the perp's behavior afterward also showed marked differences. Denning had been killed immediately while Monette had probably been controlled. Denning's apartment had been searched while Monette's apartment, though trashed, had not.

"About an hour ago," he concluded, "I took a stroll out back. This building sits flush against the buildings on the east and west, so there was no easy access, no gate left open, no alley to walk down. Plus, the doors leading to the stairwells can't be opened from the stairwell side without a key. The perp could not have been lying in wait, hoping a target happened along. No, most likely he came through the front door with the victim. That would be a big change in the killer's MO, from blitzing a victim to controlling her."

By the time Pudge lapsed into silence, the windows of the Grand Marquis were covered with snow. Captain Wideman started the car, but did not turn on the windshield wipers or the defroster. Instead, he flipped on the overhead light. Now Belinda could see her partner's face reflected in the windshield, and read his keen disappointment when the next question was addressed to her.

"Detective Moore, what's your opinion?" Carter asked. "Related or unrelated?"

Belinda let her eyes drop to her hands as she considered her response. In fact, she and her partner were in complete agreement on this one, which was not always the case. But that cut no ice here. NYPD detectives are appointed and the rank carries no civil service protections. Hence what the man freely gives, the man can take back.

"Way I see it," she finally said, "the boyfriend, Eddie Schwann, might have been waiting outside the building when Elly Monette's cab dropped her off. He might have put a gun to her head, forced her to let him into the apartment. Also, Monette hung out at Club Venez, a known gathering place for freaks of every kind and description. Club Venez has to be checked out, too."

Belinda finally raised her eyes far enough to see Pudge's reflection in the windshield. Without changing expression, he tapped the side of his nose three times.

"I think what I'm trying to say, sir," Belinda concluded, "is that within a couple of days, if we just stick to the obvious, brace Eddie Schwann, talk to the regulars and the bartenders at Club Venez, we'll be a lot closer to resolving the conflicts. Remember, we have a strong witness, Tracy Fariello, tellin' us nobody followed Monette home last night, so the club connection is a long shot."

Captain Wideman took advantage of the ensuing pause in the conversation to throw on the defroster. Apparently encouraged by the whoosh of hot air that flooded onto the glass, he tried the windshield wipers, but they proved unequal to the wet snow and barely moved. The windshield would have to be cleared by hand. His hand.

"You're a very practical woman, Detective Moore," Carter said without a trace of irony. "That's a rare trait in a detective."

"Thank you, Inspector." Belinda was unfazed by the compliment, if that's what it was. She'd given Carter a chance to avoid the decision-making process and he'd jumped at it. How shocking.

"So that's the way we'll play it. I want the two of you to pursue this as a routine homicide." Carter struggled to unbutton his coat, then reached into the breast pocket of his suit jacket to retrieve a business card. He handed the card to Pudge. "You run into any problems, need any help, just call. Now, if you'll do me one more favor, I'll let you get back to work."

"What's that, Inspector?"

"Tell Lieutenant Malden I want to see him." Carter smiled, revealing a mouthful of long yellow teeth. "If he can spare me a moment."

TEN

"THE WAY I SEE IT, the perp spent a lot of time thinking about the way he was gonna kill his victims. You know, fantasizing." Pudge eased his foot off the brake as the light at Houston Street and Broadway turned green. He was hoping against hope that the vehicles on the other side of the intersection would begin to move. No such luck. It was six o'clock in the evening, it was a weekday, it was snowing. As things stood, they'd been on the road for an hour, and the Brooklyn Bridge was not yet in sight.

"Between Denning and Monette," Pudge declared as he lit a cigarette, "our boy reviewed the playbook over and over again, adding a little bit here, subtracting a little bit there, until he had it just right."

"That's why he was so pissed off," Belinda added, "when Monette died on him. Know something, Pudge? First chance our bad boy gets, he's gonna kill again. He's probably out there right now, on skis."

Belinda paused to give Pudge an opportunity to reply, but Pudge was desperately trying to get through the light. There was a single slot open on the south side of Houston Street and two other vehicles determined to occupy it.

Supremely disciplined, Pudge feathered the gas and managed to avoid spinning his wheels in the snow. His competitors were not so fortunate. They slid sideways, drawing the wrath of a New

York City traffic agent who was already unhappy about working an eight-lane, traffic-clogged intersection in a snowstorm.

Pudge tossed his cigarette onto the slushy pavement. "The doer's taking more risks now," he said, "carrying a gun, controlling the victim."

"Yeah, how'd he do that? Control the victim? How did he get Elly Monette to allow him into that building? Because women in this town, they can spot a street mutt two blocks away."

"Maybe he put the gun to her head right after she came out of the cab."

"Gimme a break. This is a guy who in the middle of a rage doesn't break a porcelain figurine because it would make too much noise. He'd never risk confronting someone on the street. No, he talked his way in, Pudge, and by the way, it's no accident that Monette's building doesn't have any surveillance cameras. First kill, he found a way to circumvent a surveillance camera. Second victim, no surveillance cameras to worry about. This boy is very careful and very good at what he does. You said something about carrying a gun, taking more risks? My guess, the perp is white. That would make a stop and frisk unlikely. My guess is that he's reasonably well dressed, too, and that he's got some kind of patter that makes him appear harmless."

Pudge was more than happy to let his partner dominate the conversation. Belinda was upset, and he respected that. Truth be told, he was also upset. Nobody could look at the tape covering Elly Monette's face and not be upset. What you wanted to do was run out, find her killer, tear his head off. But that wasn't going to happen. Instead, you were going to drag your sorry self, in your cheap sorry suit, from place to place, from witness to witness, wearing out your cheap sorry wingtips in the process. That was just the way of it, so if you occasionally felt the need to blow off a little steam . . . well, that's what partners were for, right?

They were at the apex of the Brooklyn Bridge when Belinda regained her equilibrium. Wet snow clung to the spider's web of cables, and to the gray, rough-hewn stone of a massive tower on the Brooklyn side. The scene—cable, tower and snow—was starkly illuminated by the lights on the bridge and by the head-lights of the virtually unmoving vehicles. But when Belinda stared off to her right, toward lower Manhattan, she found her-self looking at a gray curtain through which individual flakes of snow darted as though trying to escape detection.

"Last comment, okay?" she told Pudge.

"Okay."

"Two main ways the doer gets taken down. First, he shoots off his mouth and somebody drops a dime. Second, he screws up or he gets unlucky, and is arrested at the scene. Neither is under our control. So, what can we do, Pudge?"

"We can hope he made mistakes in the past," Pudge replied. "Look at what he revealed about himself at the Denning scene. The method of entry, the search for cash—he practically told us he was an experienced thief. With Monette, though he revealed enough to link the homicides, he corrected those mistakes."

"Fine, he's still learning. What's the point?"

"The point is that he probably killed before Jennifer Denning, so that's where we need to look. The point is that if he made any fatal mistakes, before is when he made them. The point is that we have to go backward."

Belinda continued to stare out the window. They were almost at the foot of the bridge, just a few blocks from Eddie Schwann's home in Brooklyn Heights, and the snow appeared to be letting up. Pudge was still going on, defending his position as if he expected his partner to launch an attack at any minute. Belinda, however, now that she'd settled comfortably into the job at hand, the job that needed doing right now, was content to remain quiet. If her partner needed to blow off a little steam, that was fine by her.

Eddie Schwann was clearly upset to discover Pudge and Belinda on the other side of his door when they knocked at 7:08 P.M. Nevertheless, he managed a thin display of attitude by asking, "How did you get in here?"

In fact, Pudge and Belinda had waited on the street until a tenant with a key approached the town house on Joralemon Street, then followed her inside. But Pudge wasn't about to explain himself to Eddie Schwann, nor was he prepared to ask permission to enter the man's apartment. Though broad-shouldered and obviously fit, Eddie Schwann was a dwarf alongside Pudge Pedersson. When Pudge advanced, Eddie retreated.

"Mr. Schwann, do you know a woman named Elly Monette?" Belinda asked once the door was safely closed behind them.

"Is that what this is about? Elly Monette? Because I've put up with enough bullshit from Elly." In his early thirties, Schwann's fine brown hair was just a shade or two short of blond. Though his features were skewed by a square, prominent jaw, he was a reasonably attractive man.

"Mr. Schwann," Belinda repeated, "do you know a woman named Elly Monette?"

"Yeah, I know. . . . Wait a minute. I *knew* Elly Monette, okay? We're no longer in contact."

"So, you didn't speak to her last night?"

"No."

"And you didn't see her?"

"No."

"And you didn't go to her apartment, you didn't confront her?"

"No, I didn't."

"Then where were you last night, say between midnight and six in the morning?"

Clearly at a crossroads, Schwann hesitated long enough to convince Belinda that he was measuring his response. Evidence of a guilty mind? Or the act of a man trying to gauge the depth of the shit into which he'd somehow stepped?

"What's this about?" he finally asked. "What happened to Elly?"

"You don't wanna tell us where you were last night, Mr. Schwann? I have to say, I find that strange."

Schwann looked at Pudge as though expecting him to provide an effective counter to his partner's assertion. Instead, Pudge took a step to his left. Now Schwann could no longer watch both cops at the same time, and his attention finally settled on Belinda.

"I played pool last night, with a friend, Giorgio Belli, from nine o'clock until a few minutes after midnight. We play every Monday at the Supreme Billiard Parlor on Forty-second Street."

"In Manhattan?"

"Yeah."

"Forty-second and where?"

"Between Seventh and Eighth Avenues."

"That's more than a mile from Elly Monette's apartment." When Schwann didn't comment on her observation, Belinda put the interview back on track. "Where did you go after you left the billiard parlor?"

"I came back home, watched some TV, went to bed."

"Did you have company?"

"No."

"Did anybody see you come in? Did you make any phone calls, maybe go on-line?"

"No, no, and no."

Schwann's head swiveled from right to left, from Belinda to Pudge. Pudge responded by taking a second step to his left. He was now behind Schwann. "Why are you getting so upset?" he asked. "We're being polite here. In fact, we're being downright considerate."

Belinda relaxed as Schwann turned away and Pudge took charge of the interview. She could afford to relax because they'd already achieved their primary objective. Eddie Schwann did not have an alibi.

"Look, detective, I didn't go near Elly's apartment last night. For Christ's sake, I haven't spoken to Elly in months, and even then it was over the phone."

"How many months?"

"At least six. But it could have been more."

Pudge folded his arms across his chest. "Tell me, Eddie, do you keep your phone bills, maybe in a filing cabinet? Because if you do, you can check it out. Then you'll be certain."

At this point, as Pudge and Belinda knew, Eddie Schwann's best move was to demand a lawyer, then shut his mouth. But Eddie didn't see the trap coming. All he knew was that the accuracy of his response could be independently determined, so there was nothing to be gained by lying.

"In December," he finally admitted. "I spoke to Elly right before Christmas."

Pudge let his arms fall to his side. "Ya know, Eddie, if I was a mean-spirited person, I might point out that six weeks is a lot shorter than six months. But I'm not mean-spirited and I'm not gonna do that. No, the way things are, I'm gonna have to settle for placing you under arrest, then enumerating the various rights to which you are now entitled."

Pudge and Belinda did not handcuff Eddie Schwann, figuring Belinda's careful search of his person to be humiliation enough for the present. Then, too, the charge against him was not murder, but a simple violation of the order of protection generated when he first attacked Elly Monette. This was the crime to which he'd stupidly confessed when he admitted contacting Monette before Christmas.

Their aim was to control the suspect without stripping him of all hope. To get Eddie Schwann thinking, Hey, I haven't been cuffed and I haven't been hauled off to jail. Maybe I can still talk my way out of this.

"Look," Schwann said when Belinda removed her hands from

his crotch and straightened up, "I've got no reason to hurt Elly. I don't care what she said, I—"

"Stop." Belinda's expression revealed nothing. Her mouth and jaw were completely relaxed, her eyes merely curious. "What is that supposed to mean? What she *said?*"

"Well . . ." Schwann paused, his eyes blinking rapidly as the truth finally dawned on him. "What are you telling me here?"

"I'm telling you what you already know. I'm telling you that Elly Monette was murdered last night and we think you're the murderer. That should be obvious by now."

Schwann's head snapped back as though he'd been caught with a hard jab. His lips pursed and he moaned once, a cry nearly of abandonment. Pudge and Belinda watched him with the intensity of hungry snakes come upon a bird's nest. Their lives, they knew, would be made so much easier if Schwann's little drama was patently false, if those tears running down the side of his face were somehow manufactured. Unfortunately, that was not the case. Though neither Pudge nor Belinda was so prideful as to believe that he or she (or both) could not be fooled, their instincts had been honed by years of experience. From where they stood, Schwann's grief, and his surprise, were genuine.

That didn't buy him a free pass, however. Schwann had a history of assaultive behavior toward the victim. He'd vowed revenge in front of a reliable witness. He had no alibi.

"Tell me," Belinda said, "exactly what you did after you left the pool hall. Step by step. Tell me what you watched on television after you got home. I want to know everything you did after midnight."

As Eddie began his recitation, the portable two-way in Pudge's overcoat crackled into life.

Pedersson? Moore?

Pudge stepped into the hallway and closed the door behind him before responding. "Pedersson here," he finally said.

Pedersson, it's Cho. We turned up a witness. Claims he came in about two o'clock and passed somebody comin' out.

"You get a description?"

White male, about thirty, blondish, good-looking. The wit says he might recognize the man if he saw him again.

"Look, sarge, do me a big favor. We gotta stop at the house, so we're gonna be a while. Find some way to hold this guy till we get there."

Cho laughed. *Even as we speak, detective, I got two uniforms camped in the wit's living room. They're bondin' over a hockey game.*

"Thanks, Sarge. I'll see you in a couple of hours."

As it turned out, Pudge and Belinda were introducing themselves to Hobart Marcuse less than ninety minutes later. The snow had stopped as suddenly as it started, and the commuters, in all their many thousands, had finally completed their journeys. The streets of Manhattan were now dominated by empty yellow cabs tearing up and down the avenues.

Along the way, Eddie Schwann had been deposited in the precinct lockup, and nine mug shots, his among them, had been gathered. The mug shots were all of white males or light-skinned Hispanics, though not all were blond, or even blondish.

"Thanks for being so patient, Mr. Marcuse," Belinda said after shaking Hobart Marcuse's hand.

"No problem."

Formerly of Minneapolis, Marcuse was in his midtwenties, and held a master's degree in business administration from Yale University. He'd come to New York to make his fortune, despite the obstacles presented by the adverse business conditions now prevailing in the big city. Or so he told Belinda Moore while Pudge assembled the photo array on a glass coffee table.

When his big moment came, Marcuse reviewed the photos systematically. He worked from left to right, across each of the three rows into which Pudge had arranged the nine mug shots.

Then he reversed the process, working from right to left, bottom to top.

Finally he said, "It could be this one," indicating the photo of a man named Robinson Forman, presently a guest of the state. "Or it could be this one," he continued, pointing to a photograph just to the right of Forman's, to Eddie Schwann's photograph. "If I could see them in person, I think I'd be sure."

"Sure of what?" Pudge asked.

"Sure . . ." Marcuse hesitated for a moment, then his watery brown eyes dropped to the two photos he'd chosen, bouncing from one to the other as he compared them to the face in his memory. His problem, of course, as Pudge and Belinda knew, was that the face in his memory, the template, was hazy; it simply would not lie flat on either of the two faces before him. Otherwise, Marcuse's identification would have been immediate and unequivocal.

"It's one of these two," Marcuse said. "I think if I could see them in person, I'd know."

An hour later, when a set of blinds were lifted to reveal a lineup composed of eight men, seven of them cops, Marcuse was neither hesitant nor equivocal. "Number four," he declared, pointing to a very glum Eddie Schwann, "that's him."

Pudge Pedersson was not impressed. By showing Marcuse a photo array, they'd as much as declared that the face of a murderer was among the arrayed photos. Now Marcuse was looking at a second set of suspects, only this time the faces were all different. Except for one, Eddy Schwann.

On the night before, Marcuse had been waiting in the lobby for the elevator after a pleasant evening passed in a midtown sports bar named McTuff's. Though he had "a good buzz on," he was sure it was "around two o'clock" when the elevator doors slid apart and a man walked out. Apparently surprised to see Hobart, the man quickly turned his head away. Altogether, they were in visual contact for "maybe four seconds."

• • •

The lineup was over, and Hobart Marcuse on his way home, when Pudge and Belinda found a minute to huddle in the empty squad room. It was now eleven-fifteen and a decision had to be made. As both understood, the business card handed to Pudge by Inspector Carter was not merely an offer of aid, but an invitation. Specifically, if they wanted to keep him apprised of their investigation's progress, he would not object. In fact, he might even construe their courtesy as a favor to be rewarded at some later date.

"If I really thought Schwann was guilty," Belinda said, "I'd tear the inspector's card up, get on with my life. But . . ."

Pudge finished her sentence, ". . . but its only a matter of time until Elly Monette's killer does what he does best, kill women."

"Worse, Pudge. I meant what I said. The perp didn't get what he wanted from Monette. He didn't receive satisfaction and there's not gonna be any cooling-off period this time around. I'll bet my next paycheck that he's out there right now."

That was motivation enough for Pudge who took himself and his cell phone to the deserted weight room in the basement where he quickly dialed Carter's number. As he poked at the keyboard, he indulged a little fantasy in which Carter became his rabbi, in which promotion followed promotion. Pudge used this fantasy to get himself past a series of obstacles that began with a surly lieutenant who only after considerable persuasion agreed to pass a message up the line.

But Pudge was unable to clear the last obstacle, Captain Meyer Wideman, whose words cut through Pudge's fantasy like a pathologist's saw through the bony plates of a human skull.

"Inspector Carter is otherwise occupied," he growled. "Tell me what you want."

Pudge described his activities over the last five hours, mentioning his partner from time to time before firmly stating his personal opinion. "Myself," he said, "I don't think Schwann's good for it. Even with a gun, I don't see him getting Elly Monette from the street into her apartment. In fact, I don't see him as having the balls to even try. And the same holds true for the duct tape on the victim's face. The man doesn't have it in him. That's my gut reaction, my partner's, too."

"You realize," Wideman replied after a moment, "that continuing to search for Monette's killer would prejudice the case against Edward Schwann."

So that was that. Until further notice, Eddie Schwann had been consigned to the belly of the beast. The news didn't surprise Pudge, who deftly countered Wideman's attempt to shut him down.

"Right, sir, I've got that," he said, "but there's nothing to prevent us investigating the murder of Jennifer Denning. I mean, if me and my partner got the case back from Homicide."

After a very long moment, Wideman asked, "And if you had the case back, detective, what exactly would you do with it?"

ELEVEN

FINITO RAKOWSKI IS ENJOYING himself for the first time in a week. He is seated before a round table in Sal's Tavern, an Italian restaurant just a few blocks from Abigail's apartment. He is eating fried calamari, and enjoying that as well, splashing his food, from time to time, with flakes of crushed red pepper. To his left, Abigail Stoph squirms. To his right, Abigail's friend, Christine Knack, describes her recent trip to Finland. Christine is one of Abigail's best friends, a "world traveler," always on the move.

Though he has no interest in Christine's adventures, Finito pays careful attention to her rambling descriptions of the Fourth International World Music Festival. He encourages her to inflate her recitation with complicated anecdotes that reach all the way back to her college days at Duke University. Laughing in all the right places. Wagging his finger when she admits to a moment of indiscretion with a Lithuanian violinist named Danute.

Sal's Tavern, on Bank Street, is a throwback to the 1950s, the golden age of the Italian restaurant, a bit of retro in the ritzy West Village. Photos of Italian and Jewish gangsters dominate the walls. Al Capone, Abe Reles, Lucky Luciano, Meyer Lansky and Bugsy Siegel are all included in the pantheon. Bugsy's paramour, Virginia Hill, has been given a place of special honor. A poster-size photo of Hill testifying before the Kevauver crime committee hangs in the space behind the bar once reserved for the naked-lady painting.

"He took off with your passport and your train ticket?" Finito exclaims. "What did you do then?"

As Chris Knack settles into a thorough accounting of her adventures with various State Department bureaucrats stationed at the American embassy in Helsinki, Finito steals a glance at Abigail Stoph. The impatience of a few moments before has vanished. Now her round cheeks (buoyant enough to produce huge dimples when she smiles) sag like half-empty water balloons. She feels betrayed, Finito knows, and a little frightened. This pleases him immensely.

For the last six days, ever since Elly Monette escaped the nightmare he'd arranged for her, Finito has been in a rage. Unable either to express that rage (though he's walked many miles in search of another victim) or to quell it, he has blundered into the second phase of the game taught him so long ago by Patty Grogan. Abby's bliss is now to be replaced by the fear of losing her only true love, the Galahad for whom she's searched her whole life long. The Galahad she's created out of whole cloth.

Finito's tactical shift presents Abigail with a simple choice. She can cut him loose or she can hang on, make compromises, pay to play. Finito has already told her that he will be unemployed by the end of the week, that the city funds needed to run the drug treatment center have been cut from the budget. Hence their relationship is in jeopardy because he can no longer carry his share of the economic load. He can no longer keep up and is far too much the macho Latino to accept her charity.

Against the wall farthest from the entrance to Sal's Tavern, a gleaming potbellied jukebox rests in a niche of glazed brick. As

Frank Sinatra eases into "The Lady Is a Tramp," its red and blue lights begin to flash. Finito reaches under the table to stroke the back of Abigail Stoph's hand where it rests in her lap. The rush of puppy-dog gratitude that floods her eyes is so comical, it's all he can do not to laugh in her face.

When they return to Abby's apartment two hours later, Abby removes one of the most prized of her many prized possessions from its place on the wall. She seems happy at the moment, perhaps because Christine Knack is Brooklyn-bound on the N train.

"Let's smoke a peace pipe," she tells Finito. "I bought some pot today, from a friend at the hospital."

The prize possession Abby offers to Finito is, in fact, an exact replica of a Sioux peace pipe dating back to the 1830s. Little more than a hollow reed, its stone bowl is joined to one end of the stem by a thin, tightly wound strip of rawhide. Tied beneath the bowl, five white feathers scatter dust as the pipe is passed.

Finito pushes the feathers aside, then runs his finger over the blade of a stone hatchet. He finds its edge dull and rough, but nevertheless imagines, just for an instant, driving it into Abby's skull. This fantasy is due only in part to his ongoing frustration. For the past several days, as he trolled the Brooklyn neighborhoods of Canarsie, Sheepshead Bay and Gravesend, he was unable to shake the many images of knives slicing through human flesh that flooded his consciousness. That and the sense that manual strangulation is too humane for his tastes.

"You can't light it and smoke it at the same time," Abby explains. "It's too long. That's why it's called a peace pipe. Because it has to be shared."

"And what's this for?" Finito again strokes the hatchet's blade. "In case the peace don't work out?"

"The hatchet is the most interesting part," Abby lectures. "When you extend the peace pipe to your enemy, you show your trust. Just imagine it, Georgie. Imagine handing a deadly weapon to your worst enemy. Imagine you live in a world without police departments and courts, where you have to set the rules."

Although Finito is not too thrilled with part A, part B definitely has appeal. Smiling, he extends the business end of the pipe to Abby. "You first."

Abby touches the pipe to her lips, then lowers it before Finito can strike a match. "I don't wanna fight with you, Georgie," she says. "I'm so sorry you lost your job, but we can get through this together. You'll find work soon enough. You mustn't be discouraged."

Music to Finito's ears. "I have another problem," he declares as Abby takes the first hit. "My *Tía* Suzanna, she's real sick. She needs an operation, but her doctors are like sayin' she's too old. They're sayin' it's time for her to die."

Finito makes love to Abby a few minutes later, gentle love, tender love. When they finish, he tells her, "I gotta go."

Again, that look of disbelief, of betrayal. And just when it was all getting better.

Try as he might, Finito cannot imagine why he has come to this place. It is one o'clock in the morning and he is lying on a sheet that probably needed washing on the day Rosaria Montes tucked it beneath the mattress. Beside him, Rosaria lies naked, her legs splayed. She is in a deep nod and utterly indifferent to her nakedness, or to Finito's refusing her offer of sex.

Finito is quick to notice this indifference. Maybe, he thinks as he stares up at the ceiling, Rosaria is even relieved. Maybe, to her, I'm just another john, trading dope instead of money for my little piece. Maybe she thinks she got over on me.

Finito's growing resentment is accompanied by a visceral disgust with Rosaria's lifestyle and with the lifestyles of all his fellow crimeys. There was a time, he realizes, when the lives of his middle-class victims seemed far more alien than the roach-ridden apartments where he passed most of his days. But that's all changed now. He can never return to that life.

• • •

Finito rises, walks over to the window and looks out onto Avenue C. Across the street, a kid, no more than fifteen, tags the shutters covering the windows of a storefront business with a can of gold spray paint. The boy is severely obese. He wears a down-filled bomber jacket of bright orange that makes him look like a pumpkin.

Sighing, Finito glances down at his feet. All along, he has felt something special was happening, something totally unexpected. At first he tried to deny that something's existence by pretending that Darlene's murder was the product of a momentary rage. But after Marie Estevez, his eyes were finally opened. Something was growing inside him, something larger, more powerful, and there was no getting around it. Just as there is no getting away from the fact that this larger, more powerful something doesn't much care for soiled sheets and miserable junkie whores. No, Finito Rakowski's something demands better. Hence, when he reverts to his street ways, he dishonors the man he's become. He insults his own power.

A clean break with the past.

These words rise, unbidden, to capture Finito's attention, then remain in place, demanding that he consider the facts at hand. There was nobody around when he entered the building and he did not call before coming over. Nor did he have sex with Rosaria. Then, too, Rosaria has dozens of male friends, most with documented histories of violent behavior. At worst, Finito Rakowski will be one of many suspects. And that's only if the cops bypass the possibility of a burglary gone bad or that Rosaria brought home the wrong trick. Which, in a way, she did.

Finito turns away from the window and begins to undress. Rosaria watches him through sleepy eyes. She smiles as he approaches her bed, opening her legs wide enough to admit him. That she mistakes his intentions is hardly surprising in light of his rampant erection. Nevertheless, the error is fatal.

Finito has not removed his clothing because he wishes to have sex. He has removed his clothing because flesh is so much easier to clean.

The next few days provide Finito with a brief yet sorely needed respite. The tensions in his body loosen, the muscles of his back and neck especially, and he becomes more patient with Abby. Though Rosaria's death was far from perfect, it allows him to resume his hunt without the fear of doing something really stupid. Something that's likely to get him caught.

Or so Finito tells himself as he walks along Grand Avenue in the Queens neighborhood of Maspeth.

It is eight o'clock in the morning and the small delicatessens on Grand Avenue are humming. Finito picks one at random and approaches a burly counterman. The counterman wears a sweat-stained paper cap and he swipes at his forehead with a small white towel. Finally he grunts at Finito without so much as glancing in his direction.

"Yeah?"

"Gimme a toasted corn muffin and a coffee, light and sweet."

A few minutes later, he hands the old lady behind the cash register a five-dollar bill. She counts out his change and forks it over, one machine servicing another.

Finito walks the streets of Maspeth for two hours, then hops a bus running along Metropolitan Avenue. In the neighboring community of Ridgewood, he stops for lunch. As he chews on his rubbery burger and his greasy fries, he turns his attention to the police, as he has been doing more and more often. He is concerned, of course, with avoiding detection, but at the moment, self-preservation is not on his mind.

Instead, he wonders what the cops will think of him when they put it all together. They will hate him, of course, as they already hate him and anyone like him. The difference is that now they do not fear him, now he is just another mutt who needs to be slapped down from time to time. That will all change. Eventually, when his exploits becomes known, they will fear him enough to send an army of cops after his narrow ass.

But the cop army will not succeed. They will never track him from behind. He is too smart for that, too careful. If he is taken down, it will be at the scene of a fresh kill.

That settled, Finito pushes aside the very memory of the semen he left at the Estevez scene, or the small cut to the knuckle of his right index finger. Nor does he ask himself the most important question of all: Why does he make it so easy for the cops by covering his victims' eyes? Why does he virtually announce his identity? What does he hope to accomplish?

If Finito could ask himself this last question, if he were pressed, for example, by some mean-spirited psychiatrist, he would have a number of answers ready to hand. The calm evaluating gaze of the psychiatrist, for one, and the universal contempt in the eyes of the screws and the pigs who defined the outer limits of his behavior. From there he could move, with only minimal effort, to the speculative lust in the eyes of the chicken hawks who cruised the West Side piers when he'd worked that stroll as an adolescent prostitute. If you were smart, you played to their lust, fanning those fires by pretending you wanted them to tear you apart. That way they finished a lot quicker.

"Yes, yes, yes. Geeeeve eet to me."

Pressed still further, Finito might recall the dismissal apparent in the eyes of the many teachers who'd written him off, or of Judy Tannenbaum, who watched him the way a laboratory assistant might watch a rat in a maze. Still very much a little boy when he came to the Tannenbaums, Finito had entertained hopes that stretched all the way to adoption. Judy Tannenbaum's unblinking stare had quickly rendered those hopes stillborn.

Beyond this Finito cannot go, although one more set of

memories remains to be explored. These are incidents that took place early in Finito's life, before he had any framework within which to place them. He is in his mother's arms, staring up at her face. His mother rarely looks down (as she rarely holds him), but on those few occasions when she does glance in his direction, the utter loathing in her gaze inspires a terror he has carried with him for all of his life.

TWELVE

DO I HAVE BALLS? Finito asks himself later that night as he sits on Abby's couch, watching Abby's television. He knows this is what it boils down to. *Cojones*, pure and simple.

Breaking into the detached, single-family house he discovered on his stroll through Ridgewood would solve a number of the problems he's been considering over the past month. But there's a downside, naturally. For a very short time, he will be exposed to the prying eyes of neighbors while in possession of a deadly weapon. This could lead, he freely admits, to what his parole officer used to call a "negative outcome."

"Georgie?"

Startled, Finito looks away from the basketball game running on the small TV set. "What's up?" he asks.

"Can we talk?"

Finito smiles. She is wary of him now, of the off-and-on displays of what she calls "your bad temper." Little does she know how bad that temper can get.

"Hey, I'm chillin' here," he halfheartedly protests. "I'm escapin' from my problems. You should be glad I'm not self-medicating."

Abby takes encouragement from his tone. She laughs and sits on the couch beside him. "I'm serious," she declares.

Finito puts his arm around her shoulder and pulls her against him. "So tell me, what's up?"

When she says, "It's about work," Finito quickly tunes out. Over the time they've been together, he's acquired the skill of listening to Abby just closely enough to ask an occasional question, to keep her going while his own mind turns to more important matters. That she seems happy with this arrangement doesn't surprise him. It's her own voice, after all, and her own opinions that most interest her.

"I spoke to a friend at the hospital," Abby says. "Her name is Gail and she's a totally good-hearted person. She volunteers at a food pantry on Houston Street, and she's trying to adopt an orphan from Liberia. Anyway, Gail's an emergency room nurse and she sees a lot of overdoses. The overdoses get referred to the social worker, Marv Hammel. Marv's . . ."

Finito had recognized the potential almost instantly. It was five-thirty, the sun having set an hour before, and he'd been going since one o'clock, keeping at all times within a few blocks of the elevated subway on Myrtle Avenue.

His afternoon, up to that point, had been unproductive. The neighborhood of Ridgewood, on the Queens side of the Brooklyn-Queens border, was created early in the twentieth century as a residential community for the working classes. All to the good, because Finito had no interest in commercial or industrial properties. The roll he lifted from the woman on the L train six days before had totaled a bit over three thousand dollars, twenty-five hundred of which he still had.

But if Ridgewood's residential character meant lots of houses and low-rise apartment buildings, the working-class nature of that housing presented many difficulties. The apartment buildings were no taller than five stories and were served by a single stairway in the center of the building, with the apartments giving out directly onto the landings. Under these circumstances, lying in wait, as he had at Jennifer Denning's, was not an option.

The two- and three-family houses, and the scattering of single-family homes, were troublesome as well. For the most part they were attached, one to another, so that access could only be had through the front and rear, while their first-floor windows were protected by steel grates. True, the grates could be defeated with a simple pry bar, but the effort would require too much time and make too much noise to be attempted from the front or rear, which were exposed on three sides.

Though discouraged, Finito had continued on through the afternoon, doggedly persisting until everything came together at five-thirty. He'd been walking on Menahan Street off Woodward Avenue, just looking around, when a late-model Volkswagen turned into the block. The Volkswagen cruised in Finito's direction for a hundred yards before making a left into a small driveway, then coming to a stop before a stockade fence. The fence was over six feet high and concealed a narrow strip of grass between the house and a four-story apartment building to the north. Once over the fence, Finito would be shielded on three sides as he worked.

A man and a woman exited the car and walked up to the front door of the house. The man carried a bag of groceries, and he waited impatiently while the woman fished in her purse for the keys. Both man and woman were Asian, but that wasn't important to Finito. He was far more interested in the woman's age and general attractiveness, both of which he pronounced satisfactory, and in the absence of children.

If that isn't good enough, Finito tells himself as Abby winds up her pitch, he will have to give up on Ridgewood, and on a number of similar neighborhoods scattered through Queens and Brooklyn. The final judgment will be made on the following morning, when he again cruises Menahan Street.

"So what do you think? Sound like a good idea?" Abby has secured for her lover, through a friend of a friend's friend, the possibility of a job interview at a drug treatment center in Harlem. All Finito need do is phone the director, Juan Astasio, for an appointment.

Finito delivers a response prepared well in advance. That Abby would meddle was a foregone conclusion.

"Hey, baby." He pulls Abby closer, then slides his hand inside her blouse. Abby is braless, and his hand covers her small breast completely. "First, until the end of the week, I still got a job, remember? Plus, I deal with other centers all the time. I could get an interview with Juan Astasio on my own." He rolls his palm over her nipple. "*¿Comprende?*"

Abby places her hand over Finito's. "I'm just trying to help," she declares.

"I know that."

Finito slides off the couch, then lowers Abby's head to the padded armrest. He stares into her eyes, his gaze so intense they might be the only two people in the world.

"Just that you're here for me is enough help," he explains. "That you're here for me is all the help I need."

As he slowly unbuttons Abby's blouse, his eyes never leaving hers, he reminds himself that Abby has spent her whole life needing to believe in lies, and that no matter how many times life smacks her down, she will go on believing. Wanting to believe is what makes her so easy. Wanting to believe is the monkey on her back. In order to control Abby, all he has to do is offer the monkey a little treat from time to time.

"I love you, Georgie," Abby declares, her breath already coming in short heaves. "I'm crazy for you."

THIRTEEN

Wednesday, February 13

PUDGE PEDERSSON HESITATED for just a moment at the top of the stairs. Ahead of him, a short hallway led to a bathroom in which a cop from CSU was busy working. To his right, a pair of bedrooms fed onto the hallway. The first, according to the locals who'd briefed him outside, held the body of a woman named Arlene Ying. The second, at the far end of the hall, contained the body of her husband, Leonard.

When Pudge finally looked into the first bedroom, he found Arlene Ying lying prone on the room's only bed. Her mouth and eyes were covered with strips of fabric torn from a yellow sheet. A ligature mark, very thin, encircled her neck. The ligature had been created from the draw cord of the vertical blinds covering the room's southernmost window. A length of the same cord had been used to bind her hands behind her back.

Encrusted with dried blood and shreds of dried tissue, the ligature now lay on the rug a few feet from the bed. Pudge Pedersson was careful to step over it as he approached the body. Though the victim had been dead for less than twenty-four hours and the odor of decay had yet to form, he found himself holding his breath.

Arlene Ying was lying facedown with her head turned to the left. Her body was wrapped in a white comforter, from her shoulders to her knees, and her feet hung over the bottom edge of the mattress. At some point, a set of knives had been driven through the comforter into the broad muscles of her lower back, driven with such force that only their matching handles now protruded. Though the comforter was saturated with blood—abundant evidence that her heart had continued to pump for some time after she was stabbed—the room itself, including the rest of the bedding, was clean.

Satisfied with these observations, Pudge Pedersson backed into the hall, reminding himself that he and Belinda were in Ridgewood strictly on forbearance. They'd been summoned, for reasons still to be discovered, by Captain Meyer Wideman, who'd met them at the door.

"Take a quick look around," he'd ordered without turning away from a sergeant holding a plastic clipboard. "Then come back to me."

With Belinda nowhere in sight, Pudge turned his attention to Leonard Ying's bedroom. He began by scanning the berber carpeting for any item that should not be stepped on. At first glance he registered no obstacle, and he was about to enter the room when he noticed a series of faint smudges running in a line from the doorway to the bed.

A woman standing to one side of the bed turned at that moment to reveal a lieutenant's badge, its holder inserted into the breast pocket of her sky-blue coat. In her early forties, her cheekbones and jaw were very prominent, the hollows of her cheeks deep and shadowed. Only her wide, generous mouth saved her from appearing haggard. For one pregnant moment she trained her narrow blue eyes on Pudge. Then she said, "O'Neill, C of D."

Introduction enough. Lieutenant O'Neill was working out

of the chief of detectives' office. She was one of Inspector Carter's minions. "Detective Pedersson," Pudge replied, "from the two-five."

"You the one caught the priors?"

"Me and my partner, Detective Moore."

That was apparently sufficient for O'Neill, who stepped around the smudges as she crossed the room, then slid by Pedersson and walked off down the hall.

Pudge looked back into the room. Leonard Ying was under the covers, with the sheets pulled up to his shoulders and his head covered by a plush cushion. Embroidered with gold chrysanthemums, the cushion's red fabric matched the fabric covering the chairs in the living room downstairs. A hole nearly dead center in the cushion was blackened at the edges and had clearly been made by a bullet.

"Pudge?"

Pedersson turned to find his partner standing next to him. He acknowledged her presence with a nod, then turned his attention to the bathroom. Though the toilet was squeaky clean (a condition he could only envy), the basin of the sink was stained with dried soap. The label on a plastic bottle set on the sink's rim announced: *Après le Bain*/Dry Skin Formula.

Pudge dropped to his knees in the doorway and peered at the bathroom carpet. Though Belinda remained standing, she announced, "Still wet under there, right?"

"Yeah." Pudge rose and brushed off the knees of his trousers. "You check out the other vic, Arlene Ying?"

"I glanced around."

"Did you see any smudges on the carpet?" He gestured to the faint marks on the carpet in Leonard Ying's room. "Like those?"

"Nope, but I found the source."

"Where?"

"In the basement."

Pudge nodded once, then forced his eyes away from Leonard

Ying and onto his partner. The carefully neutral set of Belinda's mouth had been replaced by an obvious tension, and her eyes were blinking rapidly, as though trying to avoid a painful memory. On another occasion, Pudge might have playfully rubbed her nose in it, but not this time. This time he, too, had had enough.

"Whatta ya say," he said, "we go down the basement, take a look?"

"I thought you'd never ask."

Thirty minutes later, after Pudge and Belinda had their ducks in place, the inevitable conference took place in the Yings' basement. The basement was overheated and all present took off their overcoats and laid them on a Ping-Pong table. Then they lined up, Pudge and Belinda on one side of the table, Captain Meyer Wideman and Lieutenant Moira O'Neill on the other.

"Detective Moore," Lieutenant O'Neill demanded, "do you believe this case is related to the Denning and Monette cases?"

"I do," she told O'Neill, her mind already turning to the problem at hand. "I believe all three are linked."

"Why?"

"The doer broke through a grille covering the basement window and—"

"When?"

O'Neill was fairly barking her questions, probably, Belinda guessed, to impress her superior. "When what, lieutenant?"

"When did the perpetrator enter the house, before or after the Yings arrived home at approximately six o'clock yesterday evening?" O'Neill turned her head slightly to look at Belinda out of the corner of her eye.

"Before."

"How do you know?"

Belinda pointed to a guest bedroom thirty feet away. "Right in front of the television set, there's a patch of oily dirt. I don't know what it is exactly, but the doer stepped in it, most likely when he turned on the set or changed the channel. There are good shoe impressions all over the basement, the first floor and into Leonard Ying's bedroom, but not his wife's."

"Which means what?"

"Which means Leonard was killed first and the perpetrator's feet got wiped off in the process." Belinda hesitated for a moment, steeling herself against the next question. When it didn't come, she glanced at Captain Wideman, who had yet to speak. The captain was small and slender, with a full head of wiry gray hair, tufts of which had risen to form little canopies above his scalp. His eyebrows were also gray. Sharply angled, they ascended from the bridge of his nose nearly to his temples, somehow pulling the outer lids of his eyes into their trajectory. The end result was an expression halfway between startled and demented.

"Why don't I just run down the sequence as me and my partner see it," Belinda requested. "Then we can make comparisons."

Wideman took a Ping-Pong ball from beneath a racket and began to roll it in slow circles on the table. "Go ahead," he commanded.

"The perp entered the premises long before the Yings arrived home. He jimmied a grille covering a basement window, then broke a pane of glass to gain entry. At some point he entered the spare bedroom over there and stepped into the oily patch. Then he went upstairs and looked through the house. The Yings probably noticed the stains—the kitchen was freshly mopped and parts of the rug look as though they were recently vacuumed. But they either didn't check it out or the perpetrator was well hidden."

Belinda looked from Wideman to O'Neill, and finally over to Pudge. If Pudge was upset, he didn't show it. He seemed intent now, perhaps understanding that it really didn't matter who did the persuading, as long as the bosses were persuaded.

"At some point the Yings retired for the night. Leonard Ying went to his own bedroom, undressed and climbed into bed. We know he slept alone because there's only a single bed in the room. Arlene Ying went into the shower. The condition of the bathroom, the after-bath lotion and the open medicine chest make that clear. It was right about this time, with Leonard in his bed and Arlene in the shower, that the perp came upstairs for the second time. The smudges on the carpet indicate that he walked across the living room, straying only far enough to take a pillow from the couch, then up the stairs to Leonard's room. There he placed the cushion over Leonard's head and shot him through it."

Suddenly aware that her breathing was extremely shallow, and that she was almost whispering, Belinda lapsed into silence. She didn't, she realized, want to say the next part aloud. It was bad enough having to think it.

"Is that the whole story?" O'Neill asked.

"No," Belinda said, "there's more." She raised her eyes to meet O'Neill's. "From the bathroom, he forced Arlene Ying down the hall and into the bedroom. Most likely he used the gun because there's no sign of a struggle, not even when he bound her hands and gagged her, not even when he blindfolded her. By then, of course, she was helpless. There was nothing she could do when he tightened the ligature around her throat as he sexually assaulted her."

"You can't know that," O'Neill said. "The body hasn't even been examined."

"But I do know it," Belinda said. "I know it and you know it too. He tightened and loosened that ligature, brought her to the brink of death, then back again. How many times? Maybe until he couldn't get it up anymore. Maybe until he needed a fresh thrill, a real show-stopper, the grand fucking finale. Wrapping Arlene Ying in that comforter? Driving those knives into her back? For this scumbag, it was the perfect end to a perfect day."

Nobody spoke for a moment. They were cops, after all. They were not supposed to openly talk of the victims, of lives that would not be lived, of fear that exploded into terror, of pain that exceeded human endurance. This peculiar business of theirs wasn't about emotion. This business was about logic, and about a suspicion that cut deep into your soul, a suspicion generally referred to as gut instinct.

When Pudge Pedersson at last found his voice, it turned out to be much softer, and more circumspect, than he would have believed possible. To a certain extent, Belinda had taken the wind out of his sails. "The entire scene," he announced, "shows evidence of extreme caution. The window he broke through to gain entry, it's behind a fence and concealed even from the building next door by shrubbery. Once inside, he checked out the house before the victims arrived to make sure there were no surprises." As he warmed up, Pudge began to tick the items off on sausage-thick fingers. "He hid himself for hours, until the victims went upstairs. He brought a cushion from downstairs and shot Leonard Ying through it to avoid blowback. He wrapped Arlene Ying in a comforter so he wouldn't be hit by blood spatter. That's also why the knives were driven in once, and not pulled out."

Wideman took the stub of a cigar from the breast pocket of his gray suit, stuck it in his mouth, but did not light up. "Fine, what else?"

"The blindfold, captain. The perp didn't blindfold Arlene Ying to prevent a later ID. He knew he was gonna kill her, just like he'd already killed her husband. The blindfold was strictly for his own benefit. Like the way he covered the faces of Monette and Denning—"

"It's funny," O'Neill interrupted, "how you failed to account for the differences between these crimes. Like Jennifer Denning and Monette were presented with overwhelming force as they entered their homes while the killer lingered for hours at the Yings. Like Denning and Monette were victims of opportunity while the Yings were probably stalked. Like Denning and Monette were suffocated while Arlene Ying was stabbed and her husband shot. Like Denning's and Monette's faces were carefully covered, Monette's elaborately, while Arlene Ying was merely blindfolded and gagged."

Though O'Neill paused for breath, she did not take her eyes off Pudge Pedersson until her boss yanked her chain. "Enough already," he said, "we're wastin' time. Tomorrow morning, eight o'clock, you report to 137 West Fourteenth Street, to the task force on the third floor. There'll be printouts of all open homicides for the past two years on your desks." Wideman raised his chin and leaned toward Pudge. "You remember how you told me this guy killed before? You remember how you told me that you and your partner were in agreement? Well, you're gonna get the chance to prove your point, detective. If there's a link somewhere, I want you to find it. You'll report directly to Lieutenant O'Neill."

There followed an extended pause during which neither Pudge nor Belinda, as both understood, was supposed to speak. Nevertheless, Pudge took advantage of the momentary silence to ask a question he was not supposed to ask.

"What about Eddie Schwann?"

Wideman's eyebrows rose to such heights of agitation that they formed two nearly vertical lines on his forehead. "Eddie Schwann," he told Pudge, "is in the DA's hands, and the DA's not lettin' go. You wanna get Schwann off the hook, do your job."

"Yes, sir. Is that all?"

"No, it's not. On your way back to the two-five, I want you to make a stop, check out a homicide on Avenue C. Tomorrow morning, report your findings to Lieutenant O'Neill." Wideman took his coat from the Ping-Pong table and draped it over his arm. "And one more thing, detectives. You talk to the press, I'll rip your hearts out. Understand me?"

This time Belinda and Pudge had no trouble formulating the desired response. "Yes, sir," they declared, virtually in unison.

FOURTEEN

THE TENEMENT ON THE NORTHWEST CORNER of Avenue C and Seventh Street was a definite throwback, the exception to the Lower East Side's gentrified rule. That much was evident to Belinda and Pudge at a glance. The rotting wood-frame windows were covered on the inside, not with vertical blinds or pleated drapes, but with bedspreads and sheets nailed to the frames.

Detective Benedicto Cordova from the Ninth Precinct met them at the corner. He'd been assigned this duty by his supervising lieutenant at the request of Inspector Frank Carter, who spoke for the chief of detectives.

Fast approaching middle age, Cordova was carrying nearly as much extra weight around his middle as Pudge Pedersson. Cordova's well-lined face, though, was a good deal warmer, and his smile more ready. Rosaria Montes, the victim, he explained as he led Pudge and Belinda into a small lobby, had been murdered two days before and her body had long ago been removed to the morgue on First Avenue. Plus, the Crime Scene Unit had been through the scene, so the chaos Pudge and Belinda would view was not the chaos presented to the first responding detectives. In fact, there was no good reason why their business could not have been conducted in the precinct squad room where a mountain of paperwork awaited his immediate attention.

Though neither Pudge nor Belinda chose to dispute the facts

as Cordova presented them, they doggedly continued up two sets of stairs to apartment 3C, then waited patiently while Cordova tore away the yellow tape crisscrossing the door.

Belinda preceded her partner into the one-room apartment, certain there were no dead bodies lying in wait. Her eyes jumped immediately to the blood spatter on the lower part of the wall to her left, then to a much fainter blood trail leading into the bathroom.

"There was a mattress and box spring on the floor over in the corner," Cordova informed them, "right beneath the spatter on the wall. CSU took them, along with the bedding and a pair of bloody pillows. They confiscated drugs and drug paraphernalia as well."

"Any sign of forced entry?" Belinda asked.

"Nope." Cordova shifted from one foot to another. "The victim was beaten severely about the face, as you can see from the spatter, and manually strangled." He pointed to the blood trail on the wood floor. "At some point, the perp stepped into the blood. We got a print of his right heel that'll make a confession irrelevant if we ever get our hands on him."

Cordova pointed toward the bathroom. "The blood trail leads from the body into the bathroom, where the doer took a shower. We know because we found traces of human blood in the trap, a ton of hairs, too. I swear, the trap in the tub wasn't cleaned out in a decade."

"Any sign—"

"Wait, that's not the best part. After he showered, he went back to the vic and rolled her onto her face. At least that's the way we figure it. Montes had evidence of lividity in her shoulders and buttocks, so she must have been lying on her back for a short time after she was killed, then turned over."

"Turned her over how? How was she lying when you found her?"

"Facedown on the mattress. The impression of her face on the sheet, it was like the Turin Shroud, only in Technicolor."

Belinda nodded to herself. Now she knew why they'd been

sent over. The bosses had been covering their asses by reviewing every new homicide. "Any sign of sexual assault?"

"No trauma, but if her and the perp were acquainted, there might have been consensual sex. That's for the ME to determine." Cordova hesitated briefly, then said, "We did a few preliminary interviews with Rosaria's relatives. According to one and all, she was the black sheep of her family. Hung around with the wrong crew, did drugs, never had a job in her life. Her mother gave me a couple of names and I already checked them out. We're talkin' about serious rap sheets here, real bad boys."

Without warning, Cordova drew a breath, then clapped his hands together. "Anyway, I'm kinda late for dinner, so . . . Wait a minute, I almost forgot. A speck of tissue caught between Rosaria's incisors. Could be a piece of rare steak, but I'm betting it came from one of the perp's knuckles. The sample's off for DNA testing even as we speak."

"And how long," Belinda asked, "until you get results?"

Cordova grinned. "Now that depends. If the request originates in the precinct, we're looking at a month at least. On the other hand, if the request comes from the chief of detectives, it could be a lot shorter." He stopped for a moment, his grin expanding, as if some random thought had reached out to tickle his funny bone. "It's really not up to me, now, is it?" he concluded.

On the following morning, at seven-thirty, Pudge walked into the headquarters of Operation Intercept on the third floor of a nondescript office building on West Fourteenth Street. A harried civilian employee acting as receptionist met him in the first of a series of offices running across the southern face of the building. The civilian employee, who wore an ID from the chief of detectives' office identifying him as Clarence Thurman, was surrounded by a dozen cops of varying gender, race, and age. Like Pudge, these cops had been assigned to the Operation Intercept task force.

Thurman was dealing with them one at a time, checking each

name against a typed list, then creating an ID card on a type-writer. As Thurman's typing skills were limited at best, Pudge settled down for a long wait.

Thirty minutes later, his new ID pinned to the breast of his best suit, Pudge stepped through a door at the back of the reception room into a long hallway. Eight separate offices fed onto this hallway. In the first of these, Captain Wideman and Lieutenant O'Neill sat behind their respective desks. O'Neill looked up as he passed.

"Your office is in the back," she said. "Get settled and come back to me." When Pudge turned away, she fired a parting shot. "Your partner," she announced, "has been here for a half hour."

Pudge looked at his watch. It was two minutes after eight.

The basic setup, in Belinda's judgment, had advantages and disadvantages. As recently as two weeks before, the offices now housing Operation Intercept had been occupied by the Department of Administrative Services. Hence the furniture was in place, the phones and fax machines still up and running. There was even a computer on her desk, and one on Pudge's as well. True, the software in these computers was unrelated to their needs, but it was definitely a start. They might easily have begun with empty rooms.

But there was another side as well. Large, open spaces, she knew from experience, facilitate communication between the various elements of a task force. Now those elements would be largely self-contained and the natural tendency of cops from different units to hoard information would likely rear its ugly head. The question, in Belinda's mind, was centered squarely on the bosses: O'Neill, Wideman and Carter. It was quite possible, even likely, that they wanted to control the flow of information, and the best way to do that was by preventing information from flowing any way but up.

"So, have you been with the detectives long?"

Belinda turned to a man sitting before a desk set against the opposite wall. His name, she knew already, was Marlon Kearn, and he was a detective-lieutenant assigned to supervisory duty with the Crime Scene Unit. His job at Operation Intercept was to track evidence gathered at the scenes of the various homicides, then sent off to laboratories, public and private, including the FBI's lab at Quantico.

Kearn would, as he explained it, contact these labs daily, alternately requesting, demanding, begging or groveling in an effort to have the hundreds of samples handled with dispatch. Finally he would bring all results directly to Lieutenant Moira O'Neill.

"I've been a detective five years," Belinda replied.

Kearn smiled and cocked his head to one side. Somewhere in his late twenties, he was a light-skinned black man with a broad nose, a broader smile and a jutting chin. The tortoise-shell frames of his glasses were small and almost perfectly rectangular.

"I wanted to do investigations once upon a time," he explained. "But I don't know, there's something about lint that turns a man on." Kearn's laughter ceased abruptly when Pudge Pedersson entered the room. "Damn, man," he said after a minute, "I think I just climbed the beanstalk."

"Fred Pedersson," Pudge said. He was so distracted, he barely registered Marlon Kearn's name when the man gave it. "Lieutenant O'Neill requests our presence," he told his partner. "Forthwith."

"Why don't you handle it." Belinda held up a printout for her partner's inspection. The printout contained basic information on the 431 unsolved homicides occurring in the City of New York over the prior two years. The list had been compiled by the Homicide Statistics Section of the chief of detectives' office and passed to Belinda, along with a second copy, by Lieutenant O'Neill.

"They include everyone, Pudge. Men, women, children, black,

white, Latino, and Asian. We're gonna have to go through the list and prioritize. I'd better get started."

Pedersson stared down at his seated partner. Something was bothering her, that was obvious, and most likely that something was unrelated to their work. Well, it was her turn. Pudge had dealt with his own problem by hiring a crew, at a cost of three hundred dollars, to clean his apartment. Once they were done, he would see to a paint job and replace the worst of his furniture. On this, he and Belinda were in complete accord. When he'd announced his decision, she'd thought it over briefly, then declared, "I guess you really do love the widow, Pudge. Praise the Lord. Or Buddha, or Krishna, or whoever Annie's worshiping at the moment."

"Demeter," Pudge had replied.

"Demeter?"

"She's Greek." Pudge's tiny smile gradually expanded into a grin of such pure delight it might have come from an infant. "The goddess of fertility."

Lieutenant Moira O'Neill did not broach the subject of Belinda Moore's absence, favoring Pudge Pedersson, instead, with a very faint smile that reminded him of the testicle-shriveling sneer beloved of his Great-Aunt Margaret.

"You can assume that I'm familiar with the Montes crime scene and proceed from there," O'Neill commanded, her smile fading not a whit.

"There's only one element in the Montes crime scene that links it to the others," Pudge began. "Montes was deliberately turned facedown on the mattress at least forty minutes after she was killed. Why would her attacker do that? The blood trail indicates that he showered a few minutes after she died and that he returned to the body later. Was there something underneath her, something he had to retrieve? Or did she die with her eyes open? Was she looking at him? Did her eyes make him uncomfortable?

Did Jennifer Denning's eyes make him uncomfortable? Elly Monette's? Arlene Ying's?"

Pudge stopped long enough to draw a breath, then again sprang forward. "The difference here is that the killer probably knew his victim. There's no sign of forced entry and nothing was stolen, not even the drugs which the locals found in the apartment. More important, the perp was comfortable enough in those surroundings to shower before he left. The heelprint makes it likely he took off his clothes before he showered, and just possible that he was nude when he killed Rosaria. Since she was unrestrained at the time . . ."

Lost in thought, Pudge scratched at an eyebrow for a moment as he organized his thoughts, unaware that O'Neil's smile had broadened and now appeared almost fond.

"There's another big difference here, too. Montes's attacker made serious mistakes. He left a detailed footprint, which will eventually bury him, and probable DNA evidence. My sense is that he didn't know what he was gonna do a minute before he did it, that he went off without warning. The doer at the other scenes was much less impulsive."

"Why? What led him to be so careless?"

O'Neill folded her arms beneath her breasts and leaned back slightly. What Pudge hadn't said, because he presumed that O'Neill already knew it, was that arresting Rosaria Montes's killer would not mark the end of Operation Intercept, even if the same man had also murdered Denning, Monette, and the Yings. Given the obvious disparities among the homicides, the search would have to continue even though it was destined to produce no results. Since O'Neill's career, Wideman's as well, depended on the success of Operation Intercept, this outcome was unacceptable, a fact that O'Neill's frown clearly reflected.

"Anything else?" she asked.

"Yeah, the local who caught the case, Cordova. From what I can tell, he seems pretty sharp."

"Alright, detective, you can go back to what you were doing."
O'Neill waited until Pudge was almost through the doorway to
add, "And tell your partner that I hope she resolves whatever
conflict precluded her presence at this meeting."

Belinda didn't get around to describing the conflict in question
until she and Pudge broke for a quick lunch at noon. They'd
spent most of the morning discussing how to prioritize the list
of unsolved homicides on each of their desks. Could they
assume, for instance, that all prior killings were of females? If so,
of what age and race? Could they eliminate the septuagenarian
murdered in a Harlem apartment? And what about the eighteen-
year-old killed on the Upper East Side, and the twelve-year-old
whose body was discovered in the Bronx Botanical Gardens?
And exactly what would they look for in the cases they finally
selected? If the doer's MO was changing over time, as both
believed, a prior homicide might be hard to recognize.

Regarding the latter problem, they decided to concentrate on
the elements present in the Denning homicide simply because it
was the earliest. Those elements included the covering of the
victim's face, a crime of opportunity, a blitz attack and manual
strangulation. Of these, the printout was useful only in a single
respect, cause of death. For the rest, they would have to consult
the case files compiled by the many detectives who'd investigated the various homicides.

As an anorexic-thin waitress in a black nylon uniform set a
chiliburger deluxe on the table in front of him, Pudge watched
his partner carefully. Something was upsetting her, that was certain. She'd been out of touch all morning, concentrating on her
work to the exclusion of everything else, including his own little
witticisms which usually elicited at least the flicker of a smile.
Now she was toying with her tuna fish platter, rolling the olive
across the tomato slice.

"You wanna tell me what's up?" he asked as he grasped his burger with both hands and leaned far forward in an attempt to avoid dripping chili onto his suit, shirt or tie.

"Your chin," Belinda replied.

"My chin is up?"

"You got chili on your chin."

Pudge swiped at his jaw with a paper napkin. When it came back clean, he asked, "Where?"

"It's on your tie now."

"Forget the chili, Belinda. You're not gonna distract me. If you don't wanna talk about what's bothering you, fine. Just say so."

Belinda sighed. "It's about my cousin, Ahmed Brown." She looked down at her poached eggs for a moment, her right index finger making a little circle, as if preparing for takeoff. As usual, she was dieting. "Ahmed," she finally told Pudge, "he was gonna be the one. You know, the great success. Graduated from Stuyvesant High a year early. Got admitted to Columbia on a full scholarship. Started doin' drugs in his freshman year. Quit school for good in his sophomore year. Since then, he's been in and out of drug rehab five times, and if it wasn't for the family hiring the right lawyer, he'd be a convicted felon."

Pudge knew better then to offer an opinion without being asked. His partner was talking about her family, whose intrigues rivaled those of the Vatican. Close as he was to Belinda, there was no way he could maintain his footing on those treacherous sands, and he knew it.

"So how does this affect you?" he asked, his tone mildly curious.

"Ahmed hangs around with fashion people, club people, actors, artists. He sees himself as a talented guy who can't catch a break, not as the degenerate junkie he really is. The problem is that he's got the family eating out of his hand, including my folks. Ahmed's my mother's sister's boy."

"Same question," Pudge said when Belinda ground to a halt. "What's all this have to do with you?"

"A month ago, Ahmed comes out of a residential treatment program and announces he's seen the light. No more drugs, ever again. Now he wants to open a restaurant in TriBeCa. Never mind the boy hasn't got two dimes to rub together, is currently livin' with his mother, and never did a full day's work in his life. He's ready for the big time. All he needs is a little help which, according to my parents, the family should supply in the form of a loan."

Pudge jammed his burger into his mouth and took a quick bite, mainly to avoid smiling. "And what's your end of the loan?"

"Ten grand."

"Gimme that again?"

"You heard right, Pudge. And the thing is, me and Ralph, we're gonna lose no matter what we do. If we give him the money, he's not gonna pay us back. If we don't come across, then we're the bad guys." She shook her head in disgust, imagining the fault lines behind which various members of the clan would align themselves. Her own status was of particular concern to her. Belinda's mother was the family's acknowledged matriarch, a position to which Belinda, at least at times, aspired.

Pudge put the burger down and wiped his fingers. "You want my opinion?" he asked, the question far from rhetorical.

"Yeah," Belinda said, "I do."

"If you're gonna get hurt either way, I don't see the point in making the loan and losing the money, too."

Belinda looked at her partner for a moment, then burst out laughing. "You thought we were gonna give that junkie our money? The money that me and Ralph worked our sorry butts off all our lives to get? Is that what you thought?"

"I did entertain the idea," Pudge admitted.

"Damn, Pudge, you're even crazier than you look." Belinda picked up her fork and punctured the yolks of her poached eggs. "What I think I'm gonna do is work on Ralph's mom and pop.

They want us to go in with them on a summer house in the Poconos, but we can't do that if we make the loan to Ahmed. My folks and Ralph's are thick as thieves, so if I get them talking to each other, cause a little delay, maybe Ahmed'll screw up again before any money changes hands."

Satisfied with her strategy, Belinda dug her fork into a mound of tuna fish and began to eat. Leaving Pudge Pedersson to wonder, as men have often wondered, exactly what he was doing there in the first place.

FIFTEEN

AFTER MERELY GLANCING at the photo proffered by Detective-Lieutenant Timothy Doyle, Pudge and Belinda had no doubt, none whatever. The photo was of a murdered prostitute named Darlene Melody Crowder. Crowder was posed as the cops had found her, lying on her back, a white garbage bag covering her face. According to the medical examiner, she'd been manually strangled.

"What was in the bag?" Pudge asked. They were comfortably seated in Doyle's office at the Forty-first Precinct on Longwood Avenue in the South Bronx.

"Household garbage," Doyle replied.

"Traceable?" Pudge asked.

"There were some letters inside, unpaid bills mostly. We ran down the addressee, who has a solid alibi for the time of the murder. Plus the bag was filthy, like it'd been there for months." Doyle shrugged a pair of narrow shoulders. "People in Hunts Point, they don't worry all that much about keeping the streets clean."

Pudge glanced at Belinda who maintained a neutral expression, her hands lying flat in her lap. Though Pudge was having the time of his life, barging into lieutenants' offices, throwing around Operation Intercept's collective weight, Belinda would have been happy to return to the simple life at the two-five. They'd been reviewing homicide case files for the better part of two weeks, examining both crime scene and autopsy photos. Simply put, the carnage had begun to overwhelm her.

The pressure from above was unrelenting as well. The Break-in Killer, as he'd come to be called by the media, was an explosion waiting to happen. Thus far, the reporting had been fairly positive, limited as it was to information distributed by the Detective Bureau's Public Information Division. That would change with the next killing and all concerned knew it.

Nevertheless, at every press conference, and there had been many, the reporters were told that massive resources had already been deployed in an effort to apprehend the killer. Homicide Division was investigating the individual murders, pursuing every lead, no matter how remote. Precinct detectives were conducting massive canvasses in Ridgewood, the Upper West Side and Morningside Heights. Statistics Division, under the supervision of the Hostage Negotiating Team, was staffing an extremely active hot line on a twenty-four/seven basis. The Crime Scene Unit was collecting and collating every scintilla of trace evidence turned over to the NYPD's lab.

What the reporters weren't told—and what they'd failed to realize—was that each of these units, teams, and divisions was under the direct command of the chief of detectives, that they were merely bits and pieces of the Detective Bureau. This also held true for Emilio Venezia, the NYPD's criminal profiler.

Belinda repressed a smile at the memory. Venezia's preliminary analysis of the three murders had matched the analysis Pudge had offered to the bosses nearly point for point, without giving him any credit, or even so much as mentioning his name. The killer, Venezia lectured, was a light-skinned Latino or white male between twenty-five and thirty-five years old with good upper-body strength. He had a long criminal history consisting mostly of petty offenses, and would travel on foot or by mass transit. His verbal skills would be superior, though he was poorly educated, and he would be especially glib around women. Finally, when apprehended, he would not deny himself the celebrity associated with a public trial by confessing.

The one piece of good news in all of this, Belinda thought as she watched her partner riffle through the case file, was that the profiler had unequivocally linked Elly Monette's murder to those of Jennifer Denning and Arlene Ying. As a result, Eddie Schwann had been released without bail pending further investigation.

"Any suspects?" Pudge asked Timothy Doyle after a preliminary look at the case file.

"Only the obvious one." Doyle smiled for the first time, his pale eyelashes fluttering. "Her pimp. But there's no physical evidence tying him to the crime, and three witnesses have come forward to provide him with an alibi."

"Did you sweat him?"

"For six hours. He held up."

The issue settled, Pudge and Belinda rooted through a stack of DD5 supplemental report forms for another hour. Universally called fives, these reports include virtually anything detectives do in the course of an investigation. In theory, the progress of a case (or lack thereof) can be followed simply by reading the fives.

As Belinda read through the file, it occurred to her, and not for the first time, that her and Pudge's task would be made a lot easier if they enlisted the aid of the detectives who'd conducted the original investigations. But Lieutenant O'Neill's directions had been straightforward. They weren't to trust these detectives, who might not be competent, or even truthful. They were to examine the case files and draw their own conclusions.

There was wisdom in O'Neill's instructions, no doubt, but as the various case files were scattered across the five boroughs (and they were occasionally drafted for hot line duty), the going was slow indeed.

Nevertheless, Pudge and Belinda had proven themselves correct on the first of their predictions. The Break-in Killer had struck at least once before he happened upon Jennifer Denning. Their second prediction, however, that he was likely to have made fatal mistakes in the process, remained to be demonstrated. Certainly there was no smoking gun in the case file Belinda carefully reviewed. But a canvass of the neighborhood had turned up a few potential witnesses who would have to be reinterviewed. She forwarded their fives to her partner as they came up, then watched as he read them carefully before setting them to one side. Always a bad winner, Pudge was trying to repress a gleeful smile.

"Wasn't nobody on that street last July when I seen what I seen," Ronald Martin told Pudge Pedersson and Belinda Moore twenty minutes later. " 'Cept for that ho' and that white boy. Too damn hot to be on the street." Martin slapped the arms of his wheelchair. "Ain't that right, Yolandi?"

Martin's home health aide, Yolandi Thatcher, responded, "Uh-huh," without looking away from her soap opera.

Well into his eighties, Ronald Martin's face had the color and the texture of a walnut. Though he sat straight in the chair, his legs, beneath a green tartan blanket, were obviously withered. Belinda looked into his watery black eyes and saw, for a moment, the eyes of her grandmother in the last years of her life, by turns eager, yearning, determined, regretful and mightily pissed off.

"Maybe you could tell us what you saw, Mr. Martin," she suggested when it became apparent that Martin wasn't prepared to resume on his own.

"I told everythin' I know back then. Ain' I, Yolandi?"

"Uh-huh."

"Don't see why I got to tell it again."

In fact, the DD5 describing the interview with Ronald Martin consisted of a very few coded sentences: b/m wit approx 200 ft away; saw vic meet w/m twenty-five yrs approx 1030 hours; saw vic and perp enter railway tunnel 1035 hours; wit 84 yrs lvs w/aide.

Belinda looked over at Pudge who ducked his head for a moment, then drew a slow breath before meeting Ronald Martin's unblinking gaze.

"We're from the cold-case squad," he explained. "Homicides that go six months without an arrest automatically come to the cold-case squad."

Pudge glanced over Ronald Martin's shoulder, through the window behind him. The man had an unimpeded view of Edgewater Road and the railroad tunnel where Darlene Crowder's body had been discovered. "First thing we do, when me and my partner catch a case, is reinterview the important witnesses. Like yourself. The way it looks, you were the last person to see Darlene Crowder alive." Pudge gave it a good four seconds before adding, "Except for her killer."

Satisfied, apparently, with Pudge's dramatics, Martin grunted once, then began to speak. "Summertime," he began, "this here side of the street is shady in the morning. That's why I sit in the window early on, to get some air. Ain't that right, Yolandi?"

"Watchin' them half-naked girls is what y'all are doin'," Yolandi replied. "Lookin' out that window night and day."

Martin chuckled. "Here I am," he told Pudge, "a poor cripple tryin' to keep his mind in the world, and this is what I get. Glory be to God, but women are some kinda cold." He paused, apparently expecting Pudge to comment. When Pudge wisely held his tongue, Martin simply continued. "I know it was after ten, 'cause Rosie was on the TV. Yolandi about loves that woman, turns on Rosie's show every morning. Ain't that right, Yolandi."

"Uh-huh."

"Now, the woman got killed, she was right across the street, all by her lonesome." Martin turned his attention to Belinda. "Wasn't nobody else on the street, leastways not at first. Just cars and a few trucks goin' by fast. Too damn hot. Then this white boy walks up and she starts comin' on to him. What's her name again?"

"Darlene Crowder," Belinda said.

"Yeah, that's what the cop told me." Martin swiveled the chair so he could look across the street without turning his back on Pudge and Belinda. "The white boy, he makes like he's gonna get in the wind, but Darlene just keeps movin' her mouth and they finally make some kinda deal, 'cause he follows her into the tunnel. Course, it wasn't nothin' I ain't seen before. See it every damn day, matter of fact. Only this time, the white boy come runnin' out five minutes later, which is too quick, but Darlene, she don't come out at all. First I thought she was takin' a leak, you know, like nature calls, but then I knew somethin' bad went down. I figured she maybe got herself cut, bein' as I didn't hear no gunshot." Martin pulled at the already elongated lobe of his right ear, stretching it nearly to his chin. "Thing about it, Darlene was the onliest girl out that day. Hear what I'm sayin'? Most days, when it ain't so hot, there be three, four, five . . . hell, could be a dozen girls workin'. So that white boy, he was just in the right place at the right time. Yessir, he just got lucky."

"He was gawjus," Gladys Rosenthal told Belinda and Pudge. "Just gawjus."

It took Belinda a moment to realize the woman was pronouncing the word "gorgeous." When she did get it, she wondered if maybe gawjus put Filipo Velez's appearance in a category beyond gorgeous. They were standing, she and Pudge, in the offices of C&R Auto Parts Warehouse, conducting a group interview.

"You said he came in looking for work?" Belinda asked. "Did anyone send him?"

"Uh-uh, not that he told me."

"And you didn't think it was strange, somebody wandering in off the street?"

"Nah, it happens once in a while. Hey, you gotta look for work where the work is, right?" The fingernail Gladys thrust in Belinda's direction was a good three inches long. "What surprised me is when he said his name, Filipo Velez. I never woulda made him for no Hispanic, not in a million years." She glanced at the tall, dark-skinned man standing off to her right, then added, "No disrespect, José."

José Arellano endured the disrespect with equanimity, knowing, perhaps, that it came with the territory. Gladys Rosenthal was the boss's sister. "The man," he told Pudge, "came up to me by the loading dock, askin' me if there was any work. He spoke Spanish like he was born—"

Unable to contain himself any longer, Gus Rosenthal interrupted José with a wave of his hand. "Let's cut to the chase, all right?" He stuck a cigar the size of baseball bat in his mouth but did not light up. "I don't care if the jerk came from goddamned Lithuania, he was a mutt. Dirty clothes, built like a brick wall. This is a guy, trust me, you don't wanna meet up with him in a dark alley. And that haircut? It looked like somebody put a bowl on his head then forgot to cut on one side." He looked at Gladys. "Gorgeous? Where's that comin' from?" He snorted once. "As if I didn't know."

"Maybe," Gladys shot back, "starin' at you all day, ya slob, even dirty looks good. Ever think of that?"

"Ya know, Gladys, one day I'm gonna throw your fat ass right out that door."

"Better make sure it's after ya repay the loan I gave ya to start the business with. Otherwise, I'll be comin' back with a lawyer." Gladys turned to Pudge, her eyes widening in indignation. "I'm a junior partner here."

Pudge was tempted to guide the conversation back to Filipo Veldez's appearance on the morning Darlene Crowder was killed by asking if they'd recognize the man should they see him again. But he knew that all three had been to the precinct for a look at the four-one's collection of mug shots and failed to make an identification. What was important was that the general descriptions they'd offered—light hair, light skin, muscular build— matched those given by Ronald Martin and Hobart Marcuse. Gladys Rosenthal had even added a detail by describing Velez's green eyes as "definitely gawjus."

"So, whatta ya think?" Pudge asked his partner. If they hurried, they could make it back to Fourteenth Street before the bosses left for the day. "Time to report to our commanding officers?"

"Past time," Belinda admitted.

If it was up to Pudge Pedersson, he would've danced into Operation Intercept's offices with the words BORN TO BE RIGHT scrawled across his potbelly with a Magic Marker. Pudge was that happy. But it wasn't up to him, as it hadn't been up to him since the day he walked into the Academy fifteen years before. Thus, in lieu of crowing, he and Belinda would mince up to Lieutenant O'Neill's desk where they would maintain respectful expressions at all times. Under no circumstance would they discuss their discovery with their colleagues or with any human being outside the task force. Wideman had made the point decisively when he addressed the assembled task force within hours of its creation.

"Leaks will not be tolerated," he'd explained, his arched brows sweeping over his temples like windshield wipers. "Remember, loose lips sink careers, so keep your mouths shut. Lieutenant O'Neill and myself, as far as you're concerned, we're the only ones who need to know."

Moira O'Neill stared down at the crime scene photograph while

Belinda Moore delivered the report she and Pudge had worked out on the way over. The photo was of Darlene Crowder lying on her back, her face covered with a bag of garbage. Crowder's halter top had been torn in half and lay to either side of her body. Her miniskirt had been yanked above her waist and her red panties down to her knees.

Belinda went on for several minutes before drawing a conclusion. "The MOs in the Denning and Crowder homicides match point for point: a blitz attack, the victim killed immediately, manual strangulation as the cause of death, a hasty search conducted postmortem. Plus, from what Ronald Martin told us, I think it's safe to say this was a crime of opportunity."

Predictably, O'Neill found Belinda's weak point. She held up the photo, then asked, "Are you saying this was a search? Because to me it looks like a rape."

"I realize that." Belinda drew a breath, thinking this was Pudge's idea and now I'm stuck with it. "But we don't believe the perp would stick around long enough to rape her. Too risky. We think he was looking for drugs or money. The pathologist who did the autopsy on Darlene Crowder found no evidence of sexual assault."

With nothing more to say, not before she gauged O'Neill's reaction, Belinda settled back on her heels. O'Neill looked down at the photo, which she'd restored to the desktop, for several seconds.

"You've done good work here, Detective Moore," she finally said. "I admit I had some doubts early on, but you've erased them." She tapped the photo. "Call the four-one, tell them to copy the case file and messenger it over to us. Tell them to do it tonight. Anything else?"

"There is one thing," Pudge said. "Darlene Crowder was killed in early July, Jennifer Denning at the end of December. We think there was a murder in between."

"Is that a problem?"

"It's a problem because we covered that ground before we got to Crowder and there are no likely candidates. At least, not on our list of open homicides."

Though Lieutenant O'Neill smiled, her already narrow eyes tightened into mere slits, as if she were fighting off a headache. "Continue."

"We have to consider the possibility that somebody's been arrested for a crime our perp committed, another Eddie Schwann." Pudge's tone was very deliberate. "We think we should review all closed homicides over the past six months and we should do it right away."

"How long will it take you to work your way through them? Keep in mind, there were more than two hundred homicides in that time period and sixty percent have been closed."

"That's the beauty of it. The Crowder and Denning murders have a number of elements in common, so any murder that occurred between them is very likely to share those elements. We can eliminate males, children, the elderly, and all females who weren't strangled. That should leave us with no more than a couple of dozen possibles."

O'Neill thought it over for a moment, her smile gradually returning. When she finally spoke, she was careful to address Pudge Pedersson. "I need you and your partner," she declared, "to staff the hot line tonight. As for the printouts, I'll have my assistant phone Statistics early tomorrow, get the ball rolling. When I have them, I'll let you know."

SIXTEEN

FOR THE SECOND TIME in two days, Finito Rakowski is impressed. He is standing in the Great Hall of the Metropolitan Museum of Art, his head swiveling back and forth, just like the tourists who surround him.

The tourists, presumably, are moved by the vaulted ceilings thirty feet above, or by the towering arches that support the roof, or even by the grand floral arrangements in their marble niches. The flower of the week at the Met is the yellow rose and hundreds have been used to form the bouquets. Their fragrance permeates the air, adding to the general ambience.

Finito, on the other hand, is utterly immune to beauty or wonder, or even history, and always has been. As he approaches the ticket sellers on the far side of the hall, a single thought captures his attention: Man, this place musta cost a shitload of money.

Finito cannot stop to ask one of the many guards he passes for directions. Even if he were willing to attract attention to himself, he not only lacks the vocabulary to describe the Met's Southeast Asian Art collection, but also does not recall reading the words on the prior afternoon when Abby dragged him to her "favorite meditation space in New York."

He'd come along because they'd been quarreling for days and it was time to make up, at least temporarily. No surprise about the fighting, however. With Rosaria gone, the only alternatives to Abigail Stoph are the crimeys Finito put behind him when he killed his cousin. Now that he is no longer willing to sink to their level, he is trapped in that twenty-four/seven prison with Abby, the one his old mentor warned him against. And slowly going crazy, as his mentor predicted.

Although Finito remembers that the rooms to which Abby led him were on the second floor, he has no appreciation of the Met's vast sprawl. When he is forced to choose a direction along the balcony overlooking the main entrance, he expects to come upon the woman quickly, even if he takes a wrong turn or two. But as he soon discovers, each of the Mets galleries is divided into many smaller rooms from which there are two or even three possible exits. Hence, twenty minutes later, Finito finds himself wandering aimlessly through the bowels of the Met's largest gallery, Nineteenth-Century European Paintings and Sculptures, no longer certain whether he is coming or going.

The Met is always crowded on Sundays, especially cold, rainy Sundays in early March. But the strolling multitudes don't threaten Finito's security. Finito has worked crowds many times in the past, usually in the subway or Times Square, and he knows that crowds bring with them a near-perfect anonymity. People take great pains to mind their own business when you push them together. They move in little, self-contained groups, and nobody looks directly at anybody else if they can help it.

But the crowds do prevent Finito's expressing his intense frustration in a constructive manner, say by putting his foot through a self-portrait of Vincent Van Gogh wearing a straw hat.

• • •

Lately, Finito seems always on the verge of losing his temper. That's not the way it started out. After the Yings, Finito had entered a state of calm satisfaction familiar to him from the Denning murder. It was as if he'd passed a test, as if he'd at last graduated. He found himself content to read one newspaper after another, to watch local, network and cable news stations, nursing a bottle of beer while he searched for any mention of the Break-in Killer.

It was amazing. The reporters were talking about Finito Rakowski, the little spic written off so many years ago, and this thrilled him almost as much as the gold crucifix he wore around his neck, the one removed from the throat of Arlene Ying.

Did they believe they were done with him when he was expelled from Medgar Evers Intermediate School? When the cops tossed him into a cell? When the judges sentenced him? When the jails and prisons vomited him onto the street?

Well, they would never forget little Finito now. His name would live on long after their names were forgotten, even by their own families.

Finito's euphoria had begun to fade within a week, just as it had after Jennifer Denning. Within two weeks all that remained was a hunger for death as powerful as an addict's hunger for dope. This hunger drove him out in search of victim number eight, It kept him going day after day; it drives him even now as he wanders from gallery to gallery until he finally discovers the woman right where he left her on the prior afternoon. She is seated on a bench, pencil in hand, a sketchpad on her lap.

Except for the inky-black eyeliner and the mascara coating her lashes, the woman, in her early forties, wears no makeup. Her brown hair is drawn back along the top of her head so tightly she appears to be balding and her dark eyes are surmounted by thick, almost furry, brows. A pair of gold hoops, large enough to encircle her throat, dangle from her earlobes to the tops of her shoulders.

Yesterday, when Finito came through, accompanied by a chattering Abigail Stoph, the woman had looked away from her sketch long enough to favor him with a come-fuck-me stare so blatant it allowed for no other interpretation. Finito had been the object of similar looks often enough to instantly recognize the invitation, and the challenge.

"You're back," the woman notes, "and alone."

"What's your name?" he asks without turning.

"Ismene." The woman smiles before adding, "And your name is Georgie, right?"

"Ismene? What kind of name is that?"

"It's Greek. Ismene was a character in a Greek tragedy."

Finito leans forward to read the card next to the small plaque: The Death of the Buddha. For another moment, he studies the plaque itself. The scene carved into the stone is simple: a horizontal Buddha, who looks to Finito like a fat old lady, surrounded by vertical mourners, all male.

"You been drawing this thing for two days," he declares.

"Three," Ismene corrects.

"Why?"

"Why not?"

Finito turns to stare into her eyes, noting that she does not flinch. For some time he has been seeking a way to apply the lessons taken from his encounter with Maureen Owens in the Oriole Bar. This, he believes, is his opportunity.

Instead of answering Ismene's question, Finito squats next to her leather portfolio and rummages through the dozen sketches inside without asking permission. As far as he can tell, the sketches share only a single feature. They look nothing like The Death of the Buddha.

"I think," Finito declares, "that you got a long way to go."

Finito expects Ismene to laugh, but she does not. Instead, she turns slightly on the bench and slides the sketchpad into her portfolio before closing it. Then she pats the bench, inviting him to sit down.

"Why'd you come back?" she asks.

"For you."

"Was I that obvious?"

Finito answers her question with one of his own. "Do you think I came here to look at the pictures?"

"Not for a minute."

Ismene continues to stare up at him, her gaze frank and steady enough to convince Finito that she is trying to make a decision. Rough sex is great, her eyes declare, up to a point.

"Tell me, Georgie, is it hard to be so beautiful?"

"Only when you're a kid, before you learn to defend yourself."

Ismene's full lips part to reveal the stained teeth of a smoker. "Good answer," she admits.

Finito accepts the compliment with a nod. It's time to get the show on the road, to answer the first question. "Forget about my place," he tells her. "I'm living with the cow."

If Ismene is puzzled by the reference, she doesn't show it. Instead, she again smiles before telling him, "My roommate is away for the weekend. We'll have the place to ourselves until noon tomorrow. If you last that long."

The contrast between Ismene's statement and the reality to follow amuses Finito and he smiles to himself as he straightens. The lasting part, he thinks, is strictly up to her.

Ismene unfurls an enormous red umbrella as she and Finito emerge onto a nearly deserted Bedford Avenue at four o'clock in the evening. Williamsburg is another of those New York neighborhoods—this one in Brooklyn—seeking to become the next SoHo. More often than not, Bedford Avenue is crowded with the young professionals who followed artists like Ismene into the area, and with wannabes in search of the bohemian life. If

Ismene should run into a friend or acquaintance, maybe stop long enough to introduce him, he will lose her, painful though it might be so late in the game. But the few pedestrians they encounter as she leads him along Bedford Avenue, then down North Tenth Street toward the East River, pass by with their heads tucked firmly beneath their umbrellas.

Ismene finally stops before a two-story building on Wythe Avenue. A faded sign, hung above the barred windows on the lower floor, announces its former purpose: Williamsburg Paper and Box Company. Like many of the low-rise factories and warehouses in a dozen New York neighborhoods, it has succumbed to a housing crisis ongoing for more than a hundred years.

"Hold this," Ismene tells Finito, "while I get my keys."

Finito accepts the umbrella, which he might have been carrying all along, without complaint. The block appears to be entirely industrial and there's not a light to be seen in any window. He watches Ismene as she fumbles through her bag and thinks, Oh, you stupid bitch. You stupid, stupid bitch.

The door that Ismene finally pushes open feeds directly onto a narrow stairway. From the top of the stairs, an exposed bulb in a porcelain fixture casts a glaring light. Finito stares up at the bulb, thinking, This dump is worse than Rosaria's. But he is comforted by the belief that Ismene pays serious money for her dump, and by the knife-edged shadows cast by shards of peeling blue paint on the concrete walls.

As Finito begins to climb, he asks himself what he will do with Ismene, how he will hurt her and for how long. Perhaps, he thinks, he will allow her to recover from time to time. Perhaps he will tell her, from time to time, that he is going to release her. Perhaps he will tell her that her release depends on her sexual performance. Perhaps he will hurt her only a little bit at first, then gradually escalate until . . .

Ismene turns toward him when she reaches the small landing at the head of the stairs. The bulb is now directly overhead, and its harsh light deepens the hollows beneath her eyes. She seems a bit weary to Finito, as if she's been down this road before. Nevertheless, when she speaks, her tone is firm.

"You'll have to use a condom," she declares.

"What flavor?"

Apparently satisfied, Ismene opens the door, then flicks on a light to reveal a huge room virtually covered with paintings. There are paintings hanging from the walls, stacked against the walls, leaning against the furniture, flat on the floor. Several easels lined up before a row of windows bear half-completed canvases.

Finito looks around the room, taking his time. He has no interest in Ismene's abstract paintings. He is searching for something out of place, a reason to delay implementation of the fantasy now running like fire through his veins. He finds that reason with his ears, not his eyes, a tinkling faintly audible despite the rain pounding on the windows and the roof.

"What's that?" he asks.

"Say again?"

"That sound."

Too impatient to wait for a reply, Finito zigzags between canvases as he walks to a door on the other side of the room. If the roommate is home, he thinks, if the bitch is playing games with my head, then maybe I'll kill the both of them. Two for the price of one.

But Finito does not discover Ismene's roommate on the other side of the door. Instead, he discovers the largest pit bull terrier he has even seen, squatting on its haunches, its enormous jaws mere inches from his crotch. As black as Ismene's eyeliner, the animal wears a red collar and a red harness, both covered with small bells.

"Meet Prancer," Ismene calls out. "He's a performance artist." She pauses for a moment, her timing impeccable, then shouts, "Prancer, come."

Released by his master's command, Prancer does not so much prance, as rumble across the room, bells jingling furiously. Though he comes to a stop before Ismene, then sits, his body continues to quiver and the bells continue to jingle.

"He's well trained," Ismene explains.

Finito stares at the animal in disbelief. The dog's cheeks are as big as softballs, its head flat and large enough to support a dinner plate, its chest lumpy with muscle, its small glittery eyes blacker than its fur.

"Well," Ismene asks after giving her puppy an affectionate hug, "shall we get undressed? Or do you need a drink first?"

SEVENTEEN

"I'M NOT GOING to work today," Abby tells Finito at breakfast on the following morning. "It's finally stopped raining and I think we should do something special. I think we should go up to Central Park and welcome the new spring."

Finito pays Abby no mind. His eyes remain fixed on his plate as he sorts through his encounter with the artist, Ismene. On the one hand, all his best-laid plans had gone out the window when he found Prancer crouched behind that door. All those little details he'd rehearsed, all the pain he intended to inflict, had vanished without a trace. Now you see them, now you don't.

On the other hand, he's achieved a degree of that calm satisfaction he'd so desperately sought, and there's no saying otherwise. If he needs proof, all he has to do is look at himself. Twenty-four hours ago, he'd have lost it before Abby finished the first sentence. Now he is unruffled. Now he is above the fray. Now he can feel the power flowing through his veins. None of these things was true last night when he pulled the little .32, then shot Ismene through the right eye. When he wiped that fucking smirk off her face, for good and forever. *Adiós, chingada.*

Thinking about it now, Finito can appreciate the humorous aspects of the situation. Far from rushing to the aid of his mistress, Prancer had made a beeline across the room, scattering paintings right and left, bells jingling madly as Finito pegged round after round in his general direction. By the time the dog finally disappeared through the door on the other side of the room, Finito had only one bullet left, a bullet he did not intend to waste on a cowardly pit bull dressed up like a reindeer. A bullet for which he had a much better use.

"Georgie," Abby says, "tell me what you're thinking about."

Finito cuts through his eggs with the edge of his fork, then lays the fork on the plate. "It's my *Tía* Suzanna."

For some weeks, Finito has been using his fictitious aunt's fictitious illness to justify his bad temper. Now he is going to shift gears, to present Abby with phase three of the game. He will reach out for the big score, then take off before he goes completely insane. Before he does something to Abby that attracts the attention of the police.

"Has she gotten worse?" Abby asks.

"No, see . . . look, I'm not gonna be around for a while."

Abby's face appears to sink, her round cheeks and small double chin drooping like cookie dough in the hands of a careless baker. "Georgie, why?"

His *Tía* Suzanna's need for bypass surgery already established, Finito's gets right to the point. "Medicare will pay for the hospital, but Medicaid won't pay for the doctors."

"She was turned down again?"

Finito nods. "First they said she could be treated with drugs. Now the *maricóns* claim she won't survive the surgery." He pushes his plate toward the center of the table, though he is very hungry. "It's not like she's senile. It's not like she doesn't wanna live."

Abby reaches out to touch her lover's shoulder. "I don't know what to say," she says before adding her favorite line, "but we can work it out together."

"No, I gotta do this by myself." Finito rises and puts on his coat. "*La familia's* raised nine thousand. We need another six, and I'm gonna get it."

• • •

Ignoring Abby's heartfelt entreaties, Finito pulls on his coat and leaves. He hasn't exactly lied to Abby. He does have work to do. His first priority on this sunny morning in early March is to replace the automatic he tossed into the East River a short time after using it on Ismene. To that end, he merely crosses the island of Manhattan, from west to east, to the apartment of a gun dealer known to him as Mykola, the Mad Ukrainian.

Sitting across from Mykola in the man's small apartment on Second Avenue, Finito has no difficulty with the mad part. Between the shaved head, the beady blue eyes and the dent in the center of his forehead, Mykola looks as if he might flip out any second.

"This is what you are looking for?" Mykola asks. "This piece of shit?"

Mykola's contemptuous tone is unmistakable, despite an accent thick enough to pour into an engine block. But Finito doesn't take offense. Nor is he intimidated. Finito has dealt with many similar men in the course of his twenty-seven years.

"Yeah, that's it."

Finito points to the little .25-caliber automatic. Between its weight, under a pound, and its shrouded hammer, the weapon was obviously designed to be concealed inside a pocket. The larger weapons displayed on Mykola's bed, while more intimidating, are too easy to spot. Besides dark skin, the first thing cops look for is a telltale bulge around the waistline. That's because they get big-time brownie points for taking guns off the street.

Or so Finito thinks as he picks up the .25, then ejects the six-round magazine into the palm of his hand. When he is sure the clip is full and there's a round in the chamber, he asks, "How much?"

"Four hundred dollars." Mykola draws out the last word, nearly trilling the l's.

"You're jokin', right?" Finito continues to hold the weapon. "You're gettin' over on me? Cause I know this *pistola*, it didn't cost two hundred bucks when it was brand fuckin' new."

As they haggle, Mykola harps on the weapon's main selling point, that it was stolen from an honest citizen just two weeks before and is presumably clean. This is a claim Finito can't dispute without calling Mykola a liar, which he is not prepared to do. Finally, they settle on a figure in the upper range of their negotiations.

Finito counts out the money, then slides the weapon into his pocket. He is preparing to get up when Mykola says, "One minute you are waiting, please. I show you very interesting item."

Mykola reaches under the bed to withdraw a shoe box. He opens the box with a little flourish to reveal a hand-held stun gun the size of a small portable radio.

"State of art," he announces. "One hundred thousand volts." He places the gun in Finito's hand.

Finito presses the button marked CHARGE, and the weapon begins to hum. When the humming stops and a red light comes on, he pushes a second button marked DISCHARGE. A tiny bolt of lightning, accompanied by a sharp crack, jumps between the two electrodes.

Though Finito attempts to mask his enthusiasm with a gruff question, his smile gives him away.

"How much?" he asks.

Nine hours later, Finito occupies a stool in a pub on the Upper East Side, Manhattan's Gold Coast. The pub is called the Painted Turtle and is supposedly a match for a sister pub in Birmingham, England.

Finito's come to look for Abby's replacement, but he's not having any luck. The pub is half empty and the few women who wander inside just don't have that victim look about them. They glance at him from time to time, but their eyes reveal mere curiosity, not the aching loneliness he's hoping for.

As time passes, Finito's mood takes on a darker edge. He finds himself unable to turn his thoughts away from Rosaria and

Ismene, running through these encounters over and over again. The simple truth, which he finally admits, is that he probably made mistakes. Were they fatal mistakes? There's no way to be sure. Nevertheless, Finito briefly imagines the cops, an army of them, crashing through the door of the Painted Turtle. Cops wearing helmets and serious body armor, carrying rifles and shotguns.

Though Finito shakes off his fantasy as the barrels of those rifles and shotguns begin to rise, the fear remains, a net of paranoia through which his thoughts are continually screened. This paranoia is only heightened when he finally decides that the creature he's been nourishing all these months has a mind of its own. Even worse, like any good parasite, the creature has no concern for its host's ultimate survival. It simply wants to eat.

And he, Finito, will be the one to feed it.

EIGHTEEN

Monday, March 4, 9:00 A.M.

Lieutenant Moira O'Neill was winding up Operation Intercept's weekly general briefing. The meeting was being conducted in the largest of the task force's many offices, that of the Homicide detectives assigned in pairs to the individual investigations.

Pudge Pedersson was leaning against the wall farthest from O'Neill and could barely understand her relentless monotone. But that was okay because Pudge wasn't paying all that much attention. He and his partner's worst fears about Operation Intercept's internal structure had been confirmed. Information went up the ladder, to O'Neill and Wideman, who occasionally revealed a few tidbits (tidbits they would pass on to the media in time for the nightly news) at mandatory briefings just like the one he was attending.

From Pudge's viewpoint, the inevitable result of this policy was nothing short of depressing. Nine days before, he and Belinda had asked an agreeable Lieutenant O'Neill for a list of closed homicides going back to the prior July. On the following day, O'Neill had relayed the request to the Statistics Division. Four days after that, when Statistics got around to securing the data, a printout was forwarded, not to Pudge and Belinda, but to

Lieutenant O'Neill's personal assistant. By the time the printout was passed to the investigators who actually needed it, seven days had elapsed.

Despite his drifting thoughts, one item mentioned by O'Neill did catch Pudge's attention. The tissue found between Rosaria Montes's teeth had yielded a human DNA profile that did not match any of the profiles stored in the various state and federal databases.

Little by little, Pudge had been reworking his image of the Break-in Killer. The man was clearly not as controlled as Pudge had imagined him on the night Jennifer Denning was killed. Rosaria Montes had been attacked on the spur of the moment and there was no evidence that her death had been planned. In fact, all the evidence pointed in the opposite direction.

More to the point, the Montes killing demonstrated a self-destructive aspect of the killer's personality that Pudge had not suspected. According to the pathologist who conducted the autopsy, Rosaria had been turned onto her face between thirty and forty minutes after she died. That didn't make sense, if you assumed her killer was motivated by the passion of the moment. But it made perfect sense if her killer simply wanted to sign his work.

Hey, world, check it out: I was here.

A week before, at a very similar meeting, the NYPD's profiler had lectured the troops after linking the Rosaria Montes killing to the Break-in Killer. Many serial killers, Emilio Venezia had explained, break down as time goes by. For reasons unknown, the cooling-off period between their killings gradually contracts until their activities more closely resemble those of a spree killer. So common was this phenomenon, that it had a formal name: decompensation.

"Most serial killers go about their business for years before they begin to decompensate, and some never decompensate," Venezia had concluded, "but it's our belief that the actor in this case has already begun to break down. He might be able to slow this process, but he will not be able to stop it."

Like her partner, Belinda Moore had also tuned out O'Neill's droning voice. Belinda had reached the point where she could almost see the Break-in Killer (especially at night, when she closed her eyes in an often vain attempt to fall asleep), and she was imagining him now. Though the image she conjured was necessarily obscure, between the piercing green eyes, the almost-blond hair, and that succulent mouth, it was at the same time undeniably vivid.

Except for a single feature, the descriptions offered by the Rosenthals had differed markedly. The exception was the man's lips. They were, according to Gus Rosenthal, who'd rolled his eyes in his sister's direction, "soft enough to kiss."

Though she would have preferred not to, Belinda now envisioned that yielding mouth, the full lips so out of sync with the heavily muscled body and the determined set of the man's features. His gaze, she knew, when he thought you weren't looking, would be sharp enough to pierce your soul.

Moira O'Neill was concluding her address with a little pep talk when Captain Meyer Wideman entered the room. He ran his fingers through his already tangled hair, then made an announcement.

"It looks," he told his troops, carefully emphasizing the second word, "like we got another one, in Brooklyn."

Wideman hesitated for a couple of beats, then waved his arms impatiently when the anticipated murmur failed to die down. "Awright, awright. Enough. Whatta you, babies here?" This time his pause was met with dead silence. "We're gonna play this close to the vest until we're sure. That means no gossipy phone calls to the wife or the hubby or the girlfriend or the boyfriend. And no chatter in Murray's Tavern after work. I don't care how drunk you get, keep your mouths shut. Everybody got that?"

Another pause, another silence. Wideman tended to speak in edicts and his troops were used to him. Now he pointed to a pair of cops from Homicide. "You and you," he said. "There's a car downstairs. Get in it." His head swiveled momentarily until his eyes settled on Pudge Pedersson. "You, Pedersson, and your partner. Let's move. The ME's already on the scene. He's holding the body just for us."

Belinda folded her arms across her chest as she repressed a smile. It was lucky for Pudge, she decided, that he didn't wear a hat because it would no longer fit on his swollen head. Nevertheless, Belinda was happy for her partner. And happy, too, that Lieutenant Jerry Malden now seemed far enough in the past to be a part of some history lived by her ancestors. That she was also flattered, however, she would not admit, not even to herself. You did the job, you took the pay. The ego part could only get you into trouble.

Having done her duty, Belinda Moore was standing on Wythe Avenue outside Ismene Farrier's loft when Moira O'Neill came through the door. O'Neill's brows arched momentarily, then she took out a cigarette, lit it up, finally sucked the smoke down into her lungs. It was after four o'clock, and the March sun had dropped behind the commercial buildings on the far side of the block, leaving Wythe Avenue in deep shadow. Across the street, a forklift driver raised a pallet loaded with fifty-gallon drums into the air, then tilted the pallet before hurrying off.

"Seen enough?" O'Neill asked.

The simple truth was that Belinda Moore had seen more than enough, given the fact that she would play no part in the subsequent investigation. But she wasn't about to announce her squeamishness to her superior. What would be the point?

"It was nice of him," she told her superior, "to leave us his calling card."

"Tell me."

"Well, it's not just that he blinded her by shooting her through both eyes. It's how he did it."

"Which is?"

"There's no stippling around Ismene Farrier's right eye, but there's tight stippling around her left eye. That means he leaned in close before he fired the second shot. He wanted to make sure we got the message."

Belinda was referring to the small particles of gunpowder embedded in Farrier's skin. The stippling pattern surrounding her left eye was consistent with a small-caliber round fired from a distance of three to six inches.

O'Neill took another hit on her cigarette. Again, she drew the smoke deep into her lungs, holding it there briefly before forcing it between her lips in a thin flat stream.

"I think it was like Elly Monette," she finally told Belinda. "He thought he had Ismene where he wanted her, then something went wrong. Probably the dog."

Belinda allowed herself a smile. Earlier in the day, when the locals broke out the locks on Ismene Farrier's door, they were met by what they'd first taken to be an apparition, the hound from hell. Several had reached for their weapons, jingle bells or not, fully intending to shoot the animal. But Prancer was too quick for New York's Finest. He was down the stairs and out onto Wythe Avenue before a shot was fired.

"Dogs," Belinda said. "Push comes to shove, you never know what they're gonna do."

"Not unlike the men in my life," O'Neill observed.

Belinda looked around for Pudge, hoping he'd come through the door. The last time she'd seen him, he'd been subjecting an assistant medical examiner named Baker to what amounted to an interrogation. Well, Pudge would have to miss out. O'Neill's last statement was as close to bonding as the woman was likely to get, at least with Belinda Moore. It was now time to make the request suggested by Pudge on the way over.

"We've got a theory," Belinda said. "Me and my partner."

"Which is?"

"The way the perp was described by the witnesses in the Bronx—dirty clothes, powerfully built, raggedy haircut—we're thinkin' maybe he just got out of jail."

"Why?"

"Gladys Rosenthal made a big thing out of the perp's body. She said he looked like he spent half his life in a gym. But that doesn't make sense, because he was dressed like a street thief and street thieves don't go to gyms."

"Unless they're doing time."

"Exactly."

O'Neill let it rest for half a beat, then asked, "Why a jail? Why not a prison?"

"Only felons go upstate. Misdemeanor time is served on Rikers Island."

"And the perp couldn't be a felon?"

"All convicted felons have to submit DNA for profiling. That started in 1996. Since we didn't find the perp's DNA profile in the Department of Corrections database, its not likely he came out of a prison. Besides, all along we've made this guy for a petty criminal. It makes sense that he was doing misdemeanor time at Rikers."

"Alright, so where does that leave us?"

"It leaves us," Belinda replied, "meaning me and my partner, hoping we can get our hands on a list of all male prisoners released from Rikers Island between June 15th and July 9th of last year."

Two days later, with Pudge still subdued, Belinda finally decided that maybe something else was bothering him, something more than hurt feelings at being left out of the negotiations. They were on their way to review a case file at the eight-three in Bushwick, Brooklyn, coming off the Williamsburg Bridge just a few blocks from Ismene Farrier's loft.

"Pudge?"

"Yeah?" Pudge blew a dense plume of smoke through his open window.

"Is something up? Maybe with Annie?"

"You're reading minds now?"

"Well, as far as I can tell, this case and Annie are the only two things going on in your life. The case seems to be doing alright. . . ."

"You think so?" Pudge turned the car onto Broadway just as a train rattled over the elevated tracks above their heads. With greater patience then he would have expected, he waited for the train to pass before continuing. "The way I see it," he told his partner, "we're coming to the end of the list, and we haven't found that smoking gun, that fatal mistake. Being as it's our credibility on the line, I don't see what use the bosses are gonna have for us if we come up empty. As for the Rikers Island thing, there's no reason O'Neill has to give it to us. She could assign it to anyone at Homicide. And that's only if she and Wideman go for the idea in the first place."

"That's too pessimistic, even for you, Pudge." Belinda shook her head. "Why don't you just tell me what's bothering you and get it over with? Don't make me beg."

Pudge settled back against the Chevy's plastic upholstery as he pulled to a stop at a red light. He waited just long enough to make it plain that she was already begging, at least in his humble opinion. Then he said, "Annie and me, we're not speaking."

"And how long has this been going on?"

"Ten days."

"Ten days? And you didn't say anything?" Belinda waved off her partner's reply. "Never mind. Just tell me what happened."

Pudge finally cracked an embarrassed smile. Now that he'd been persuaded to open up, he was already feeling better.

"Okay," he said, "you know how we're always working late?"

"Sure."

"And I haven't been tryin' to get out early, even when I have a date with Annie?"

In fact, it was inevitably Belinda who was first to suggest they call it quits. As far as she could tell, Pudge would have been happy to work around the clock. Annie be damned.

"My problem," Pudge continued, "is . . . I mean, my problem *was* that the dinners Annie cooked were either cold or burned by the time I got back to Staten Island. So what I suggested was that I give her a call as I'm comin' over the Verrazano Bridge, and she can order Chinese from Hop Lin's. With a little luck, the food will arrive about the same time I do."

"Makes sense."

Pudge made the left onto Myrtle Avenue, following the path of the el. When he hit a red light, he threw the Chevy into PARK and turned toward his partner. "First thing I did wrong was I offered to pay for the food. Annie got insulted right there. That's her thing, ya know. She won't let me chip in when she does the cooking, but she always splits the bill if we go out. She tells me it's about her independence, but I don't see what's independent about paying more than your fair share—"

Belinda cut her partner off, knowing that Pudge, if left to himself, would ramble on for the next hour. "We're coming up on the eight-three," she said. "In case you haven't noticed."

"Alright, I'll get to the point." Pudge dropped the gearshift into DRIVE and turned onto Knickerbocker Avenue. "The dinner comes to $29.50 with the tip. My share is $14.75, right? So I give her a ten and a five, and I make a joke. I say something like, Keep the change. I mean, we're talkin' about a quarter. But no, she won't have it. She's gotta make it even. Meanwhile, she only has twelve cents in her wallet. So what does she do? She goes searching through the house, feeling under cushions. I keep telling her I don't care about the quarter, but she keeps looking. She won't even answer me when I'm talkin' to her."

Pudge stopped long enough to back into a parking space a

block away from the precinct. He shut down the engine, tossed his smoke into the street, then turned to his partner. "I'm tryin' to keep a handle on my temper, but finally I tell her that I'm not gonna take the quarter even if she comes up with it."

"What'd she say?"

"Nothin'. She just kept lookin' until she found a dime and fifteen pennies. I mean, she's holdin' the change in the palm of her hand and her hand's under my nose. It's like, take it or else." Unable to meet his partner's gaze, Pudge fumbled for the button that controlled the window. "Man, I was hot," he told Belinda. "I stomped off into the kitchen, threw the dime and the pennies into the garbage. Naturally, Annie was standing by the front door when I came back into the living room and the door was open. I haven't heard from her since."

Belinda opened her own door. Time to go to work. "I hope you're not gonna say this was about the principle of the thing."

"No," Pudge replied as he climbed out of the car, "it was definitely about the quarter. I was tryin' to buy her affections and she caught me at my game."

NINETEEN

THE TWO PHOTOS PUDGE PEDERSSON STUDIED were, to his mind, unambiguous. Taken five months before, on October 15, they were of a murdered prostitute, Maria Estevez, lying on her back in a vacant lot. In the first, Maria's head and throat were covered with rubble, broken red bricks for the most part, the remains of a demolished tenement. In the second, the bricks had been piled off to the side, revealing the woman's face. And what jumped out at Pudge was that Maria's features were undamaged in the second photo. The bricks had not been used as weapons.

Pudge and Belinda were seated in the eight-three's squad room. Aside from a single detective sitting behind a desk placed against the opposite wall, they were alone. The detective, though he hadn't introduced himself, had pointed Pudge and Belinda toward the case file when they'd come in ten minutes before.

"Lieutenant Braciak's not in the house and it wasn't my case," he'd announced before returning to the paperwork on his desk.

Belinda removed a small magnifying glass from her purse, lifted the second photo and carefully studied Maria Estevez's face. She stayed at it for a few minutes, pausing only to wipe the lens of the magnifying glass.

"It's hard to be sure," she finally told her partner, "because there's brick dust on her skin, but I don't think her face was even bruised."

"It wasn't." One step ahead, Pudge held up the autopsy report for his partner's inspection. "No contusions, no lacerations, a few minor abrasions. The cause of death was asphyxia due to manual strangulation." Pudge continued on, knowing that what he had to say would come as no surprise. "He didn't just dump those bricks on her face, Belinda. He took the time to place them carefully, maybe one at a time, despite the obvious risks. It's cold, you know what I mean? A contradiction. Cold passion."

Belinda nodded agreement, though she would have put the observation less dramatically. "What we're looking at here is the next step in the great experiment. He liked what he did to Crowder with the bag of garbage, so he embellished his performance, like he did later, with Denning and Monette."

Though Belinda's tone was assured, she was not overlooking the obvious. On November 12, about one month after the slaying of Maria Estevez, a man named Arthur Vandover had been charged with her murder. Subsequently arraigned and indicted, Vandover was now in the Brooklyn House of Detention awaiting trial.

"Hey."

Pudge looked over at the unnamed detective on the other side of the room. The man had a long face dominated by a heavy nose, and a five-o'clock shadow dark enough to be mistaken for a beard. "What?"

"I got the lieutenant on the phone. He wants to know how long you're gonna remain on the premises."

Belinda responded without hesitation. "Until he gets back," she said. "Whenever that may be."

By the time Lieutenant Teodor Braciak arrived ninety minutes later, Pudge and Belinda had thoroughly reviewed the case file. On the surface, the evidence against Vandover was compelling. Swabs of the victim's cervix had produced enough semen for DNA testing. When the resulting profile was run through the

Department of Corrections' database of known felons, Vandover's name had popped out. There was no doubting that he'd left the sample.

Taken into custody at his home, Vandover initially denied all knowledge of Maria Estevez. Only when confronted with the DNA evidence did he finally admit to having unprotected sex with her. But then he lied about the time this sex occurred, first backing up a day, then several hours, before admitting that he'd run into Maria on his lunch hour, at twelve-thirty, on the day she was murdered. That put their subsequent interactions within the ME's estimate of the time of her death.

Were the lies evidence of a guilty mind? Or the standard reaction of a mope who's been through the system? Though Vandover's yellow sheet revealed a felony drug conviction eight years in the past, he'd never been charged with a violent crime. Nor had he confessed to Estevez's murder, insisting on his innocence in the face of an aggressive interrogation.

But that was the least of it, the part that made for reasonable doubt. There were also problems of a higher order to be dealt with, problems sufficient to prompt a phone call to Moira O'Neill shortly before Braciak's arrival.

"Keep the son of a bitch entertained," O'Neill had told Pudge, "until we show up. And don't be awed by his rank. As far as you're concerned, he's just another sinner in need of confession."

Short and powerfully built, Braciak had an already florid complexion made even redder by acne scars in the hollows of both cheeks. A thirty-year-man, he'd come to the job fresh out of the air force at age twenty-three.

"C'mon in." Braciak's warm smile belied the intensity of his gaze, which swept over Pudge and Belinda, as palpable as a frisk. "What can I do ya for?" he asked.

"We've been looking through the case file while we were waiting," Belinda said, "and there's a couple of things we don't understand." Her objective was to get Braciak's version on the record, then let the anomalies speak for themselves. To that end, she maintained a deferential tone.

"I didn't actually work the job." Braciak's smile expanded as he spread his hands in front of him, palms up.

"Are you telling us, sir, that you're unfamiliar with the case?"

Belinda settled back as a flush rose into Braciak's cheeks. He was being questioned by a subordinate and he didn't like it. Still, he had to know that his responses would be forwarded to the bosses running Operation Intercept. If he didn't put Belinda's questions to rest, they would be asked again by a higher authority.

"No, I'm not saying that." Braciak's smile returned. "Look, tell me what's bothering you and I'll do the best I can."

Belinda dropped a crime scene photo onto Braciak's desk, then gave him a few seconds to look it over. The photo was of Maria Estevez as she'd appeared when the cops found her. Unsurprisingly, Braciak's eyes went first to the pile of bricks covering the victim's head, to the bizarre.

"The way I read the file," Belinda said, "Vandover's semen was found in Maria's cervix. That would mean they had genital-to-genital intercourse, right?"

"I guess it'd have to."

"So how come her shorts are pulled up?" Belinda pointed to Maria Estevez's passion-red short shorts. "Those are latex and they're tighter than the woman's skin. It's hard takin' 'em down, and even harder yankin' 'em back up. So when exactly did she do that?"

Braciak's smile finally evaporated. "Maybe after they had sex," he speculated. "Or maybe the perp raped her postmortem."

Nodding agreeably, Belinda continued on. "As to the latter, sir," she said, "the pathologist who performed the autopsy says there's no evidence of sexual assault, that the sex was consensual."

"Fine, so she pulled them up herself."

"But that would mean that Vandover waited until Estevez was dressed to launch his attack? Me and my partner, we can't understand why he'd do that."

"Obviously the guy's a psycho." This time Braciak managed a short manly chuckle. "You have unprotected sex with a New York street whore," he observed, "you gotta be a psycho."

Pudge watched his partner with undisguised admiration, wondering if Braciak knew what was coming. Braciak was a detective and had most likely used deflection to loosen up his suspects. You start with a hanging curveball over the heart of the plate, then follow with a two-seam fastball aimed at the batter's helmet.

"Alright," Belinda conceded, "even though Vandover has no violent history and has worked the same job in Bushwick for the past two years, let's say he's a psycho. It's not up to us to supply motive, anyway."

"No," Braciak agreed, "it's not."

Belinda leaned back in her chair and crossed her legs. "But it isn't really Vandover that's bothering us," she confided. "No, it's the crime lab reports, or the lack thereof, that caught our attention."

When Braciak failed to respond to her pregnant pause, Belinda explained herself. "The AME who did the autopsy"—she riffled through the file for a moment—"Hamani Babangida, that's his name. Well, he dispatched two sets of samples containing what he thought were bodily fluids off to the NYPD Crime Lab for analysis. One set was taken from the victim's cervix and vagina. The other was taken from her mouth. Now the first set led to Vandover, this we already know. But the other one? Well, there's no report on the other one, nothing in the file. In fact, if it wasn't for the autopsy report, produced by the office of the medical examiner, you'd never know that sample existed. Why do you think that is, sir?"

"I have no idea," Braciak responded without hesitation. "I'll have to ask the detectives who ran the case."

Pudge repressed a smile. Never mind the fact that Braciak had signed off on the file before sending a copy to the Queens DA, or that it was his job to make sure the file was complete and accurate.

"Are your detectives in the field? Can you call them back to the house?" Belinda's gaze was steady yet mild, a trick she'd been perfecting for years. "I need something to tell my superiors."

Teodor Braciak wasn't biting. "They're both off today," he announced. "Mandatory compensation for last month's overtime."

"How about calling them at home?"

A good question, in Pudge's opinion, but a question that was never to be answered, as the door to Braciak's office opened at that minute to reveal Inspector Frank Carter standing on the other side. Lined up behind him, like penguins approaching the sea, were Meyer Wideman and Moira O'Neill.

Most of the bosses Pudge had come across in the course of his career had an intimidating air about them, but Carter was in a class of his own. His full mouth had a pronounced downturn at the corners, rendering his expression perpetually sour. This effect was augmented by a mustache that curled around his lips and a pair of eyes as dark and merciless as those of a predatory insect.

"Detectives Pedersson and Moore," he finally said before stepping back, "I'd like to speak to you outside." He waited until they scooted past like the obedient little children they were before addressing Teodor Braciak. "I'm Inspector Frank Carter," he said with just the hint of smile. "Do you want to see my identification?"

Braciak swallowed twice before finally managing a brave smile. "Should I be talking to my lawyer?"

"Not if you want to keep your pension."

• • •

Pudge Pedersson jammed a cigarette between his lips and lit up the minute he and his partner stepped through the doors of the Eighty-third Precinct. Despite his troubles with the widow Mac-Dougald and his partner's garnering the lion's share of the credit, his life had taken a definite turn for the better and he was properly appreciative. Thus he hadn't resented Carter's ordering them to wait outside. What was important, in Pudge's mind, was that they'd been listened to at all.

There was a second element contributing to Pudge's general air of contentment as well. Initially, Pudge was disappointed when the media settled on "Break-in Killer" to describe the monster who'd already slaughtered eight people. Pudge would have much preferred Night Stalker or Hillside Strangler, something more in line with the perp's true nature. But over time he'd come to believe there were no words (not in the English language, anyway) to describe the man responsible for the murders he and the task force were investigating.

As a child, Pudge had been told about a war between good and evil raging throughout the universe, a war in which he was expected to play a part. It was a lesson he'd eagerly embraced, conducive as it was to the superhero fantasies that preoccupied him at the time. But now he understood its deeper significance. He understood that evil wears an aspect suitable to its environment. Out in the far galaxies, it may take on forms unimaginable; on Earth it bears a human face. Maybe the Break-in Killer was small potatoes alongside the big killers, the Hitlers, the Stalins, the Maos. That didn't mean he was any less evil.

There was an upside to this reasoning, for Pudge Pedersson. Because if the Break-in Killer was evil's representative on Earth, then he (and the rest of the task force) had to represent the other side. It was only logical.

This was a juxtaposition that suited Pudge nicely as he stood outside the Eighty-third Precinct. In fact, at that moment, only one thing stood between Pudge and a contentment rivaling that of a well-fed cat napping in a patch of sunlight. Though he was dying to reveal his insights to his partner (to let her know that she was a living embodiment, not just of the good guys, but of the *absolute* good guys), he was reasonably certain she'd laugh in his face if he did. It was a risk he was not prepared to take.

"You know what I think it is about cops?" Belinda said. "I think we can only take it up to a point."

"Okay." When he had no idea where his partner was going, Pudge had long believed it was best to limit his exposure.

"We have two false arrests in this case, one of which we made ourselves, right?"

"Right."

"So how did that happen?"

"Beats me."

"Pudge, it's simple. We can accept murder when it's motivated by a reason we understand. Money, love, revenge . . . we can even imagine being tempted ourselves if the stakes were high enough." Belinda stopped abruptly, then looked at her partner. "In fact, Pudge, if Ahmed doesn't pay back the money Ralph and me loaned him? Well, I might just catch up to him one night and blow his brains into the vichyssoise."

Under intense pressure from her family, Belinda had finally contributed to the pool of money loaned to the newly rehabilitated Ahmed Brown. Though the amount given was far less than the amount requested, Belinda seemed no less resentful.

"The restaurant's not open yet," Pudge reminded. "It's too early to get worked up about the loan."

"Don't change the subject. We were talking about why two men were charged with crimes they didn't commit." Belinda stuck her hands in her pockets. The night was rapidly growing colder. "I don't know about you, but I can't imagine killing somebody for the thrill of it. And I think that's true of cops in general. You catch a homicide like Estevez, you don't wanna look it in the eye. You don't wanna think too hard about those bricks covering the vic's head because the image gets burned into your brain and you find yourself studying it at three o'clock in the morning. So what you do is jump at the first opportunity to close the case."

"That doesn't justify dumping that lab report."

"You telling me you don't carry two notebooks?"

In fact, Pudge Pedersson, like his partner and almost every other New York detective, was never without a pair of small pads. One contained the notes he kept for himself. The other went into the case file, and eventually to the defense.

"Defense lawyers," Pudge groused, "they take your notes and twist 'em into knots."

"Don't they just."

Pudge thought about it for a moment, then said, "Belinda, you're gonna feel much better when we take this guy down."

"I know that's what you believe, Pudge. But me, I got a little problem here. Uncovering Maria Estevez, it's a definite feather in the old cap, no doubt about it. But I didn't see anything in the case file that puts us closer to an arrest. And you didn't, either."

Ten minutes later, Moira O'Neill walked out of the precinct. She buttoned her coat as she approached her detectives, leaning slightly forward against a steady breeze. When she drew within a few feet, she looked from Pudge to Belinda, then lit a cigarette.

"What I have to tell you," she announced, her words accompanied by little puffs of smoke, "it stays here."

The message fully explained why O'Neill had come alone, at least to Belinda Moore. Later, if Pudge or Belinda proved themselves untrustworthy, Carter and Wideman (and the chief of detectives, naturally) could plausibly deny all knowledge of the conversation.

"On the way over," O'Neill continued, "I contacted a senior supervisor at the crime lab. According to the case records in their files, the fluid taken from Estevez's mouth was semen, and yielded a DNA profile which did not match the DNA profile from the sample left by Arthur Vandover."

"What about the DNA from the Rosaria Montes scene?" Pudge asked. "The tissue found between her teeth. Was it compared?"

The withering glare O'Neill focused on Pudge Pedersson had an immediate effect. His mouth closed almost as fast as his eyes widened.

"DNA found in tissue taken from Maria Estevez's mouth, when compared to DNA taken from the tissue between Rosaria Montes's teeth, produced a match that excludes 99.97 percent of the population. We've now linked those killings with hard physical evidence."

Done with Pudge, O'Neill turned to face Belinda. "Lieutenant Braciak has decided to retire. He'll be gone by the end of the week. The detectives who worked the case will soon be patrolling a housing project in Brooklyn. The charges against Arthur Vandover will be dropped before the end of the month." Finally, O'Neill smiled. "The alternative requires that we hand the missing lab reports to Vandover's Legal Aid lawyer, along with an explanation sure to be questioned when the detectives we demoted have to testify."

O'Neill waited long enough for Belinda to nod in agreement, then turned back to Pudge. "The public's been terrified ever since Ismene Farrier's body was found and the media's not helping matters. We don't need to make things worse by adding police misconduct to the mix. That said, you've done great work here, even if you haven't turned up that fatal mistake you promised. I want you to return to what you were doing and take it a step farther. Maybe there was a killing before Darlene Crowder. We won't know if we don't look, so back it up to the beginning of last year. I'll have printouts of all closed or open homicides on your desks by tomorrow morning."

"What about the other list?" Somehow, Pudge managed not to flinch as he asked the question.

"What list?"

"The one of prisoners released from Rikers just before Darlene Crowder."

"It was unmanageable, Detective, more than a thousand names. I've asked Statistics to refine their search. Specifically, to exclude all women, all black males, all Asian males, all whites or Latinos with brown or black eyes, and all white or Latino males under eighteen or over forty. If the printout isn't in your hands by the beginning of next week, remind me again."

TWENTY

As HE DRIVES ALONG Queens Boulevard, Finito Rakowski finds himself in the best of moods. This strikes even him as strange. Here he is in a stolen van, without a driver's license, carrying a set of burglar tools designed to facilitate the crime of grand larceny, auto. Given his record, he could do a solid nickel for this alone. Factor in the stun gun in his pocket, he could be looking at maybe eight. Then there's the little gym bag in the back, the one containing a roll of duct tape, ten feet of clothesline rope and three plastic drop cloths.

The cops make a routine traffic stop, find the bag, they'll know right away who he is. And this can definitely happen because cops from the local precinct sweep the Queens Plaza stroll from time to time, hassling johns and whores alike. Plus, there are the outright stings, with female Vice cops done up in latex miniskirts, playing at being whores.

Finito's hand rises to the gold crucifix at his throat, Arlene Ying's gold crucifix. Yeah, he thinks, that would be good, too, if the cops found the fuckin' cross.

A moment passes before Finito stumbles on a reason for his composure. All the jerks out there, he decides, the good citizens, if they were in his shoes they would've shit their pants ten minutes ago. Finito Rakowski, on the other hand, is in a place beyond fear, a place you get to by taking the risks good citizens fear. Risk is the key to the kingdom. No risk, no gain.

Content for now, Finito doesn't give a thought to the nightmare which awakened him at three o'clock on the prior morning, the cops blasting through the door, the courtroom, the steel walls, the execution chamber, the IV, the gurney. In his dream, the gurney had risen to a sitting position, then beckoned him forward.

A block before Stillman Avenue, Finito bears left, onto Thomson Avenue. He is on familiar ground here, in a neighborhood of squat warehouses, shotgun tenements and low-income housing projects. Just a few blocks away lies Queens Plaza, where the Rikers Island bus deposited him eights months ago, a day before he murdered Darlene Crowder.

Finito turns on the defroster to clear the van's rapidly fogging windshield. New York is in the midst of a late-season cold snap, with the temperature expected to drop into the single digits by morning. This is good. He will have no trouble luring any of the whores who work the area surrounding the Fifty-ninth Street Bridge into the van. On a night like tonight, they'll practically give it away for a chance to get warm.

Though his head doesn't turn, Finito watches both sides of the street. It's whore heaven in Queens Plaza, as it should be on a Friday night, with johns cruising almost every block. The whores call to Finito from time to time: "Yo, baby, I got what you need. C'mon over here." But Finito does not respond. There are too many eyes out there, too many potential witnesses. He will bide his time.

The whores are a definite compromise, a step back, or so Finito believes. He is substituting quantity for quality. In his heart of hearts, he would much prefer another Arlene Ying, squeaky-clean from her shower. When he'd pushed the door open, when she'd pulled aside the shower curtain and seen who it was, she'd frozen for a moment, her eyes blinking furiously, as if she couldn't process Finito Rakowski and the little gun he was pointing at her head.

It was a moment to treasure, no doubt about it. But now the idea is to grab somebody who won't be missed, use her for a few hours, then dump what's left of her where it won't be found. Only a whore satisfies the first part, the won't-be-missed part. The windowless van and the East River serve for the rest.

Finito is driving along Eleventh Street when an ambulance streaks past, sirens screaming, lights flashing madly. A moment later, the ambulance is followed by a police cruiser, then another. Though the cops obviously have a fixed destination, the spooked johns turn right and left at the next corner, headed for parts unknown.

With the streets virtually empty of traffic, Finito becomes instantly more bold. This is his chance, the opportunity he's been waiting for. He pulls to his left, to the curb, in front of the first prostitute he finds standing alone, then rolls down the window.

"Hey, baby, you lookin' for a date?"

Finito's eyes wander across the whore's body in an attempt to answer the most basic question. Is she a little girl, or a little boy? Though the whore's body is slender, her shoulders narrow, her hips suitably rounded, Finito decides to make sure.

"I don't want no man," he announces. "If you're a man, it's best you don't get in this truck."

After a quick smile, the whore raises the hem of her faux-leather miniskirt. She is not wearing panties.

"Good, good," Finito says. Now he is certain of two things:

that the whore is, indeed, a girl, and that she is not a cop. Dumb whore, smart Finito.

"So, wha'chu after tonight?" she inquires.

"A little bit of each."

"You talkin' about half and half?"

"More like a third, a third, and a third."

The whore leans into the window. "That's gonna cost ya, baby. You got a mattress back there?"

Finito lays the tip of his fingers on the whore's shoulder and gently but firmly pushes her away. "How much?" he asks.

The whore rubs her shoulder. "Don't be touchin' me." When Finito doesn't respond, she says, "A hundred."

"Uh-uh." Finito raises his left hand to display a fifty-dollar bill tucked between his index and ring fingers. "This is what I got. I already told ya what I want."

The whore looks at the fifty, then into the van. If it was any colder outside, she'd have frost on her eyelashes. Finally she walks around the van, opens the door on the passenger side and gets in.

"Wha'cha wanna do is take a right, head down to the river. I know a quiet spot under the bridge." A white woman in her thirties, she has an accent straight out of Bensonhurst.

"What's your name?"

"Angelique. What's yours?"

"Finito."

"Finito, huh?" Suddenly she reaches over with her left hand to grab his erection. "Guess who's ready," she teases, snuggling closer. "I like a man who's ready."

"You think that's for you?"

"Baby, it can be for anybody you want. Take another right. Yeah, that's good. Pull over in the middle of the block."

The block they turn onto, Tenth Street, is edged with low-rise warehouses, the tallest three stories high. The warehouses are closed, of course, and the globe on the streetlight in the center of the block has been shattered.

"You can pay me now."

When Finito complies, dropping the fifty into her extended palm, Angelique unbuttons her jacket and shrugs it off. She is all business now, sliding between the seats and onto the rug covering the open floor in the back. Her sweater follows her coat, her skirt follows her sweater.

"C'mere, baby," she says. "Let momma fix."

Suddenly Finito is on fire. He owns this woman now, mind body and soul, past, present and future.

"Tell me, Angelique," he demands as he slides into the back, as he presses the stun gun to her ribs, "have you ever been tortured before?"

Some three hours later, Finito squats in the rear of the U-Haul van, awaiting the reaction shot. This is what Abby calls the double takes in the comedies she loves to watch late at night on the classic movie channels. Reaction shots.

While he waits, Finito recalls past reaction shots: Darlene Crowder's defiance, Jennifer Denning's resignation, Rosaria's shock, Arlene Ying's confusion.

As these images proceed through his consciousness, they arouse him sexually. Finito needs arousing because he pretty much spent himself on whore number one, giving no thought even to the possibility of whore number two until much later when he'd happened on her standing a few doors away from Gentleman Johnny's, a local titty bar. Far from reluctant, she'd made a run for the van before he even came to a stop, throwing herself into the passenger's seat.

"Oh, baby, I am sooooo mutha-fuckin' cold."

Now that he has whore number two secured in the back of the van, Finito intends to get his money's worth. He is parked in the industrial neighborhood of Long Island City, one vehicle among many. It is three o'clock in the morning and the streets are deserted.

Impatient, Finito prods whore number two with the sole of his foot. He has tied her so that her arms and legs embrace a long cylindrical object wrapped in plastic. At first glance, the object appears to be a rug. In fact, it is the body of whore number one carefully prepared for disposal.

Finito's prodding is rewarded with a gag-muffled groan, a noise resembling the hum of a bee. Pleased, he settles back to watch whore number two's arms flex against the ropes that bind them. When she tries to kick out with her legs, they barely move.

A silence follows, a time of testing as whore number two regains control of her faculties, as the movements of her arms and legs grow more controlled and purposeful. In a minute she will figure it out; in a minute she will raise her head to discover her worst nightmare sitting not three feet away.

As Finito hefts the roll of duct tape in his hand, his eyes remain fixed on his victim. Though whore number two will remain alive for another few hours, his face will be the last thing she sees. She will carry his face all the way to hell.

At seven o'clock, some four hours later, Finito rides a crowded D train from the Bronx into Manhattan. Though it is Saturday, the car in which he travels is filled with mostly Latino workers traveling from the tenements of the Bronx to the basements and subbasements of Manhattan's office towers. Every seat is taken and people stand in little knots, their hands gripping the vertical steel poles like kids choosing up sides for a game of baseball.

Finito doesn't spare a thought for the working lives of these men and women. He's too busy maintaining his sanity. As the train accelerated on the long straightaway beneath the Harlem River, he'd become more and more certain that it was going too fast, that a crash was imminent. Now, when the car jerks suddenly to the left and right, he breaks into a sweat and becomes nauseated. His legs wobble beneath him and he struggles to draw a breath. Worst of all, some demented voice in his head demands that he make his escape before it's too late.

But, of course, there's nowhere to go.

When the train finally pulls to a stop at the 155th Street Station, Finito heaves a sigh of relief that vanishes before the train reaches the next station. This time he becomes convinced that his fellow passengers, almost as a group, are casting inquisitive glances in his direction. From this perception it's only a hop, skip and a jump to the belief that some part of his body is spattered with enough blood to attract attention. Despite all his fucking precautions.

Finito's nerve deserts him altogether on the three-mile express ride from 125th Street to Columbus Circle. Fighting his way through the crowd, the gym bag with all its incriminating evidence clutched in his right hand, he advances to the next car, and the next, and the next, until the D finally pulls into the station. Then he jumps onto the platform and heads up to the street as fast as his legs will carry him, finally emerging miles north of Abigail Stoph's Greenwich Village apartment.

Finito walks south, maintaining a steady pace, the pressure in his chest gradually easing. By the time he reaches Forty-second Street, he finds the courage to enter a diner, order a container of coffee, then visit the rest room. With the door shut and locked behind him, he turns to the mirror and inspects his reflection until he finds a tiny spot of what could be blood on the collar of his jacket.

After a moment's consideration, Finito makes a firm decision. The jacket must go, the rest of his clothing as well. This will present no challenge. Already he has dumped the bodies of his victims in the river, their personal effects in a dumpster, the van on a side street in the Bronx. He is an expert on dumping.

And that seems to be the end of the matter, at least for the present. Finito marches along Ninth Avenue as though he owns it. Not once does he think of the various items nestled within the gym bag, or of what might be demonstrated by an analysis of that little speck of blood on his collar. Instead, he feels the beast within him curl around his brain, a contented kitty in need of a good snooze after a hard night's work. This buoys him still further, until he becomes convinced, against all the evidence, that it's going to be okay.

Finito is still asleep when Abby returns from Mount Sinai Hospital at six o'clock in the evening. Like most nurses, even in the hospital's administrative division, she is required to work occasional weekends. When she discovers Finito in her bed, she is at first surprised, but then decides not to disturb him. Too late, though. His instincts honed by a life rarely without danger of one kind or another, Finito comes instantly awake.

"Hey," he says, "when did you get home?"

"Just a minute ago."

Finito sits up long enough to stretch and yawn, the covers dropping to his waist in the process. Then his head falls back to the pillow and he smiles. "How was your day?" he asks.

"Hectic."

Abby sits on the edge of the bed, her expression, in Finito's eyes, cautious if not outright suspicious. That she no longer appears hopeful does not surprise him. He's been watching her make up her mind for the past week. Now she just wants him out of her life.

"Where did you get the ring?"

The ring Abby points to surrounds Finito's right pinkie. It came from the middle finger of whore number two and has a cluster of small purple stones in an elaborate setting.

"My *tía*," he says, "gave it to me."

"Oh."

Finito shrugs. The last time they spoke of his ailing aunt, Abby had given him a little talk about letting go, one she'd undoubtedly picked up from the grief counselor at the hospital. It was her way of telling him that she wasn't gonna cough up the six grand for the operation. Well, if compassion wasn't motivation enough, he would just have to make her realize that six grand is the price to be paid for his departure.

"There's something I need to talk to you about." Abby turns to look into Finito's rapidly hardening eyes.

"What?"

"Well, I have a sister, Thelma, she's married to a man named Jack Slater and they live in Saginaw, Michigan. I mean, now they live in Michigan, but they used to live in New York, just a few blocks from here. Thelma has a daughter named Dawn and every year Dawn comes to stay with me for a long weekend during her spring break at school. We go to the park and to plays and the museums. You see, Dawn and I were very close when she was younger, before Thelma took her to live in Saginaw. I used to baby-sit all the time and—"

"When is this weekend happening?" Finito interrupts.

"Dawn will be flying into LaGuardia on Thursday, the twenty-first. She'll be staying until Sunday evening."

"And you don't want me around when she gets here." He keeps his tone flat, making it a pure statement of fact, and immediately knows that he's hit the nail dead center. Abby's eyes betray her, as usual. But Finito isn't overly troubled. The question is whether she's got the balls to confront him directly.

"No, no, I'm not saying that." Abby shakes her head twice, the gesture sharp and well defined, as if she's trying to convince herself. "I just want you to come with us, to the museums and things. I want to make it like a family weekend."

Finito reaches up to stroke Abby's shoulder. "Sure," he declares, "it'll be fun." A smile follows, a softening of the eyes. "I'm lookin' forward to it."

TWENTY-ONE

Monday, March 11, 1:45 P.M.

THE FIFTY-NINTH STREET BRIDGE, connecting midtown Manhattan with the borough of Queens, lacks the graceful and delicate silhouette of New York's suspension bridges. Supported by a complex network of girders, its superstructure appears to have been assembled by a precocious child from an Erector Set. Nevertheless, at a distance—especially at night, when the span is lighted—the intersections of the vertical and angled girders produce a lacy effect. Close up, however, this illusion is quickly dispelled. Despite more than twenty years of rehabilitation, eruptions of rust speckle the white paint covering the steel, as obtrusive as mushrooms on a suburban lawn.

Both these views, from far and near, are familiar to New Yorkers, millions of whom pass over the bridge each year. But there is still another view of the Fifty-ninth Street Bridge, this one relatively unknown, but which occupied Belinda Moore's attention on that late winter afternoon. This view, from beneath the bridge, is to be found on Roosevelt Island, a knife blade of land in the East River.

Belinda was on the west side of the island, standing between a pair of massive stone columns that rose fifteen stories to support an arch bearing much of the bridge's weight. Constructed from blocks of granite, columns and arch, like most of New York's architectural wonders, were reduced by the very scale of the city. The skyline of midtown Manhattan appeared nearly solid on the far side of the river. Nevertheless, if you moved the whole business, say to the steppes of Russia—the locals would fall down and worship it.

Comforted by the thought, Belinda finally worked up the courage to approach the bodies. She threaded her way through and around the city vehicles blocking the crime scene until she found her partner in conversation with Lieutenant Marlon Kearn, the CSU officer who shared their Project Intercept office. Farther away, a cluster of ranking officers, including Inspector Frank Carter, were holding a very heated conversation.

"Hey, Belinda." Kearn was smiling, as always. As always, his smile was apparently sincere. Even his black eyes, swollen behind his glasses, were warm and welcoming.

"Marlon, what's up?" For Belinda, the question was purely formal. What was plainly up, a mere fifteen feet away, was a pair of bodies visible beyond a circle of cops. The cops had gathered close to the bodies in an effort to shield them from the media helicopters hovering above the river.

Belinda doubted that the cops would succeed. She could see the bodies plainly. Bound at the ankles, knees and wrists with rope, the two naked women had been gagged and blindfolded with silvery duct tape.

"They came out of the river thirty minutes ago," Pudge interrupted. "Here, lemme show you."

Kearn's already broad smile broadened still further as Belinda nodded to him before walking off to join her partner. Even though Kearn had undoubtedly been the one to show Pudge in the first place, Kearn made no move to join the party.

"They were down there," Pudge said, "up against the seawall, maybe fifteen feet apart. Caught up in the rocks."

Belinda leaned over a waist-high railing, following Pudge's finger as it traced a line across the jagged boulders ten feet below. Obviously not the best place to dump a pair of bodies, but you wouldn't know that if you happened to arrive when the tide was up.

"We're thinking the bodies were dumped at high tide," Pudge said. "They sunk to the bottom, got trapped in the rocks, then the tide went out. Up close to the seawall, they would've been hard to spot from the walkway."

Belinda glanced to her left. The walkway in question was a long promenade running south past Goldwater Memorial Hospital. The promenade was lined with hundreds of cherry trees. Within a few weeks, their tightly wrapped blossoms would burst open, presenting the owners of the waterfront apartments across the river with a soft pink addition to their already spectacular views.

"How'd they get found?" Belinda asked.

"Guy walking along saw all these seagulls milling around. He looked over the railing to see what they were eating."

Belinda buttoned the collar of her coat. Though the temperatures had moderated overnight, the winds along the East River were predictably brisk. "How long were they down there?"

"Two, three, four days. With the water and the air this cold, it's anybody's guess."

"What about cause of death?"

"There are ligature marks around their necks, and probable knife wounds. But the crabs and the gulls also did a lot of damage. Plus, the vics might have been alive when they went into the water. Until after the autopsy, there's no way to know."

Belinda shuddered, then changed the subject. "He took a lot of risks here," she said. "He snatched two women, almost certainly off the street, and given his MO, it's likely he stole the vehicle he used. How many hours you think he was riding around after he picked up his first victim? If he'd been stopped, just at random, because some cop didn't like his face, it'd be all over now."

Belinda lapsed into silence. The disposal site was no more than ten minutes from Queens Plaza, where street prostitutes were eager to jump into vehicles driven by men, especially if those men were young and gorgeous. If it was her job to identify the victims, that would be the place she'd start.

But it wasn't her job and it wasn't going to be her job. She and Pudge were wasting their time, spinning their wheels when they could be out reviewing autopsy and crime scene photos.

"We have something else to do here?" Belinda asked her partner.

"Besides attend Her Highness, I can't think of anything." Pudge winked at his partner. "I'll bow, you scrape."

Lieutenant Moira O'Neill appeared haggard to Pudge Pedersson. Her eyes were noticeably bloodshot and the puffy flesh beneath them was the unhealthy brown of smoked tofu. O'Neill's mouth had slackened as well, softening her general expression in a manner that excited Pudge's sympathetic instincts. Still, he wasn't fool enough to believe these merely physical changes indicated any softening of his superior's heart. He stood respectfully before her, his hands behind his back, and waited for her to speak.

"I'd ask you what you think," O'Neill said after a moment, "but it doesn't matter. Too many people already saw them."

Pudge merely grunted an affirmative response. The first cops had rolled up on the scene to discover that personnel from Goldwater Hospital, including at least one physician, had retrieved the bodies, carrying them up off the rocks. In the process, they'd naturally observed certain details that one or more would reveal to the media. A half-dozen press vans were already parked along Vernon Boulevard at the far end of the bridge connecting Roosevelt Island to Long Island City in Queens.

Those were the facts on the ground, the sad facts, the unalterable facts. The homicides would have to be investigated by Project Intercept. The public would demand it, not to mention the mayor, the commissioner, and the chief of detectives.

"For the record," Belinda said. I'm certain this is the work of the perp who killed the others. And what I'm hoping, since he didn't expect the bodies to be found, is that he left something incriminating behind.

"Something long washed away by the tide, no doubt."

O'Neill was standing with her back to the water, to the East River, which wasn't a river, at all, but an arm of the Atlantic Ocean separating Manhattan from Long Island. The tides along its length, going and coming, reached seven knots, too strong for the barges and tugboats to fight. Commercial traffic went with the tides or stayed home.

Unsurprised by O'Neill's pessimism, Pedersson shrugged. "Anything else, lieutenant?" he asked.

"Yes, I need you to work the hot line tomorrow and Wednesday, eight to midnight."

Pudge glanced at Belinda. Lately, she'd taken to poking around whenever they were assigned hot-line duty. This was easy enough because the cops manning the phone lines typed summaries of incoming data into a central computer, which sorted the facts into files and prioritized them. The files were readily available to these same cops, who were incidentally charged with discouraging pranksters from calling repeatedly. The initial data, including the caller's name, address, and phone number, could be matched to a database of all prior callers.

"Anything else?" O'Neill asked.

"That list of released prisoners, the Rikers Island list," Pudge said, just beating his partner to the punch. "You told me to remind you if I didn't find it on my desk by today."

Lieutenant O'Neill's response was more explanatory than harsh, perhaps because of Pudge's deference. Or maybe she was just tired. "Look, this whole business with Rikers Island, it's based on three facts. Fact one: the man who stopped in at C&R Auto Parts on the morning Darlene Crowder was killed wore old clothes. Fact two: he had lots of muscles. Fact three: he had a bad haircut. I can't make any one of these, or all together, a priority. Not when we're getting a hundred phone tips a day. No, my judgment is that we're better off, the whole task force, if you keep on doing what you're doing. Understood?"

O'Neill waited for confirming nods before adding, "I'm not saying we won't get to it. I'm saying this is something you do after you do everything else. Now, it might please you to know that we're in the process of contacting all sex offenders released from jail or prison in the six months prior to the Crowder homicide. You can be sure we'll be taking a hard look at each of them."

Twenty minutes later, Pudge and Belinda were topping a quick lunch at the Midway Diner, on Twenty-first Street in Astoria, with cups of hot coffee. The best diner in Queens according to a *Daily News* poll, the Midway's apple pie, which Pudge was enjoying with a generous scoop of vanilla ice cream, was indeed delicious. As their next stop was the One Hundredth Precinct in Far Rockaway, where they would review the files on six unsolved homicides, perusing dozens of photographs in the process, neither was anxious to get rolling.

"I ever mention my Uncle Coltrane?" Belinda asked as the waiter refilled her coffee cup. She picked up two packages of sugar and gave them a vigorous shake.

"Coltrane?"

"Coltrane Montgomery." Belinda smiled. "What could I say? His father played tenor sax in college. So did he, come to think of it."

Pudge swirled a chunk of pie through his melting ice cream. "So, what about him?"

"He's a deputy warden. On Rikers Island."

"Belinda . . ."

"Please listen, okay? Then make up your mind. My uncle can get that list, just the way O'Neill described it to us. No females, no black or Asian males, no whites or Latinos with brown or black eyes, no whites or Latinos younger than eighteen or older than forty. He says he can do this without it being traced back to him, or even to his computer terminal, and he can supply their mug shots, too."

"Damn."

"Damn?"

"Yeah, exactly." Pudge held a napkin beneath his fork as he brought it to his mouth, catching most of the ice cream that dripped between the tines. "See, what you're gonna do is paint yourself in a corner. People like Carter, Wideman and O'Neill, you go behind their backs, they'll make you pay for it. Even if your hunch is right."

"Even *if?*"

Though Pudge was putting forth his best arguments, he was in many ways a man waiting to be persuaded. As both knew.

"The incident at C&R Auto Parts?" he asked. "O'Neill's analysis wasn't far off the mark. But even if she's wrong and you're right, it doesn't mean the guy who walked into C&R looking for work killed Darlene Crowder." Pudge folded his arms across his chest. "From where I sit, what you wanna do is take a very big risk when there's very little hope of a reward."

"But don't ya see, that's the whole beauty of it, Pudge. If we're wrong, so what? Nobody'll ever know."

Stubborn as ever, Pudge returned to his original argument. "O'Neill finds out we got the list after she ordered us to leave it alone, she'll send us home in a box."

"Are you telling me you wouldn't make that sacrifice to get the man who tossed those women into the water? Is that what you're telling me, Pudge Pedersson? That you fear the wrath of O'Neill and Wideman more than you fear the next crime scene?"

• • •

What could Pudge say to that? What could he say that would leave his integrity, not to mention his manhood, intact? Especially when he considered the risk his risk-averse partner was prepared to take.

Though Belinda hadn't grown up in dire poverty, her parents had both worked at low-paying jobs and there'd been times when money was scarce, when she'd been acutely aware of her parents' fears as they huddled around a table piled with bills at the beginning of every month. During recessions, the family had lived under constant threat. The phone, the gas, or the electricity was about to be shut off, or they'd come home to find an eviction notice taped to the door of their tenement apartment. There were even times when they'd been forced to choose between food and her brother's asthma spray.

From very early on, Belinda had been determined to escape that fate, to move up in the world, to make a secure life for herself and the family she'd one day have. She'd begun by postponing marriage while she worked a full-time job by day and attended Queens College at night. Then, after three long years, when she'd finally accumulated the sixty college credits required by the NYPD, she'd abruptly quit school and joined the cops, much to the consternation of her family.

"What was I supposed to do with a B.A.?" she'd told Pudge on more than one occasion. "Become a personal assistant? Maybe an HRA case worker at thirty grand a year? In the meantime, I would've picked up another ten thousand dollars in loans."

With overtime, Belinda had knocked down close to seventy-five thousand on the prior year. Her package included twenty-five vacation days and virtually unlimited sick leave. In a bit over seven years, at age forty-five, she could, if she chose, hand in her papers and collect a pension to the end of her days, along with lifetime medical and dental benefits. That wasn't bad, even when compared to various relatives who'd fulfilled their parents' ambitions by getting that college degree.

• • •

What captured Pudge's attention, as he considered his partner's challenge, wasn't the sacrifice she'd called on him to make, but the risk, to her family and herself, that she was taking. Belinda was putting decades of bullheaded effort on the line. She was turning her priorities on their head.

"Tell me what you wanna do here," he finally said.

Belinda took a deep breath. Her smile was warmer now that she'd gotten her way. "First, I don't think the list is gonna be that long. Whites and Latinos with green, blue, or hazel eyes, between eighteen and forty, released over a period of three weeks. There can't be a lot of them."

"Agreed."

"So what we're gonna do, when we get the list a few days from now, is show their mug shots to the folks at C&R."

Suddenly Pudge realized that he'd been hoodwinked. This wasn't an either-or proposition. This wasn't either O'Neill and Wideman don't find out, or Pudge and Belinda get their man. This was racing down blind alleys, hoping nobody tossed a garbage can off the roof.

"Homicide's running the Crowder investigation, not us," he pointed out. "No doubt they've touched bases with José and the Rosenthals. That's a given." Pudge stopped long enough to finish the last of his ice cream with a coffee spoon. Then he put down the spoon and leaned over the table. "For all we know, Homicide might walk into C&R ten minutes after we arrive, while those mug shots are lying on somebody's desk. That would definitely provoke a display of professional resentment."

"You done, Pudge?"

"One final point. You lay a photo spread before three witnesses, any three witnesses, one of them will make an ID. We know that from experience. Just like we know the resulting ID, which in this case is more than eight months old, will be totally unreliable. So what are we gonna do when someone at C&R

says, I *think* that's him? Or, that *looks* like him? Or, that *could* be him? Go directly to O'Neill? Keep it to ourselves? If we keep it to ourselves, it could take us a year to run the guy down. If we take it to O'Neill and the ID's wrong, we could find ourselves in the hump seat at a departmental hearing."

Belinda stood up, started for the cash register on the other side of the diner, then suddenly turned back to Pudge. "You remember what Ronald Martin told us? Shortly after ten o'clock, while his aide was watching *Rosie*, he saw a light-haired white man approach Darlene Crowder. According to Martin, they went into the tunnel together, but the man came out alone. That's less than two hours after the C&R gang had their surprise visitor. Somehow I don't think the two incidents were unrelated."

Fighting his bulk, Pudge gradually worked his way across the bench, then rose to his feet. Belinda's failure to respond to a single one of his points came as no surprise. That didn't mean those points would vanish, or that Belinda wasn't taking them seriously. It only meant that problems would be handled as they arose, that risks would be assessed before chances were taken.

As he started after his partner, Pudge was acutely aware of the long road Belinda had traveled in the past few months. Taking the man's pay and doing the man's job had always been the source of her pride, and it was pride that had kept her going, despite the obstacles. But she wasn't doing the man's job now. She was on her own. Except for him, of course.

TWENTY-TWO

"HOT LINE, DETECTIVE PEDERSSON."

In an effort to shut out the din of a half-dozen ongoing conversations, Pudge Pedersson leaned forward in his office chair, placing his head squarely between the panels of his minicubicle. It had only been two days since the recovery of the bodies on Roosevelt Island, and the reward for the Break-in Killer had been upped to a hundred thousand dollars. For the past three hours, the hot line had been jammed with hundreds of callers, most of whom immediately hung up when placed on hold.

"This reward, you are still having it?" The man's tone was low and conspiratorial, his Russian accent thick enough to pour into an engine block. Ziss for this, haffink for having.

"No one's claimed it yet," Pudge replied evenly. "It's still up for grabs."

"Well, I am knowing who are committing these murders."

"Great. Why don't we start with your name?"

"Why you are wanting my name?"

"Well, sir, it's gonna be hard to give you the reward if we don't know who you are. I mean, do me make out the check to cash and leave it in a phone booth somewhere?"

After a brief hesitation, the man said, "You are recording this, yes?"

"All hot line calls are recorded."

"Then you will know from my voice who I am."

Pudge hit the Tab key, then typed ANON into a box on the monitor bearing the legend Witness. Satisfied, he used the mouse to scroll past the fields for address and phone number, to an open space at the bottom of the electronic form.

"Alright, sir," he said, "what do you have to tell us?"

"This is who has done these murders. Sergei Abromowitz."

"Would you spell the name?"

As the caller reeled off the letters, Pudge dutifully pecked away at the keyboard. Then he brought the cursor to the task bar at the bottom of the screen and clicked the mouse, sending the computer off on a search of the files in its hard drive.

"Sir, could you tell me where Mr. Abromowitz lives?"

When Pudge typed the response, a window popped up on the right side of the monitor to display a dated list of eight prior calls naming Sergei Abromowitz as the Break-in Killer. Pudge chose one of these calls at random and retrieved the data. Sergei Abromowitz, he read, was a fiftysomething naturalized citizen of Russian origin who worked nights in a Canarsie bagel factory. When he wasn't being extremely cruel to small birds, kittens, and butterflies, he was being extremely cruel to his wife, children, neighbors and coworkers.

"Sir," Pudge said, "have you called us before?"

"You are not investigating. This is why I am calling back to you."

"How do you know that?"

"Know what?"

"How do you know we're not investigating? Say, you're not Sergei, are you? Because what I'm thinkin' is that you're Sergei and you wanna keep an eye on the case, see how close we're gettin'."

Pudge drew a contented breath when the caller hung up. Now

that it was past eleven, things were settling down. Pudge was seated one cubicle away from his partner, who was using the last in a long row of workstations lined up against the southern wall of the office. The stations were separated by freestanding panels designed to deaden sound. Before the panels were brought in from a city warehouse on West Thirty-third Street, the din had been nearly overwhelming.

"Hey, Pudge, come check this out." Belinda waited patiently for her partner's head to come around the partition, then for him to read the information on the monitor:

W/F Wit met H/M Sub 1st time Oriole Bar Bway/W.73 on 2/4. Sub mid-20s, grn/light brn, light skin. Gave Spanish name, spoke Spanish. Acted weird. Left bar approx 0130 hours.

"You see that date?"

"That's the date Elly Monette was murdered." Pudge leaned in for a closer look. "The subject is a light-skinned Hispanic male in his midtwenties with green eyes and light brown hair. He met the witness for the first time in the Oriole Bar at Broadway and Seventy-third Street. He spoke Spanish and acted weird. At one-thirty he left the bar, five blocks from the Monette scene."

"The ME estimated time of death between midnight and three o'clock in the morning. A witness at the scene, Hobart Marcuse, described a white man with light hair exiting the elevator around two o'clock, but it could have been a light-skinned Hispanic."

Pudge favored his partner with a frankly admiring glance. When it came to detail, Belinda was by far his superior, a fact long established. That's why he drove the car and she did the paperwork.

"How'd you find this?" he asked.

"Way I saw it, Pudge, the hot line didn't get started until after the Ying killings, so there was a lot of backed-up information out there. Also, you remember how many times the computers went down that first week? The operators were writing out the information in longhand, then entering it between calls when the computers started working again."

"Mostly," Pudge admitted, "it was pure chaos."

"Exactly." Belinda slid the mouse across the monitor and clicked once, bringing up the caller's demographics. "See, I kept thinking how easy it would have been to overlook something important in those first few days. Especially because we had no clear idea who we were looking for at the time. The witnesses in Hunts Point didn't turn up until February twenty-second, eight days later, and the wit at the Monette scene, Hobart Marcuse, was discredited when he made a false ID of Eddie Schwann."

"That still doesn't explain how you found—" Pudge glanced at the screen—"Maureen Owens."

"Simple, Pudge, I started with a search of all the files dated February fifteenth, the day the hot line went up. Then I began with the lowest-priority files, the ones I was sure hadn't been reviewed, and worked my way through them."

"And how many files would that be?"

"I don't know. A few hundred." Belinda's grin was quick and spirited. "I been goin' at it for the past two weeks."

On the following morning, at nine-fifteen, Pudge and Belinda were met in the reception area of New York Life's Overseas Division by Maureen Owens. Tall and notably attractive, Owens wore a pearl gray business suit over a lighter gray blouse. A small pin depicting an angel in full flight hung from the lapel of her jacket. Belinda initially assumed it was made of silver, but when she complimented Owens, the woman smiled, stroked the pin and announced, "It's platinum."

That fact established, Owens led them to her thirty-fifth floor office. The office was nicely appointed, with a spectacular view of midtown Manhattan, but Belinda's attention was drawn not to the Empire State Building, which seemed close enough to touch, but to a folded garment bag hanging over the back of the leather chair behind Owens's desk.

"Are you leaving town?" Belinda asked.

"I'm going to London. Be back next Tuesday. In fact, I'm in a bit of a hurry. How long will this take?"

"That depends on what you have to tell us. All we really know is that you met this guy who spoke Spanish and acted weird on the night Elly Monette was killed."

"George Espinosa."

"Pardon?"

"That's what he called himself."

"I see." The man who'd walked into C&R Auto Parts seven months before had called himself Filipo Velez. Two different people? Or was he playing the Hispanic part of the perp's basic MO? "Maybe you should just begin at the beginning. What was there about George Espinosa that you think we should know?"

Maureen Owens smiled, revealing a pair of crossed lower incisors. "How about the way he wore a shearling jacket?"

"How about it?"

"Most men in New York," Owens explained, "they put on a suede-out shearling coat, they look like cowboy wannabes. Like maybe they should be considering a testosterone patch. On this guy, the jacket was an understatement."

"A stud?"

"You could say that."

"Could you say he was rough trade?"

Owens thought about it for a moment, then shook her head. "First, he wasn't trade of any kind. The Oriole Bar isn't a meat market. It's a place where everybody knows your name, even if you happen to be unattached and over thirty. Second, he had a good line, very smooth, and he knew how to cover you with those green eyes. When he turned them on you, it was like you were the only thing in his world. He told me that his grandmother was a witch."

"A witch?" Belinda's eyes widened encouragingly.

"A witch in Santeria," Owens continued. "He told me his grandmother made potions and that she worshiped some goddess or other. I don't think he was making it up, or that he read about it in *New York* magazine. I think at some time or other, he lived it."

"Did he have an accent?"

"No, and I never would have taken him for Latino, either. Not in a million years. The guy was practically blond." Owens smiled. "I was amazed when he came on to me," she admitted. "Which is not to say I can't compete with the ladies at the Oriole. But this guy was in his twenties and he was beautiful." Owens leaned a little closer. "The mystery was what he was doing in the Oriole at all."

"Do you remember how the conversation went?"

"You know, back and forth. He offered to buy me a drink. I accepted. He asked me what I did for a living. He told me he was a social worker and his job was helping people with advanced HIV." Owens laughed. "The signals we were sending each other, Detective, were mostly nonverbal. If you take my meaning."

"I do, Ms. Owens. Trust me, I do." Belinda glanced at Pudge, who was staring out the window. The day was clear, the sunlight intense on the glass office towers to the north. "Still, I don't quite see what made you so suspicious that you decided to call the hot line."

Owens walked to a small closet and retrieved her coat. "Okay," she said, her smile now somewhat embarrassed, "what I've told you so far, it doesn't amount to much. But here's where it gets strange. I asked George where he lived and he gave me this sad story about his impossible roommate and how he's planning to move as soon as he finds an apartment. That made it the moment of truth, right? It's my place or it's not happening?"

"That's what it sounds like."

"Well, Detective, girls get horny, too. Me, I'm not given to one-night stands, but . . . but I'd had a few drinks and this was a chance that wasn't gonna come my way again. So I told him that I lived alone."

"And what did he do?"

"He paid his bill and left without another word."

Two thoughts jumped into Pudge's mind as he and Belinda left Maureen Owens's office. Owens was pissed off and her motive for making the call was hurt feelings. Nobody likes being rejected, especially after an hour of flirting. But then there was the artist, Ismene Farrier. For sure, the man who smooth-talked Maureen Owens into offering her apartment for a night of indulgence could've done the same to Ismene. But why would he walk out on Owens when he'd achieved his goal? Unless, of course, he was just practicing.

Curiously, this was exactly what his partner told him a minute later. "He was only practicing, Pudge. It was an experiment, a learning experience he eventually applied to Ismene Farrier. He knew from jump street that even if Owens made him an offer, he couldn't accept because too many people got a look at him."

Pudge nodded once, then lit a cigarette. "So where do you wanna go with this?"

As Maureen Owens did not expect to return from London until the following Tuesday evening, six days hence, there didn't seem to be much of a rush. Still, Pudge put the question forcefully. By contrast, Belinda's reply was tentative. Clearly, she wanted to hear his response before she committed herself.

"You think there's a connection between George Espinosa and the Break-in Killer?" she asked.

"Could be. Could be coincidence, too." Though Pudge, by an act of will, maintained his silence for a good five seconds, his urge to pontificate quickly rose to the fore. As he began to lecture, he noted Belinda's eyelids drop to half mast. From boredom or relief, he couldn't be sure.

"It's the physical part that jumps out at you," he declared. "The light hair and the green eyes. But it also works psychologically. The man who killed Darlene Crowder in Hunts Point obviously knew the mean streets because he took Darlene off one of the meanest. Meanwhile, the man Hobart Marcuse saw come out of the elevator at the Monette scene was so presentable that Marcuse took him for a tenant. Now skip to Maureen Owens. George Espinosa, as she describes him, fits either side of the equation. He's well dressed and smooth, but he talks about Santeria and growing up in the Bronx. That also accounts for the way his MO changed, from the early blitz attacks to the later controlled attacks on Elly Monette, Ismene Farrier, and the two prostitutes from Roosevelt Island whose names we learned this very day."

Belinda winced. The bodies of Angela Ciccarella (a.k.a. Angelique) and Earline Thomas (a.k.a. Jamaica Moon) had been positively identified the night before. The bad news was that Belinda and Pudge had learned about the IDs over breakfast that morning. From an article in the *Daily News*.

"So," Pudge concluded, repeating his earlier question, "where do you wanna go with this?"

"What are the choices?"

Pudge replied without hesitation. "Nowhere and directly to O'Neill."

"I was afraid you were gonna say that." When her partner failed to respond, even with a smile, Belinda continued. "I think we have to take it upstairs, Pudge. If George Espinosa and the Break-in Killer are one and the same, we don't have the resources to exploit the fact."

"What about your Uncle Coltrane?"

"Sometimes people tell you what you want to hear. They make promises they can't keep."

"And you think your uncle is one of those people?"

"The jury's still out, but I'm not holdin' my breath. Meanwhile, here's my story, the one I'm gonna stick to. Nobody told me I couldn't look through the files when I wasn't answering calls. Nobody said, Don't interview a witness if you turn something up. I was just doing my job to the very best of my ability.

Pudge looked over at his partner. "We," he said.

"What?"

"*We* were looking through the files when we weren't answering calls. *We* were just doing our jobs to the best of our abilities."

When his partner didn't respond, Pudge finally grinned. "In fact," he admitted, "if you wanna say the whole thing was my idea, I'll be more than happy to take the credit. I mean, finding Maureen Owens? Now that, Detective, is what we mean by detecting."

Much to Belinda's surprise, Lieutenant Moira O'Neill listened to her story (which fully reflected the *we* insisted on by her partner) without changing expression. Not so Captain Meyer Wideman who was standing behind his subordinate. Wideman's bushy eyebrows rose to within a few degrees of vertical, a position Belinda associated with the threat display of a tropical bird. This illusion was strengthened by the many cowlicks in his graying hair and the reddened wattle beneath his chin.

"I don't know what disgusts me more," he said. "To discover that you're not team players or that you're actually incompetent." He leaned a little closer to O'Neill. "Explain it to them, lieutenant," he told her. "I've got better things to do."

O'Neill waited for Wideman to walk off. Only then did her expression soften. Watching from his partner's left, Pudge got the distinct impression that if O'Neill had her way, her response would be different.

"Yes," she said, "if the wit's account is untainted, George Espinosa behaved strangely. Yes, he fits the description offered by the witnesses at C&R. Yes, the bar is five blocks from the Monette apartment and the time frame works. George

Espinosa could have killed Elly Monette. The problems, Detectives, are twofold. First, a hundred thousand people live and play on the five blocks between the Oriole and the Monette murder scene. Second, while Monette could have been killed around the time Espinosa walked out of the Oriole Bar, she could have been killed earlier or later as well."

O'Neill fended off Belinda's response by wagging a finger, if not in Belinda's face, not all that far from it. "In the future, you are to confine yourself to the jobs assigned to you. Under no circumstance are you to approach any witnesses. That's a direct order. As for Maureen Owens, I want all the paperwork on my desk within half an hour. Where and how she fits into this investigation is no longer your business."

Belinda and Pudge were on their way back to the small office they shared with Marlon Kearn when Belinda stopped before the open door to the office given over to Homicide. She paused long enough to stare across the room at a long corkboard running along the far wall. Virtually covered with the bits and pieces of the various cases, with photos, impromptu maps, detectives' notes, and lab reports, the board was a senseless jumble of shapes and images. Only the names of the victims were clear enough to read. That was because someone had taken the time to print them out in bold capital letters: DARLENE CROWDER, MARIA ESTEVEZ, JENNIFER DENNING, ELLY MONETTE, ROSARIA MONTES, LEONARD YING, ARLENE YING, ISMENE FARRIER, ANGELA CICCARELLA, EARLINE THOMAS.

A moment later, when they walked into their office, Lieutenant Marlon Kearn spun in his chair to face them. "What's new?" he asked.

"Not a thing," Belinda replied as she walked to her desk and began to sort through her notes. Though she didn't sit down, Belinda persisted at this task for a moment before turning back to Kearn.

"Marlon," she said, "I wanna ask you a question. That be okay?"

"Sure."

"We're friends, right? We call each other by our first names?"

"Is that the question?"

"No."

Enlarged by his glasses, Kearn's brown eyes sparkled. He was clearly enjoying himself. "In that case, the answer is that you and I are definitely friends."

"Well, I'm asking you this question as a friend who really needs to know the answer. Have you handled any evidence likely to reveal the perp's identity?"

After a moment, Kearn's expression grew more somber. "You bring him in," he finally said, "and I'll nail him to the wall."

"That's not what I asked, Marlon." Belinda's gaze was steady, her expression neutral. If he was going to refuse her, he was going to have to say it out loud.

"If you're thinking," Kearn finally said, "we've got a name and address, put it out of your head. It's like I said, you bring him to me, I've got the DNA evidence to convict at trial. But there's one thing you might look for. We recovered white animal hairs at two of the crime scenes, Monette's and Farrier's. They're wool. Like you might find on a sheepskin rug or a coat."

"A shearling coat?" Belinda's heart jumped into second gear, then third.

"Maybe, or maybe from the lining of a leather jacket, or any of a dozen other sources. That's not the point, anyway. The most you can say from a comparison of undyed animal hairs is that they don't exclude each other. There's no such thing as a match. It's just something you might wanna keep in the back of your mind in case you get lucky and come across the source."

"Does O'Neill know about this?"

"No. I'm saving it to surprise her on her birthday."

If Kearn's sarcasm was meant to discourage further questions, it missed its mark by a wide margin. Perhaps realizing this, he instantly clarified his position. "I'm not gonna sit for an interrogation, Belinda. Friends don't interrogate friends."

"One more question, Marlon. Then I'll shut up, I promise. And I definitely owe you for this."

Kearn sighed. "Let's hear it."

"What did O'Neill do when you brought the animal hair evidence to her attention?"

"The only thing I know for sure is that she took it to the Monette witness, Hobart Marcuse, and Marcuse didn't remember what kind of coat the man he saw coming out of the elevator was wearing. Or much of anything else, drunk as he was at the time."

TWENTY-THREE

THE CRYING GRATES on Finito's nerves. True, he'd known it was coming, that sooner or later she'd break down altogether. But it's her own fault; *La Puerca* should've paid him off a long time ago. How is it his responsibility if she's too cheap to come across with a few dollars? One thing he knows for sure, *La Puerca* has tons of money. Just a few weeks ago, she told him that her shitty one-bedroom apartment was worth a half-million dollars. Not only that, but when she bought it ten years ago, she only paid a hundred and ten thousand. So what's six grand to *La Puerca*? If she wants to be rid of him so bad, why doesn't she just cough up the fucking money? He can't understand it.

Finito's thoughts tumble in a circle, rising and falling through his mind as he nurses a beer and tries to concentrate on more important things. Abby is in the bedroom, crying because she found the gun where he'd hidden it beneath his underwear, as she was meant to do. The .22-caliber automatic may have been small in comparison to the 10-millimeter and .50-caliber behemoths on the market, but the bulge it created was unnatural enough to get *La Puerca*'s attention when she put the laundry away.

But then it went wrong. What *La Puerca* was supposed to do, after Finito explained that his aunt's worsening condition was driving him to desperation, was say the magic words: I'll lend you the money for the operation. That would've been the perfect way to finish the relationship. *La Puerca* pretends that it's only a loan, while he pretends that he's going to pay her back. Then they never see each other again. What could be simpler?

Instead, she carried on about her niece coming tomorrow, and what if Dawn found the gun, and she couldn't have this in her life, this horrible violence. God, how he wanted to smack her in the face.

Finito's thoughts continue to run on automatic for some time, alternating currents of blame and anger that eventually become faint enough to reveal the volcano beneath. The discovery of the bodies he dropped into the East River, imagining them gone forever, has shaken him to the core. Already, he has shed the stun gun and his shearling coat. At the time, as he tossed the bag into a dumpster on West Street, he'd wished that he could simply abandon his own skin, that he could resume as someone else. Now that the cops have the bodies, they will eventually discover exactly what he did with the stun gun. As they will eventually discover that both women were prostitutes, then blanket every stroll in New York City with undercover cops.

For three nights after the bodies were recovered, Finito dreamed the same dream. He was running through a subway train, chased by three boys, all older, who steadily gained ground. Finito knew what would happen if they caught him, what they would do to him, what they would make him do to them. He ran for his life. He ran until he awakened.

Finito's not used to fear. Fear is something he put away long ago, an emotion he associates with childhood, and with his victims. This is why he compensates with the epithet, *La Puerca*, which means fat sow, and why he keeps tightening the screws when it's at least possible that he will drive them in too deep, that Abby will change the locks, maybe even call the police. Finito desperately needs to control something and Abigail Stoph is the only game in town.

In an effort to somehow balance his fears and his needs, Finito has decided to leave New York. Leaving town has become his anchor, the only thing holding him in place. If it weren't for this solution to his problems, he'd . . .

And that's as far as he is willing to go. He will leave New York and start over. He will not make the same mistakes again. He will survive.

Satisfied, Finito's mind drifts to the practical. What are the rules, he asks himself, in the barrios of Los Angeles, Chicago, Boston, or even nearby Newark? How will he find a place to live when he has never legally rented an apartment in his entire life? Or possessed a driver's license or a credit card? In fact, the only reason he has a Social Security number is because the juvenile authorities forced it on him the first time he got busted.

Well, the obvious thing to do, he decides, is to find somebody who can show him the ropes. And Finito knows just the man to seek out, Rosaria Montes's cousin Raul, who left New York one step ahead of a robbery indictment about a year ago. According to Rosaria, the robbery indictment went away after the victim died of a heart attack, but Raul was doing so well in his Florida digs that he wasn't even tempted to return.

Finito doesn't know either Raul's address or phone number. But he knows who to ask: Rosaria's mother, Maria Gomez-Cardilla. His failure to show up for Rosaria's funeral doesn't worry him. That's because the principal emotions associated with death—grief and sympathy—are unknown to Finito. As he can't imagine his presence at Rosaria's wake and funeral having any positive effect on Maria Cardilla, he can't imagine his absence being an obstacle to her granting his request. He will make some weak excuse, and she will accept it. He will say he's sorry that Rosaria's dead and she will say, *"Gracias."*

Nevertheless, there is one aspect of the long subway ride he begins some thirty minutes later that does bother him. When he attacked Rosaria, he'd imagined himself breaking free of the sordid life he'd known up to that moment. Breaking free was his justification before and after the deed. But now he is returning to the Melrose section of the Bronx where he spent so much time as a child, where he suffered humiliations beyond counting. The gang bangers will be out, the punks and the wannabes, the stone-eyed drug dealers, the stumbling piss bums.

Finito is afraid of being like them, afraid that all his fantasies of growing into something larger are the dreams of a fool, that he is still that desperate little boy awaiting an opportunity to fill his stomach.

Of all the futures that Finito can imagine, this is the one he fears most. Better the gurney and needle, he tells himself again, than the mean streets of the South Bronx.

Maria Gomez-Cardilla's three-bedroom apartment on Eagle Street bears no resemblance to Finito's sordid imaginings. Working-class proper in every respect, it is testimony to the fact that Rosaria was the black sheep of the family. A green velvet sofa, flanked by oversized armchairs, rests on a white shag rug. Dominating the wall farthest from the sofa, a projection television set is virtually surrounded by speakers, leaving only enough space in the corner for a small shrine bearing a statue of the Virgin Mary. The Virgin wears blue robes and holds the heart of Her Son in Her upraised hand. Before Her, votive candles flicker behind red glass.

Maria's youngest son, fourteen-year-old Tino, sits at a computer workstation placed against the wall behind the couch. He stares at the monitor of an IBM desktop, his left hand resting on the mouse. Tino is doing his homework, an onerous task made necessary by the presence of his mother, who works the late shift at a nursing home in Washington Heights.

"So, Finito, I haven't seen you in a long time. *¿Qué pasa?*" Maria Cardilla is in her early forties, an attractive woman with a customarily assertive air that sets Finito's teeth on edge. Finito is wearing his best, a white turtleneck sweater over designer jeans, and a brown leather coat that drops to midthigh. His hair has recently been cut short and he now sports the beginnings of a beard, which is coming in darker than the hair on his head.

"You know," Finito says, "like I'm sorry I missed Rosaria's funeral. I was . . . you know, incarcerated. I couldn't do *nada*."

Two cups of Bustelo coffee sit on a glass table in front of the couch, along with a plate of small cakes and a bowl filled with cubes of sugar. Maria lifts her cup, then says, "You lookin' good, *hombre*." She gestures to his wardrobe. *"Muy bueno."*

"I'm workin' now," Finito responds. *"Estoy enmendando mis costumbres y doblando la hoja."*

This promise to reform has tumbled from Finito's lips many times in the past and Maria does not react to it. Instead, she sips at her coffee, then returns the cup to the table.

"How is Miguel?" Finito asks, referring to Maria's current husband.

"Miguel hurt his knee, but the Transit Authority won't give him time off. They say he sits all day when he drives the train so his knee don't matter. The union's gonna file a grievance but you could wait for them until you're dead. *Eso es la vida*."

The mother of five children, Maria Cardilla is a third-generation New Yorker, and more comfortable in English than in Spanish. Her husband is a motorman with the Metropolitan Transit Authority, while she has been a nurses' aide for many years.

"I'm sorry to hear that," Finito says, his tone so mechanical that he's sure he's not fooling anyone, certainly not Maria who knows him from way back, who from time to time gave him shelter, who is as close to a *Tía* Suzanna as he will ever get.

Nonetheless, Finito doggedly persists, inquiring about each of Maria's living children, about her siblings, about favored nieces and nephews. In so doing, he stakes a claim to a place in Maria Cardilla's extended family. That he does this after having slaughtered Maria's daughter not only doesn't trouble him, it never crosses his mind. Once he expressed his regrets for Rosaria's passing, she simply became irrelevant, neither an impediment, nor an aid, to the realization of his goal.

Finito is still at it twenty minutes later, when Maria's son-in-law Martin Butler enters the apartment. He is carrying a CD burner which Tino eagerly takes from his hands. Butler is an electronics wholesaler who supplies merchandise to the Cardillas from his warehouse on Bruckner Boulevard at slightly above cost.

"Hey, man, thanks." Tino demonstrates his appreciation with a complex series of high and low fives. Then he opens the box, removes the manual and begins to read.

Smiling, Butler turns to Finito and Maria. "Hey, Finito," he says as he kisses his mother-in-law's cheek, "I saw you the other day. In the Village. You were with a woman and I didn't wanna cut into your action."

"You should've said hello." Finito tries to smile but doesn't quite succeed. In the past he's made a number of attempts to hustle Martin Butler, all unsuccessful.

Butler takes a seat on the couch, then crosses his legs. "So, what's up?" he asks.

For just an instant, Finito indulges a fantasy in which he takes the pistol he carries from his coat pocket, then kills them all. Butler, Maria and Tino, one after another, bang, bang, bang. Though brief, Finito's fantasy is vivid, resulting in a slight sexual arousal, a familiar tingling in the groin. Suddenly he is feeling better.

"I'm thinkin' about leavin' town," he declares. "About startin' over somewhere else."

"Are you planning to leave soon?" Butler asks.

Finito ignores the question. "The last time I saw Rosaria, a couple months ago, she told me that Raul was in Florida and he was doin' good, so I figured I'd look him up. Only thing, I don't know exactly where he's at."

"Raul's in Orlando," Maria replies, "but he might not be doin' so great. When I spoke to him last week, he asked for money."

"*Mira*, if I had his phone number, I could call him and ask him how it's goin'." Finito shrugs. "It ain't no big deal. Raul and me were always close. Raul's like *mi hermano*.

As if Finito could ever be a brother to anyone. As if Maria Cardilla and Martin Butler don't know it. But Finito is not counting on his words standing any test of truthfulness. What matters is that Finito and Raul are committed *delinquentes*. What matters is that *la familia* will not be upset should Finito leave New York and Raul never return.

Finito's feeling much better when he finally leaves Maria Cardilla's apartment, Raul's address and phone number safely tucked into his wallet. A weight has been removed from his shoulders, and he suddenly believes that anything is possible, that his horizons are limitless. It's time to play.

Eight hours later, Finito draws a thin line of heroin up though his nose, just enough to confer a light buzz. Then he watches his former roommate, Janice Hunt, probe for a vein near her left elbow with the point of a disposable syringe. Hunt is a handsome, well-fleshed woman who lives on the small income generated by a trust fund inherited from her mother. This income is sufficient to pay the rent on her Hell's Kitchen apartment, put food in her stomach, clothes on her back. But it is not enough to put dope in her veins and she has alternated between a series of junkie lovers and periods of abrupt withdrawal for the better part of a decade. Finito was lucky enough to meet her, quite by accident, three days before, and to find her in her desperate phase. Knowing he'd arrive with a gift, she'd practically begged him to come by.

A thin plume of blood filters into the syringe. Janice has finally hit a vein. Eyes narrowing in anticipation, she eases the plunger down a bare quarter of an inch, then hesitates, then another quarter inch, then hesitates, again and again until the syringe is empty. Sighing, she finally withdraws the bloody needle, drops it beside a candle on the night table, and falls backs onto the bed, eyes open. Only the rise and fall of her chest indicates that she is even alive.

Finito watches Hunt for several minutes before he opens a drawer in Hunt's double dresser and removes several silk scarves. Approaching the bed, he runs the silk over her cheek.

"*Mira*," he whispers, "you remember the little game we played on that Sunday when it rained?" He leans down to nuzzle her throat. "You remember?"

After a very long moment, Hunt's lips part in a slight smile. Janice does remember and she would like to play again.

Finito starts to remove her blouse, then stops himself. It will much more fun, he thinks, to cut her clothes away. Later, when she's awake enough to know what's happening.

Hunt's left arm, when Finito lifts it, offers no resistance, not when he turns one end of a scarf several times around her wrist, nor when he ties the other end to the brass headboard. And why should she resist? Finito is quite right. They have played this game before. All he has done is modify the rules.

The first evidence of these modifications, from Janice Hunt's point of view, comes just a few seconds later when Finito stuffs a washcloth into her mouth, then ties it down with a scarf.

Shortly before sunrise, as Finito walks toward the shower, he catches sight of himself in a mirror hanging on the inside of the bathroom door. He is naked, his body smeared with blood, from his scalp to his feet. As he pauses to admire his reflection, he thinks the same thought three times. I am death. I am death. I am death. Then he turns on the water, adjusts the temperature, steps into the shower and begins to lather up. Within seconds, as if all the terrors of the past week have simply taken flight, he is daydreaming of Orlando, imagining sun-washed beaches, palm trees, bikini-clad beauties to be had for the asking.

TWENTY-FOUR

Friday, March 22, 4:40 P.M.

PUDGE PEDERSSON WAS HAVING a very bad day and there was nothing his partner could do to cheer him up. First thing, he'd been jilted by the love of his life, the widow Annie MacDougald. Pudge had called her shortly before one, intending to put his foot down, to demand she accept his apology. Far from submissive, Annie had coolly informed him that she was now involved with somebody else, that for the time being she was committed.

Disoriented by the news, Pudge asked who that somebody was. "John Taggert," Annie replied, "if you must know."

As John Taggert regularly attended Pudge's church, Pudge could now look forward to seeing the happy couple every Sunday morning. He could look forward to bearing witness.

"Methodism," he told Belinda, "is lookin' better and better."

But Detective Moore was not impressed. "A few days ago," she pointed out, "you were makin' noises like you wanted to end the relationship."

"Yeah," Pudge admitted, "but not this way."

Blow number two came at four o'clock when Pudge and Belinda waltzed into the office only to discover that another body had been found early that morning. This time they hadn't been invited to the crime scene, nor had their opinions been sought. Instead, they received the news as a gift from Marlon Kearn, who'd been working the scene since early in the morning.

"The apartment," he told them, "it's only one room, a studio. There was blood everywhere."

An hour later, they were summoned to a general briefing. Moira O'Neill, flanked as usual by Meyer Wideman, told the assembled that victim number thirteen was named Janice Hunt and she'd died within an hour of being found at 7:00 A.M. by the porter who noticed her door ajar.

And that was that, the very news that would soon be revealed to the press was now revealed to the police. Pudge was burning to know the details; not knowing offended him to the core. But there was nothing he could do except feign indifference while his partner wheedled a few details out of Marlon Kearn. As usual, Kearn seemed amused by the exchange.

"The perp took a shower and the victim used heroin. We found a set of works and a couple of bags lying on the night table. According to the porter, she had a lot of junkie boyfriends. He says he knows because he used to be a junkie himself. That was before he found Jesus."

"A heroin-dependent victim with multiple lovers? Sounds like Rosaria Montes."

"That's what the profiler said."

"The profiler say anything else?"

"He said the perp's freaking out. The way he butchered . . ." Suddenly Kearn's eyes grew remote as he ran the fingers of both hands over his closely cropped hair. "Christ," he said, "there was blood everywhere."

They'd come into the office to catch up on their paperwork before the weekend, and that's what they did until Belinda received a phone call at six o'clock.

"Belinda, sweetheart," her Uncle Coltrane told her when she answered, "can you make it out to my place tomorrow morning, round about ten? You say you're comin', I'll have breakfast on the table when you get here."

"See you at ten," Belinda replied without hesitation. As she turned to her partner, she struggled with a rising agitation. This wasn't like walking the edge. This was like walking the god-damned plank. Meanwhile, there was no doubt in her mind that she would go forward, with or without her partner. Just as there was no doubt that what she felt at that moment was far more pleasant than the conversation she would have with her husband when she got home.

"Bingo," she told her partner at seven o'clock when they stepped out onto Fourteenth Street. Then she repeated what her uncle had told her, word for word. "So, whatta you wanna do here, Pudge? Now that we've been warned and our jobs are on the line?"

"Where's your uncle live?"

"In Queens. Elmhurst." Belinda rattled off the address.

"Fine. I'll meet you at ten, take a look. Could be there's no gorgeous, green-eyed white men on the list. Then it won't matter."

But it did matter, as Pudge Pedersson discovered on the following morning when he examined the photos arrayed on Coltrane Montgomery's kitchen table. Only a few years older than Belinda, Coltrane was tall and well built, as were most of the Corrections officers Pudge had run into over the years. His wife, on the other hand, who'd been introduced to them as Lily, was sitting in a wheelchair in the parlor, listening to the Marcus Roberts Trio explore the Cole Porter songbook while she read the newspaper.

There were twenty pairs of photos on display, but a number of these could be eliminated immediately. Two were of black men, another of an Asian, while several more were of dark-skinned Latinos very unlikely to be described as white. Another five, though of green-eyed white men, revealed countenances that not even the most charitable would deem "gawjus." That left nine possibles.

"What's this about?" Belinda displayed the mug shots of the two black men and the Asian to her uncle.

"Our data processing unit is understaffed," Montgomery said without a hint of apology. "When you gotta work all day at top speed, you make mistakes."

"Does that swing both ways?"

"Say what?"

"Does it mean that some green-eyed white men have been classified as black-eyed Asians?"

Montgomery laughed. "Most likely," he admitted.

Laying the photos to one side, Belinda arranged the possibles into three lines of three photos. "You makin' anybody here?" she told her partner.

Pudge answered without looking up. "I don't claim," he said, "to know how women think, but I don't see anybody who'd impress Maureen Owens. She's a pretty tough cookie."

Belinda noted the underlying bitterness in the little preface to Pudge's answer and was, for once, sympathetic. Her conversation with her husband just a few hours before had not gone well. Ralph was as even-tempered as any man Belinda had ever known, but not this time. In fact, if it weren't for the kids in the other room, he might have started throwing things.

"Nobody looks good in a mug shot," Belinda finally said. "Here, check this guy out." She leaned forward and read off the man's name: "Jorge Rakowski. Who do you think got to him?"

A pair of mug shots, full front and left profile, revealed a young man with two swollen eyes, the right nearly shut, and a split lower lip. As the mug shots were taken the day Rakowski arrived at Rikers, twenty-four hours after his arrest, Belinda's first suspicions naturally fell on the arresting officers. But the beating seemed too severe, too wanton for cops. More likely, she was looking at the end result of vigilante justice.

From the living room, a series of piano arpeggios cascaded into the kitchen as Marcus Roberts dug into a decidedly uptempo "Paper Moon." Like most of the younger jazz musicians, Roberts was a virtuoso, his touch as delicate as it was precise. Coltrane Montgomery nodded once and said, "I'm gonna go inside, sit with Lily. You take all the time you need."

Belinda waited for the door to close before returning to the nine photos. In her more optimistic moments, she'd believed the perp would leap at her the instant she looked at his photo. But it hadn't happened and now she was faced with sorting through the possibilities, imagining one man photographed in a more flattering light, another freshly shaved, another dressed in something more presentable than a torn and dirty Black Sabbath T-shirt.

"I know I keep repeating myself," she finally told her partner, "but what do you wanna do here?"

Pudge made no response initially, his eyes jumping from one photo to another, and Belinda was sure he was going to put a halt to their little rebellion. But then he finally turned to her and asked, "You remember what we decided about Rosaria Montes's killer, right?"

"Remind me," Belinda said.

"At the time, we both figured it was probable that the killer knew his victim. The shower afterward, the obvious rage, no sign of forced entry . . . that's what it added up to."

"True enough."

Pudge took a couple of steps toward the kitchen door, then spun around to his partner. "The local who caught the Montes case, what was his name?"

"Detective Cordova," Belinda said.

"Yeah, Benedicto Cordova. He was the one who told us that Rosaria was the black sheep of her family. He said he knew because he spoke to her mother. You recall that?"

"I do."

"That means Rosaria has a family."

"And?"

"And I think it's possible that if Rosaria knew her killer, her family did, too, so that's where we oughta take the mug shots." Pudge rushed on as if he expected his partner to voice an objection. "Maureen Owens is still in London and I don't trust the witnesses at C&R. It's been too long and they've already given conflicting descriptions, not to mention the fact that the Rosenthals are actually insane. Plus, Lieutenant O'Neill told us to stay away from the witnesses, but Rosaria's mother isn't a witness."

"Not yet."

"Not yet?"

"Well, Pudge, if she were to make an identification, that'd change her status in a hurry. By the way, Rosaria's mother, I assume we're gonna wheedle her name and address out of Detective Cordova."

Pudge Pedersson's grin exposed two neat rows of small teeth. "C'mon, Belinda, be fair. We wouldn't wanna take up Project Intercept's precious time when we have another way to go. That would be wasteful."

TWENTY-FIVE

PUDGE PEDERSSON WEDGED HIMSELF into an armchair in Maria Gomez-Cardilla's living room and basically expounded the same line his partner had run on Ronald Martin. Their mission was routine, a backward look at ground already covered. He was, of course, very sorry to be taking up their time, especially on a Saturday evening, but Project Intercept was working a twenty-four/seven schedule, sparing no effort to nail the Break-in Killer.

To Pudge's left, Maria Cardilla sat next to her husband, Miguel. Behind them, his hand resting lightly on his mother's shoulder, Tino Cardilla watched Pudge intently. Tino favored his father; his skin was dark and his features had a pronounced African cast. By contrast, Maria's nose was aquiline, her hazel eyes folded in the corners. Her olive skin might have been found anywhere along the Mediterranean Sea.

"Alright," Pudge said when Belinda walked back into the living room, "we're ready. Now, I want you to go in there, one at a time, and take a close look at the photos we've arranged. If you see anyone you recognize, don't say anything until after everybody's had a chance. Okay?"

Though all present nodded, it was a matter of seconds before Maria Cardilla broke the agreement. "¡Dios me salve!" she shouted, "they got Finito here." Whereupon her son and husband charged into the kitchen.

In that moment, Pudge felt something rise within him, a chill that bore with it more than a tinge of the overtly sexual. All that hiking around, pickin' 'em up, puttin' 'em down on sidewalks as gray as the civil service world in which you functioned. It was wearying, it was drudgery, it was almost always frustrating. Well, this was the payoff, the validation. This was why he packed that gun every morning, why he put the badge into his pocket, why he stuffed his corn-studded feet into a pair of scuffed, worn-at-the-heels wing tips.

Pudge looked over at his partner, only to find her staring back at him. Though neither smiled, Pudge curled his right hand into a fist and tapped his chest.

"We did it," he whispered. Then he got up and walked into the kitchen where he took back the photo Maria held. It was Jorge Rakowski's photo, black eyes, split lip and all.

"I want you to look at the rest of the mug shots," he instructed. "*Carefully*. Don't jump to any conclusions. Just take your time."

After that, it was just a matter of waiting for the charade to be over, for Tino, Miguel, and Maria to grow bored with the game, to return to the living room and resume their respective places. When that was finally accomplished a few moments later, Pudge handed the Rakowski mug shot to Maria, then leaned back in his seat. His aim was to gather as much information as possible without asking pointed questions.

"Finito, man," Tino said as he took the photo from his mother's hand, "they really whipped on his head that day."

"He got caught robbin' a car," Maria explained, "by the owner and his brothers." She hesitated for a moment, then presented Pudge with a question he'd been anticipating. "Do you think Finito killed my Rosaria?"

Pudge stared into Maria's eyes for a moment, then shook his head. "Actually, we were looking at somebody else, but I guess we'll have to check him out. Those photos, by the way, they're all of people who were released from Rikers Island around the same time."

Tino was the first to respond. "Finito," he pointed out, "spent half his life on Rikers. He musta been busted like fifty times."

Maria briefly considered this fact, then turned to her husband. "Finito, he's not like . . . *un asesino.* He's like–"

Miguel finished her sentence. "He's *un pillo.* He steals little things. Once he done a robbery and they sent him to prison. Since then, he's too much afraid. He don' mess around with guns."

"But he'll steal anything that's not nailed down," Tino observed. "When he was here the other day, I watched him every minute."

"That's right," Miguel said, "you tole me Finito came around." He looked at Pudge. "Finito's gonna move to Florida to be with Maria's cousin Raul."

When the family grew silent long enough for Pudge to be sure they were waiting for him to speak, he retrieved the photo and stared at it for a moment. One thing was immediately apparent. If he needed to do a canvass at some point, he'd have to secure a better likeness, perhaps from an earlier arrest.

"What does . . . you said, *Finito?*"

"That's what everybody calls him," Maria responded, "since he was a little boy."

"Well, what does Finito look like? When he's healthy?"

"Like a *maricón,*" Miguel replied with a laugh. "Like a *pato.*"

"*Deja eso.*" Maria gave her husband a little push. "Finito is beautiful. When he was growing up, he had any girl he wanted. Miguel is only jealous." She gave her husband another poke. "Wait, I'll show you."

Maria went into her bedroom, returning after a moment with a photo album. "My daughter, Teresa, from her wedding," she explained as she opened the album and flipped through the pages. "Here, this is Finito."

Pudge glanced at the face Maria indicated, then looked at his partner. Belinda was drinking in the sandy hair, the green eyes, the silky eyebrows, the sensual mouth, the arrogant chin. Vindication for her, too, for the logical inferences she'd drawn from the available evidence, and for her gut instincts. After a moment, she sat back, crossed her legs, and smiled.

"A pretty boy," she announced. "I can't wait to meet him."

The cross-talk continued long enough for Pudge and Belinda to learn that Maria's son-in-law Martin Butler had recently come across Finito somewhere in "the Village." The East Village? Greenwich Village? The West Village? Martin Butler and his family lived on Leonard Street so it was probably the West Village.

But the Cardillas weren't certain, as they weren't certain that Finito had any residence at all. What little knowledge they had of his life had come from Rosaria. She and Finito were close as children, and they'd maintained their friendship as adults, though they saw each other infrequently. In fact, the infrequent contact and the general perception that Finito was physically harmless were the main reasons he hadn't been included in the list of Rosaria's male associates given to Detective Cordova.

It was past dark when Pudge and Belinda left the Cardillas' apartment. Although Belinda had asked that their little visit be kept a secret, neither was at all sure the Cardillas would comply. Almost certainly, they would call Martin Butler. It was the least they could do after giving his address and phone number to the cops.

They were approaching Pudge's car, a battered Ford Taurus less likely to be vandalized than Belinda's Jeep, when Belinda broke the silence.

"He's gettin' ready to skip," she said. "Finito."

"I know the point you're makin', okay?" Pudge unlocked Belinda's door, then stepped back.

"Which is exactly what?"

"Finito has to be taken down fast, before he kills anybody else, before he runs. The way you do it is you get every cop in the city looking for him and release his photo to the press."

Belinda slid into the Taurus, then waited for her partner to take his place behind the wheel before stating the obvious: "That first item you mentioned? We can't accomplish that, not by ourselves."

When Pudge didn't answer, when he pulled away from the curb and headed off down the block, she clarified her position. "I don't care about winning. I don't care about being right. I don't care if the job tosses me out with the garbage. I just wanna take Finito down before he kills anybody else."

"And that means we have to go to the task force."

"First."

"First?"

"Yeah, first we go to O'Neill and Wideman, give them a chance to do the right thing."

"And if they don't?"

"Then we call CBS, NBC, ABC, CNN, Fox, and every damned newspaper in the city."

Neither Wideman nor O'Neill was in the office they shared when Pudge and Belinda entered at eight o'clock. Instead, Detective-Sergeant Michael Crouch was seated behind O'Neill's desk. In his midfifties, Crouch had long ago hitched his wagon to Meyer Wideman's star, a move designed to get him off the street and behind a desk for the remainder of his working life.

"This better be good," Crouch said.

"We know who he is." Pudge was standing in front of Crouch's desk, leaning slightly forward. "The villain," he quickly added when the sergeant's expression tracked the line from suspicious to confused, "the bad guy, the perpetrator."

"You've got him?"

"I didn't say that. I said we know who he is."

"And you're sure?"

"I am."

"And you, Detective? Are you also sure?"

"Me, too," Belinda replied. "I'm also sure."

Crouch smiled for the first time as his fingers riffled through a black Rolodex. Then he picked up a telephone and said, "O'Neill's gonna be pissed. What she told me when she left this afternoon, she's goin' to a wedding tonight. Deputy Commissioner Monroe's daughter."

When she made her appearance an hour later, O'Neill was resplendent in a black cocktail dress complemented by a necklace of thin silver chains that spilled to the top of her considerable décolletage. As she crossed the room on four-inch heels, her silver earrings tinkled faintly.

"This better be good," she announced.

But it wasn't good, not as far as Pudge could tell, not after he admitted that they'd secured that list of Rikers Island prisoners on their own. No, when Pudge announced that little fact, O'Neill's face lit up as though it had been slapped. But Pudge was undaunted as he laid a mug shot of Finito Rakowski on the table. The full-front color photo had been taken thirteen months before when Finito was arrested for boosting a radio at the Kmart on Astor Place. No longer worried about leaving an electronic trail, Belinda had used a task force computer to secure and print the photo while awaiting O'Neill's arrival.

The color drained from O'Neill's cheeks as fast as it had appeared. "Go back over it again," she commanded.

The leap of faith, Pudge freely admitted, was the association of the perp's ragged appearance and highly defined physique with someone who'd recently been in jail. But once you made that leap, the rest was easy. The general description first provided by the witnesses at C&R was confirmed by Ronald Martin who saw the perp with Darlene Crowder, by Hobart Marcuse who bumped into him coming out of an elevator, by Maureen Owens who flirted with him in a bar. As for their belief that Rosaria Montes knew her killer (the belief that had taken them to the Cardillas' apartment in the Bronx), that conclusion was fully justified by the evidence at the crime scene.

After a moment, O'Neill picked up Finito Rakowski's mug shot and carried it to a high-intensity lamp resting on a filing cabinet. She turned on the lamp and bent forward to examine the photo closely.

Belinda suspected that O'Neill wanted nothing more than to reject Pudge's every argument. After all, though the inferences she and Pudge had drawn were reasonable, they were not the only inferences that could be drawn from the evidence. But there was no getting around Finito Rakowski. Despite the harsh lighting and the predatory look in his vivid green eyes, it was clear that Gladys Rosenthal and Maureen Owens had been accurate in their insistence on his physical beauty. He was gawjus.

"I have no reason to believe," O'Neill finally said, "that you'd obey a direct order, so consider this a request. Would you please go back to your office and wait there until I sort this out?"

Pudge started to reply, then felt Belinda's hand on his elbow. Her touch stopped him before he could echo O'Neill's sarcasm by saying what he'd been wanting to say from the beginning: We were right and you were wrong. Instead, he turned and walked away, leaving the field to his partner who, as it turned out, was up to the task.

"Do you think," she asked, her demeanor and tone neutral enough to be insolent in their own right, "that we might run down to the diner, pick up some burgers? What with all the running around, we didn't have time to eat."

TWENTY-SIX

IT'S ABBY'S NIECE, DAWN SLATER, who makes all the difference. Within an hour of her arrival on Thursday, Finito grasps Abby's vulnerability. In eight-year-old Dawn's eyes, Abby is the favorite aunt who treats her favorite niece to fancy restaurants and Broadway shows, or takes her shopping in the boutiques along Madison Avenue, or down in SoHo, or even in hip, shabby Williamsburg. In Dawn's eyes, Abby is way cool.

They are returning from the airport, Finito sitting in the back and not saying much of anything. Up front, Dawn chatters away, her excitement and pleasure obvious. Abby's own pleasure is equally obvious. And why not? To her niece, she's Abby the competent, the successful. She's all the things she can never be in real life.

Phony is the word and contempt the emotion Finito puts to this basic perception. In his world, kids are weak and pathetic, without the ability to protect themselves. They're nothing and adults never seek their approval, or even their permission.

Abby's need for Dawn's approval is more evidence of Abby's vulnerability, of the fear that rules Abby's life, the fear that people won't like her. This is the conclusion Finito draws as they crest the Kosciusko Bridge connecting Brooklyn and Queens, as aunt and niece ooh and aah at the skyline of Manhattan to their right. That leaves only one real question to be addressed: Is a child's approval worth six thousand dollars? Because Abigail Stoph is going to suffer a loss before the weekend's over. It's just a matter of what.

Whenever the kid looks at Finito, he smiles his most ingratiating smile. His aim is to charm Dawn, to claim her approval for himself. But it's a nonstarter. The kid watches him the way a bird watches the progress of a snake. Will he bite? Or will he he curl up under a rock and fall asleep? Time for plan B.

Once the bags are unpacked and the car returned, they go out to a neighborhood Japanese restaurant where Finito flirts openly with the waitress, drinks too much, and uses the word "fat" at every opportunity. On the way home, he shifts his weight to bump the shoulder of a middle-aged man walking in the opposite direction.

"Watch where the fuck you're goin'," he calls over his shoulder. Then he winks at Dawn and adds, "Maybe we oughta walk single file. The way it is, we're takin' up the whole sidewalk."

Later that night, after Dawn goes to bed, when Abby finally makes the offer, she can't bring herself to look Finito in the eye.

"I've been thinking," she says, "about your Aunt Suzanna. I've been thinking that I could lend you the money for her operation. You can pay me back when you find a job."

Finito can barely contain himself. "Oh, baby," he says. "*Gracias, gracias.* You don't know what it's been doin' to me. Worryin' about my *tía.*"

He lays it on thicker than necessary. He rubs Abby's nose in it. And later, when he slides beneath the sheets, when he lays his hands on her thigh, when he climbs on top of her, she doesn't resist.

In the morning, Finito, now the good boy, makes herbal tea

and cinnamon toast for the ladies. Then he excuses himself when Abby announces a shopping trip to the exotic boutiques of the Lower East Side.

"I don't think," he tells the ladies, "they carry my size."

Two hours later, Finito sits before the television, watching NY1, the cable news station. As the anchor introduces a trio of pro-filers, he plays with a key chain in his pocket. The chain, once the property of Janice Hunt, has a silky rabbit's foot attached to its clasp.

For just an instant, Finito considers the possibility that once Dawn is gone, Abby will renege on the deal. Then he laughs, imagining just how many pieces he will cut her into, just how long he'll keep her alive.

From this fantasy, Finito's thoughts jump to his prior victims. He recalls his disappointment with the deaths of Elly Monette, Darlene Crowder, Jennifer Denning and Ismene Farrier. By com-parison, the deaths of Janice Hunt and the two whores were as good as it got, which is exactly the opposite of what he'd figured at the time.

Finito stays with this contrast for another fifteen minutes, ignoring the images on the television until Rosaria Montes's photo suddenly appears on the screen. After Rosaria's death, Finito had decided that he made a mistake. But that wasn't so, as Janice Hunt proved. Hunt was the pinnacle and the hours they spent together were greatly intensified by the simple fact that he knew her. By his knowing, absolutely, that Janice Hunt was a cockroach, just like Rosaria, just like the two whores. That they were made to be crushed.

Finito maintains his positive attitude into Sunday morning, when he decides to run out for bagels. The bagels are to be a little treat for the girls before they traipse off to Central Park, where the daffodils, according to Abby, are in full bloom.

Outside, the air is chilly, the sun still low in the east, but the sky above is a deep blue and nearly cloudless. A beautiful day for a murder, Finito decides. And he has the perfect victim in mind, another ex-girlfriend. Does he have the balls to slip in and out of her little apartment in Flushing between the time Abby and Dawn leave for the park and the time they leave for the airport? Does he have the balls for a farewell performance? The best part is that he hadn't seen this girlfriend in almost a year, not until he ran into her on the street a month before. If he calls her now, out of the blue, if he gets lucky and she happens to be home alone, there will be nobody to connect him to her death.

Though the boldness of the deed appeals to Finito, capturing most of his attention, it fails to override his innate caution. This fact is made clear when he approaches the bagel shop on Sixth Avenue. Like virtually all of the retail businesses clustered along the avenues of Manhattan, the bakery's front is dominated by a large window. Through this window, Finito sees two men approach the counter. He knows these men are cops before they flash their shields, before they present a photograph for the counterman's inspection.

Finito turns and walks off. Not too fast, not fast enough to attract attention, but not taking his time about it, either. He tells himself the cops might be searching for anybody, but that theory is blasted into a thousand pieces when he discovers a second pair of cops, a black woman and a giant of a man, on Seventh Avenue.

Finito runs his hands over his beard. Still fairly short, it has nonetheless thickened. The beard has remained dark as well, much darker than the hair on his head. If he keeps his wits about him, if he makes himself invisible as he has hundreds of times in the past, he will survive.

Strategy and goal, to become invisible and to survive, propel Finito forward until he enters the deserted lobby of Abby's building. Then he drops to his knees, his fingers trembling, all his joy turned to panic, his bravado to abject terror. His mind spins as he tries to cope with the transition. Only a few moments before, he was in perfect control; he was planning his future. Only a few moments before he was the shoe, now he is the cockroach.

TWENTY-SEVEN

Sunday, March 24, 10:15 A.M.

BELINDA MOORE IGNORED her partner's sulk with practiced ease. Pudge had been forced to compromise twice in the course of the prior evening and compromise was definitely not his thing.

The first compromise was taking the Montes ID to Project Intercept, but that one had been necessary. They simply could not accomplish what had to be accomplished in order to bring Finito Rakowski down, not on their own. Pudge might've lived with that. But not the compromise suggested by Detective Emilio Venezia, the NYPD profiler. Trained by the FBI at Quantico, Venezia had spoken with maddening assurance when he addressed the hastily assembled task force at one o'clock in the morning.

"Some serial homicides," Venezia explained, "are characterized by cooling-off periods that go on for years. The men who commit these homicides are rarely apprehended. Other serial killers, like the D.C. snipers, hunt more or less continually."

Venezia hesitated briefly as his eyes swept the room. Commanded to appear on a Saturday night, the senses of more than a few of Project Intercept's detectives were obviously dulled by alcohol.

"For various reasons," Venezia continued, "certain killers begin to lose control after a number of successful kills. As I've explained in the past, the breakdown process accelerates with each additional kill and is generally referred to as decompensation. The perpetrator in our case has been decompensating for some time. That means he suffers episodes of extreme anxiety. In my opinion, faced with the knowledge that he's been identified, he will decompensate further. When Ted Bundy escaped from jail and made his way to Florida, he abandoned the control associated with his prior homicides. No more elaborate ruse, no more carefully prepared killing and dumping grounds, no more taking his sweet time. Bundy killed as fast as he could whenever he could until he was finally arrested."

Bottom line, if Finito Rakowski's photo appeared on the little screen (assuming he was the perp; Venezia would only say that Rakowski satisfied most of the elements listed in the profile), it was probable that he'd indulge in a final spree. On the other hand, if they didn't put his face out there, if they kept the search low-key, there was the less likely chance that either he'd kill again before he was found or flee the jurisdiction.

What settled the deal, for the bosses, was the profiler's belief that Finito's talk of running away to Florida was symptomatic of his need to relieve the pressure. It did not necessarily mean that he would desert New York where he knew the streets like the back of his hand.

It was O'Neill, after Venezia finished, who revealed the strategy they would pursue. Pairs of detectives would canvass the three Villages, plus the adjoining neighborhoods of SoHo, Chelsea, and the Lower East Side. The selection of this territory was justified by Maria Cardilla's son-in-law, Martin Butler, who'd already been contacted. Butler had seen Finito on the west side of Sixth Avenue near Tenth Street on a Saturday evening at about seven o'clock. At the time, Finito had been walking south on the other side of street, in the company of an older woman.

"It wouldn't be so bad," Pudge groused to his partner, "if we had any real idea where Rakowski's holed up. I mean, Butler saw Finito on Sixth Avenue near Tenth Street. So what? It was Saturday night in Greenwich Village. There's gotta be like twenty thousand people come to the Village on Saturday night. We got no reason to believe he lives in the neighborhood or even in Manhattan."

Belinda nibbled at the crust of her tuna fish sandwich, leaning far forward to avoid dripping mayonnaise on her coat. They were standing on the edge of a concrete pier jutting a hundred yards into the Hudson River, taking an early lunch. The air was calm, the sky cloudless, the sun to their backs.

"They way I see it, we should be glad we're still on the job." Belinda shuddered, remembering O'Neill marching into the office she and Pudge shared with Marlon Kearn. O'Neill had given them their assignment, followed it with a little lecture, then left. "Besides, it's only for a day, two at the most."

"What makes you so sure?" Pudge leaned over the railing to look out on a long string of yellow kayaks making their way north over the flat water. Bright as toys, their wet hulls reflected a myriad of tiny suns, as did the spray kicked up by a dozen windmilling paddles.

"There's fifty detectives out there showing the same photograph to thousands of people. I wouldn't be surprised if some enterprising reporter wasn't on her way downtown even as we speak." She tore off a piece of her sandwich and tossed it to a hovering gull. Seemingly without effort, the gull dropped a few inches and caught the tidbit in its bill.

"One way or another," Belinda continued, "it's *finito* for Finito." She looked down at her sandwich, thinking that she should eat something. But her stomach was queasy, as it usually was after snatching three hours' sleep in a room with four snoring males who passed gas every fifteen seconds. Meanwhile, her partner, a few feet away, dug into a bacon and egg sandwich with obvious gusto. As she watched, a ruby-red drop of ketchup appeared at the corner of his mouth, only to be snatched away by his darting tongue.

Silently, Belinda broke the remainder of her sandwich into pieces and began tossing the bits to the gulls.

The territory assigned to Pudge and Belinda ran west to east from the Hudson to Seventh Avenue, and south to north from Fourteenth Street to Christopher Street. Home to perhaps twenty-five thousand people, the area was small enough to thoroughly canvass its many retail businesses, including the clubs which they would work into the night.

They got their first break in one of the many boutiques on the far western edge of Fourteenth Street after two hours of unsuccessful canvassing. They were in what remained of the Gansevoort meat district, now mostly relocated to the market in Hunts Point. The district covered just a few square blocks on the border of the West Village and the trendy neighborhood of Chelsea. Up for grabs, it was universally understood to be the choicest plum in the developers' pie.

Accustomed to the bustle of the department stores at the mall on Flatbush Avenue, Belinda was first impressed by the silence as she entered Ameriana, then by the open space. The floor was green marble, the walls covered with brown silk. A matching silk canopy rippled in a light breeze generated by a fan recessed in the far wall.

Belinda hesitated before a display of handbags. Like sculptures in a museum, the bags were set apart, each in its own pool of light. The cheapest among them, she knew, would set her back four hundred dollars.

The sales associate who approached Belinda was a young and

stunningly attractive brunette. A model, no doubt, or an actress in the making. Though she must have realized that neither Belinda, nor her mountain of a partner, was likely to produce a commission, her smile was friendly when she asked if she could help them.

Belinda displayed her shield. "We're lookin' for this man," she said, as she'd said a dozen times that morning. "Would you tell me if you've seen him?" Her expectations were low. Ameriana was not the sort of place she associated with Finito Rakowski, the petty thief.

"Yeah," the woman replied, "I did see this guy."

"Are you sure?"

"Almost positive."

"When did you see him?"

"Let's see?" She tilted her head back and momentarily gazed at the rippling fabric above. "Friday," she finally said. "He was with an older woman and a child. Wait a sec, let me show this to Stefano."

Belinda watched the woman cross the store, then present the photo to an associate, a short, barrel-chested man who wore a shiny black suit over a white-on-white T-shirt. The man caressed the tuft of hair beneath his lower lip as he listened to his colleague, from time to time glancing at the detectives. Finally, he nodded once, then came forward.

"I am Stefano Peridi," he announced, "and I remember this person very well." He rolled his eyes. "A beautiful boy. Above his station, though. In Ameriana's."

Peridi continued on, his gestures growing broader as he presented Belinda and Pudge with the details. Glancing over his shoulder, Belinda watched Peridi's colleague nod from time to time. She found the confirming gesture reassuring enough to kick her pulse up several notches.

What quickly became clear was that both Stefano and his associate, Sarah Cole, evaluated Finito Rakowski in the same way. He was a sexual object, a boy-toy, not someone you'd take seriously but worth a very brief, very vulgar fantasy. They were equally in agreement about the woman who'd accompanied him. "A dishrag," was the way Peridi described her. "At least ten years older and dumpy to boot. I can't imagine what they were doing together. She didn't even have money. She was strictly a tourist."

Not that Peridi meant that literally. Tourist was the word he ordinarily employed to describe shoppers who entered Ameriana never intending to make a purchase. Boy-toy and his sugar mommy were definitely of this type.

"So, you're saying they were local?" Belinda asked.

Sarah Cole spoke up for the first time. "They might be," she said, "except for the child. She was about nine or ten, a pretty girl, looking at the price tags and giggling. That's very Minnesota. Which is where I'm from, incidentally."

The door opened and a middle-aged woman in a red leather coat stepped through. Peridi was off in an instant, clapping his hands as he crossed the showroom. "Marvelous Martha," he shouted, "that coat is you, absolutely *you*."

Cole winked at Belinda. "Duty calls," she said. "Anything else?"

"Yeah, one thing," Pudge Pedersson answered. He was standing before a display of shoes and boots, all for the right foot. "This boot here? This red one? The little tag on the heel says $625. And what I wanna know is if that's $625 apiece, or do you throw in the left one free?"

TWENTY-EIGHT

BELINDA GOT ON THE CELL PHONE within seconds of leaving Ameriana. Wideman's instructions had been specific. Probable sightings were to be reported to command and control without delay. Though detectives in the field would be allowed some leeway in their definition of probable, they were strongly advised to err on the side of caution. Under no circumstances, unless the subject was observed on the street and alone, was he to be approached without specific authorization.

Cigarette in hand, Pudge Pedersson watched Belinda from a distance of fifteen feet. There was a slight flaw, he'd already decided, in the bosses' strategy. Given that Finito Rakowski was the street thief Pudge had all along believed him to be, there was an excellent chance that he'd spot the cops before the cops spotted him. Mutts like Rakowski, they could not only smell a cop from two blocks away, they knew how to melt into the shadows, to become invisible. That was how they survived.

Pudge stared at his reflection in Ameriana's showroom window. There he stood, a great lumpy mountain sandwiched between a pair of glistening red shoulder bags. Nobody, not even a cloistered nun, would make him for anything but a cop.

"You alright?"

Pudge looked away from his reflection and toward his partner. "Yeah, fine, what'd the bosses say?"

"I spoke to O'Neill. She says we're gettin' hits all over, especially in the East Village."

"Anything solid?"

"Rakowski's been seen from time to time, usually out buying dope. Nobody knows where he currently lives, but all agree that's he's lookin' sharp these days." Belinda gestured toward the window. "You in the market for a new bag?"

"No," Pudge said, "I'm not. I was checkin' myself out."

"And what did you decide? About yourself?"

"That I look just like a cop."

"And . . . ?"

"And we better get to work." Pudge tossed his cigarette into the street. "You comin'?"

"After you, Cisco."

The predominant mode of transportation in much of New York City, and virtually all of Manhattan, is walking. Cars are out of the question; there's no place to park when you arrive at your destination even if you're willing to brave the traffic. No, the humdrum of life, the routine errands that keep a household up and running, are accomplished one step at a time, which is why New Yorkers walk so fast.

It's also why stores of every kind locate within walking distance of residential neighborhoods. Dry cleaners, drugstores, laundromats, barber and beauty salons, supermarkets and liquor stores, restaurants, movie theaters, banks. If you're able and willing to cover a radius of ten blocks, a mere half mile, you can buy almost anything.

Within the territory assigned to Pudge and Belinda, commercial establishments fronted Seventh and Greenwich Avenues, as well as Christopher and Bleecker Streets, hundreds of stores presenting a solid front to the bustling pedestrians. Forbidden to split up, Pudge and Belinda moved from one to another, flashing tin, flashing Rakowski's photograph. By four o'clock in the afternoon, with a half-dozen solid hits under their belt, they'd concluded that Rakowski was living somewhere in the neighborhood. That somewhere, however, remained unknown. Only once had they come close, when a Latino delivery boy pointed them at a town house on Horatio Street. Pudge and Belinda had approached a woman sitting on the stoop, a long-time resident as it turned out, who claimed to know everybody in the building and who'd never laid eyes on Finito Rakowski.

False alarm or not, the sighting had set Pudge Pedersson's heart to racing, and he'd yet to calm down. As he and Belinda made their way along Christopher Street, he gazed at the features of each male he came across, regardless of age or race, hoping against hope. Though it was rapidly growing dark, the sidewalks were still crowded, the outdoor cafés packed, and Pudge's eyes jumped from one face to another, restless as butterflies. His partner's eyes, he noted, were doing the same dance. This was a skill they'd learned in their first years on the job, patrolling the mean streets at a time when they were about as mean as streets can get. Everybody received a look, a pointed evaluating glance.

They labored on until five o'clock, when the cell phone in Belinda's purse began to ring. They were inside a porno bookstore at the time, enduring the attitude of a clerk who stubbornly refused even to glance at Rakowski's photo.

"We don't look at the customers," the clerk repeated as Belinda stepped outside to take the call. "They got a right to privacy. That's our policy."

"Okay," Pudge said after the door closed behind his partner, "it's still a free country. You don't wanna look, you don't have to. No hard feelings."

Pudge demonstrated his sincerity by offering his massive right hand for a quick shake, an offer the clerk could hardly refuse, but which he quickly came to regret. Pudge squeezed down hard and held on for a count of five, a slow count. He did this not only because the clerk failed to cooperate, but also because he,

Pudge Pedersson, was offended by the very idea of pornography. Except for a single gasp, the clerk was wise enough to hold his tongue.

"Anything important?" Pudge asked his partner a moment later. One thing about Pudge, he didn't mind being mean-spirited, as long as Belinda didn't catch him at it. The business with the clerk had definitely elevated his mood.

"More sightings, no address. Ya know something, Pudge, what I'm beginning to think, you could show this mug shot in Chicago and get hits. I mean, 95 percent of the people we talked with claim they never saw the guy before. Why are they wrong and those clerks in the boutique right? You think maybe it's because we want them to be?"

Pudge waved off Belinda's pessimism. "The reason we believe the wits in the boutique," he pointed out, "is because they identified Rakowski without hesitation, saw him just a couple of days ago and recalled significant small details. Plus, there's the wit in the bagel store. He also ID'd Rakowski the instant he looked at the photo. He says Rakowski's been a regular customer for months, that Rakowski's got a thing for garlic bagels and vegetable cream cheese."

"Alright, I'm convinced," Belinda declared, though her tone of voice indicated otherwise. "Where do you wanna go from here?"

Pudge looked around. They were standing on the corner of Christopher and West Streets, across from the river. In the last nine hours they'd covered virtually every open store in the territory assigned to them. There were the clubs, of course, but it was far too early for the clubs.

"What we could do," he said, "is rework Seventh Avenue and Hudson Street, concentrate on restaurants that make deliveries. The delivery boys will just be coming on duty now."

It was a reasonable strategy. Though a small army of men pedaled their bicycles from restaurant to residence and back again, delivering every sort of cuisine, from Peruvian to Malaysian, on a twenty-four/seven basis, the hours between six and midnight were by far the busiest.

"We could do that, Pudge," Belinda admitted, "but I think we oughta skip to the chase, work the side streets, talk to the doormen and the supers."

"O'Neill give you the okay?"

"I didn't ask."

Their job, as strictly defined by Moira O'Neill, was to canvass the commercial establishments in their territory—the small businesses by day, the clubs by night. Once Rakowski was located, traffic would be closed off and the surrounding blocks flooded with cops before contact was made.

"Ya know, Belinda," Pudge said after a moment, "you and me, we still got our feet in the fire. We do this, we'll be in up to our ears."

It was a decent bluff, or seemed so to Pudge Pedersson. Belinda, however, dismissed it out of hand. "Say that again, Pudge, only this time look me in the eye."

Instead, Pudge looked down at his shoes. "My feet are killin' me," he admitted.

"It's those flat shoes. You got no arch support. I told you that a hundred times."

Pudge tried to imagine Eliot Ness in sneakers, chasing after Al Capone. "Let's give it a couple of hours," he finally said, "see what turns up."

Luck is a matter of perseverance, a cop truism long ago embraced by Pudge and Belinda. Did you catch that break? Or did the break catch you? In the end, it didn't matter. As long as the investigation was closed with an arrest, nobody gave a damn.

It was fully dark, the streetlamps casting an unforgiving light over a short industrial block of West Tenth Street, when Pudge and Belinda, after nine hours of perseverance, finally got lucky.

The light, of a nameless color located at the intersection of pink, amber and beige, cut through the shadows to reveal two men sitting on the loading dock of a closed warehouse. The men were African Americans and they sat with their legs extended, their backs against the overstuffed trash bags that held their possessions. Apparently settled in for the night, they were sharing a pint of cheap wine which they'd cleverly concealed in a paper bag.

These men were not happy to be approached by Pudge and Belinda, and they did not so much as glance at the shields offered to them, erecting instead a sullen shield of their own. Public drinking was a crime in New York, a quality-of-life crime, and they were subject to arrest. Failing that, they would most likely be encouraged to remove their ragged asses from the West Village. Just when they were getting ready for bed.

But then Pudge displayed Finito Rakowski's photo and the men quickly brightened. Whoever this white dude was, he wasn't either of them. The older of the two fumbled through the pockets of his coat until he found a pair of reading glasses. Settling them on this nose and ears, he briefly reexamined the photo, then said, "There a reward for this dude?"

In fact, the reward money was up to $175,000, a fact that Pudge was not at liberty to reveal. For a moment, he calmly evaluated the old man with his tightly curled, white-on-white beard, his rheumy bloodshot eyes. Then he made a show of removing his wallet and withdrawing a ten-dollar bill.

"Sure," he said, "and here it is."

Belinda stepped to the man's right, putting some distance between herself and her partner. The gesture was threatening and meant to be so. "What's your name?" she said.

"Jimmy Smith."

"Jimmy *Smith?*" Belinda rolled her eyes. "Lord, give me patience."

"I ain't done nothin'. Why you goin' on like this?"

Pudge shook his head and answered the man's question with

one of his own. "Why don't you wanna tell us whether you know the man?"

Jimmy shook his head in disbelief. "Ain't this some shit? Here you ain't even axed me the question and you wanna know why I ain't answered it."

"Well, do you, Jimmy Smith?" Belinda said. "Do you know this man?"

"Matter of fact, I do. Okay? And I know where he's livin' at. How you like that?"

Smith grinned, folding his arms across his chest. Now that he had the stage to himself, he wasn't about to rush his performance. First, he launched into a complaint about the city's new recycling policies. For the past several years, he told Pudge and Belinda, he'd been salvaging redeemable cans and bottles from the recylables set out for pickup, carefully opening the blue plastic bags, retying them once they'd been picked clean. But then, without any warning, the mayor simply announced the end of plastic and glass recycling in New York City. This change had negatively impacted Jimmy's bottom line and he was severely pissed off.

"Seems like they wanna snatch what little a man's got," he lamented. "Seems like nobody don't want a man to have nothin'."

Belinda was far from sympathetic. "You're not jerkin' us off, are you, Jimmy? Because that wouldn't be in your best interests."

Jimmy's lip curled at Belinda's reference to masturbation, but he understood well enough to comply with her request. "Okay," he said, "check this out."

Though only peripherally related to his problem with the city's recycling policy, Jimmy's story put his questioners on full alert. Jimmy, it seemed, had been collecting recylables a few months ago when his work was interrupted, first by a voice that said, "Hey, bum, have another one," then by a flying Pepsi can that bounced off his shoulder.

"Now me," he told Pudge and Belinda, "I ain't no punk. I been inside, done the whole bit, ya know what I'm sayin'? But ah'm a old man now and what I seen in that boy's eyes was somethin' I didn' wanna fuck with. So I let him go his way."

"Which was exactly where?"

"Into that same buildin' where I was standin'. Yessir, had his own keys. Walk in like he own the damn place."

"You ever see him again?"

"Seen him plenty of times, seen him go into that buildin' again. Yessir, that's where he's livin' at. Right there. You want, I'll take you to that very spot."

When Pudge dropped the ten into Jimmy's outstretched hand, the old man chuckled. He turned to his comrade and nodded twice. "Done killed two birds, Clyde," he announced. "Made myself ten dollars and I get to even up with that knucklehead. I musta stepped in the good shit, uh-huh. When I get back, we gonna celebrate."

TWENTY-NINE

FINITO'S MIND REELS from thought to thought, unable to find a single point of rest. One minute he decides to flee, to get out, to run from his crimes as he's run so many times in the past. The next minute he is certain that if he opens the door and steps into the hallway, he'll be paralyzed with fear, that he'll literally stop moving. A minute after that, he's telling himself that the cops are looking for somebody else, not him at all, that as long as he doesn't do anything stupid, he has nothing to worry about.

After a long struggle, Finito is finally able to grasp this last idea. Are the cops looking for him or not? It's a question, he realizes, that might be answered. He'll call around, check in with his bros in the Bronx and on the Lower East Side. Those are the first places the pigs will look if they're really searching for him.

Finito's third call, to an associate living on Third Street near Avenue D, produces the result he'd both expected and feared.

"Hey, Leander, *qué pasa?*"

"Who this?"

"It's Finito."

"Finito? Oh, shit, the poe-leese be steady lookin' out fa yo ass. Like, the man is *everywhere.*"

So, that's that. They know, they are coming. Finito's fears now explode in his brain, clamoring for attention, demanding to know why he didn't listen before it was too late. He recalls every mistake he made, the details passing in and out of his consciousness with a great roar. He is finished. *He is finito.* They will put him in a cell and keep him there until his appeals expire. They will strap him to a gurney and stop his heart and he will be dead. Running will not help him as it has so often in the past when his crimes were minor. No, the man will never stop looking. There is no way out. That's what happens when you make yourself powerful. That's what happens when they come to fear you.

These last thoughts, though he stumbles across them accidentally, ripple through Finito's body. In a way, he tells himself, the beast has delivered what he promised.

No, not in a way, but absolutely. The cops will hunt him forever *because* he is powerful. They're *admitting* that he's powerful.

Finito carries a chair from the dining room table over to the front window. He sits and carefully arranges his shirt to cover the pistol tucked beneath his belt. Then he peers out onto the street through embroidered curtains that flutter in a noticeably cool breeze. The window is open several inches on the bottom, but he makes no move to close it. Maybe, he tells himself, execution is the price of power, at least for people like him. If you aren't willing to pay the price, you end up crawling through the muck until you drown.

Already feeling better, Finito goes on to remind himself that the road between arrest and execution is a long one, and that he might still have some fun along the way. He tells himself, also, that it doesn't really matter what he does between now and his arrest. After all, they can only kill you once.

By the time Abby and Dawn return from their Central Park excursion at four-thirty, Finito has settled down. Now that he knows his fate, he can concentrate on the fate of *La Puerca.* In Dawn he has no interest, outside of her potential value as a hostage. She is no more attractive to him than was Leonard Ying. On the other hand, *La Puerca* has been the subject of many a blood-drenched fantasy. Hurting *La Puerca* would do him no end of good.

"Are you okay?"

Abby's voice drags Finito into the present. He smiles at her, nods to Dawn. "How was the park?"

Dawn speaks up before Abby can respond. "Why are you sitting by the window?"

Finito briefly considers driving the toe of his shoe into her forehead by way of explanation. "I'm enjoyin' the breeze," he announces. "What a day, huh?"

"Well," Abby tells her niece, "if we're going to be out of here in an hour, we better pack up. Are you coming with us to the airport, Georgie?"

Though Abby's eyes communicate a fervent wish that he remain behind, Finito says, "Wouldn't miss it for the world."

For the next forty-five minutes, Finito sits calmly while Dawn and Abby hustle from one predictably messy room to another, gathering Dawn's possessions, her books and CDs and computer games, her coats, hats and sweaters. Twice they pronounce the job done. Twice Dawn's bags are zipped shut. Twice some new article is found.

Finito watches the performance with half an eye. He has seen it all before, the fumbling inadequate *La Puerca*. He thinks that if she'd only paid him off a month earlier, when he first told her about his *Tía* Suzanna's operation, he'd be long gone. But generosity was obviously beyond her, even though the money was chump change, even though, at the time, she swore she was in love with him.

What bullshit. *La Puerca* was never in love with her little Georgie. No, no. It was all about greed, about dragging his pretty face to restaurants and movies and plays, showing him off like he was some kind of trophy. Look at me, everyone, I got the man I could never get. The man I dreamed about in high school when I had to settle for pimple-assed faggots who only asked me out because they couldn't do any better.

The sex was the worst of it. *Georgie, Georgie, I didn't know it could be like this.* What'd she think, that he was turned on by her fat ass?

One look in the mirror and *La Puerca* had to know it was about the money. But she was too greedy to pay her debts, clinging to her pennies the way she clung to his ass when she pulled him on top of her. Like she owned it.

Well, they'll just have to settle up. Once the kid is gone, when they are safely returned, when they are all alone and the door is locked behind them. Then they will have a final reckoning.

But it's not to be. At five-fifteen, as Abby picks up the phone to confirm her reservation at the car rental agency, the *mondo* cop and his *negrita* partner turn onto the block. They are with a shorter, older man, a bum, who points directly at Finito's apartment house before walking away. The two cops hesitate long enough to exchange a few words, then cross the street.

A moment later, Finito yanks the receiver from Abby's hand. When she protests, he pulls the gun and places it against her forehead. Though the weapon is small, a .22 automatic, Abby freezes in place and tears start from her eyes. A few feet away, Dawn makes a low keening sound in which Finito can detect shock, confusion and fear.

So far, so good.

THIRTY

PUDGE INSISTED ON making the call. It was his turn, he explained. Belinda had taken enough heat for one day. Plus, he wanted to stake out the ground he would eventually have to defend, to put his story on the record.

As he made these points, Pudge removed his coat, laid it on a shelf beneath the mailboxes, then unbuttoned his suit jacket. The fingers of his right hand slid to his hip, briefly touching the butt of his weapon, a 9-millimeter Sig-Sauer. A few feet away, his partner took her own weapon, a Glock, and stowed it in her shoulder bag. Then she crimped the bag's flap so it rested against her hip, leaving the bag open. Finally, she retrieved her cell phone and passed it over.

"Be my guest."

Pedersson's eyes darted from the elevator to a door that lead to the building's only stairwell, then to the phone's keypad as he dialed a familiar number. Fearing his partner's caustic tongue, he maintained a studiously neutral expression. As if he hadn't been waiting for this moment all his life, as if he didn't fully intend to enjoy it, as if Belinda didn't know him better than he knew himself.

When Moira O'Neill came on the line, Pudge said, "Lieutenant, we got Rakowski," even though he knew this was, at best, an exaggeration.

"You have him under arrest?"

"No, but we know where he lives."

"Didn't you just say you *had* Rakowski? Did I mishear?" O'Neill gave it couple of beats, then said, "I want you to be precise, Detective. If you need a few moments to collect your thoughts . . ."

But Pudge was undaunted. Despite every roadblock thrown up by the bosses, he and Belinda had won. Quite deliberately, he allowed his tone to convey that triumph as he described his activities over the past thirty minutes, laying special emphasis on three points as he proceeded. First, Jimmy Smith did not know the physical address of the building in which Rakowski lived; he could only take them to Bethune Street and point. Second, to accomplish part one, for Smith to raise that finger, they'd been forced to expose themselves to the view of anybody watching from the windows. Third, Smith was an old man, his eyesight poor, and he'd been drinking. Of necessity, they'd sought out the building's porter, Mathias Calaveris, who lived in the basement and confirmed Smith's story.

"It was a good thing we did," Pudge concluded. "According to Calaveris, Rakowski's living with a woman named Abigail Stoph. There's a kid there, too, a weekend guest."

O'Neill asked only a single question: "But you don't know if he's inside the apartment right now?" When Pudge admitted that he did not, she ordered him to wait, then dropped the receiver onto something hard.

"What's up?" Belinda asked without looking at her partner.

"They put me on hold."

Like her partner's, Belinda's eyes jumped back and forth, from the stairwell door to the elevator. At that moment, she expected O'Neill to order them to remain where they were until the cavalry showed up. In fact, this was her most fervent wish; hero was her partner's game. Belinda slid her fingers beneath her blouse and ran them over the light body armor she wore against her skin. An assault team, she noted, would be draped in body armor thick enough to stop a bazooka.

O'Neill was back on the phone within a minute, demanding that Pudge again describe the building's exits.

"There's three ways out besides the windows," Pudge explained for the second time. "One through the lobby and two through the basement. You can reach them by the stairs or the elevator." After a moment, he added, "There's no fire escape."

"And where are you now?"

"In the lobby."

"Which leaves the basement uncovered."

"You want us to split up?"

"No, I want you to secure the fifth-floor hallway until the professionals arrive, which should take no more than ten minutes. Do you think you can handle the assignment without starting a war?"

"Roger that."

Pudge hung up, stuck the phone in his pocket and turned to Belinda. "We gotta go upstairs," he explained. "Keep an eye on things until our backup arrives."

Belinda sighed. Containing Rakowski made good sense. If he was at home, you'd naturally want to limit the damage he could do. Abagail Stoph might not agree with that, but the greatest good for the greatest number was an idea that never did hold much appeal for the minority whose interests were being sacrificed. According to Calaveris, Abagail Stoph, a longtime resident, was a good woman who'd fallen for a bad man.

"How do you wanna handle this?" she asked.

"Let's take the elevator up to the fourth floor, use the stairs for the final flight. What I'm thinking, if we can see the door to 5B from the stairwell, we won't have to show ourselves. One thing we don't wanna do here is spook a guy who's already breaking down."

A good idea, both agreed, but the stairwell door on the fifth-floor landing had only a tiny window which looked out on the opposite wall. Though Belinda craned her head in both directions, neither the elevator, nor the entrance to 5B at the end of the hall came into view. They would have to physically occupy the corridor, to expose themselves to the peepholes cut into every door, including 5B's.

Resigned to her fate, Belinda reached into her bag, settling her fingers around the butt of her weapon. "You ready?" she asked.

"After you."

As her feet settled into the tightly woven carpet and her eyes adjusted to the softer light from a set of tulip-shaped sconces mounted high on the wall, Belinda told herself that Rakowski had used a gun to control his victims and to murder Leonard Ying. She told herself to be on full alert, that Rakowski's behavior could not be predicted and that there were other families on the fifth floor who might get in the path of a stray bullet. She told herself that everybody's welfare, not least her own, depended on maintaining control of the situation.

Nevertheless, when the door to apartment 5B flew open a few seconds later and a bearded Finito Rakowski materialized in the doorway, when he fired the weapon in his right hand three times, then slammed the door closed, when the wail of a terrified child ripped through the corridor, Belinda did nothing at all. For several long seconds she did not move, did not breathe, did not blink. Then her legs gave out and she dropped to her knees. A few feet away, her partner was bringing his Sig-Sauer to bear on the door of 5B.

"Don't," Belinda said. "Don't shoot."

Pudge looked at her, his small eyes as wide and round as the eyes of a terminally stoned crackhead. "What?"

"There's a child in there. Don't shoot. Are you alright?"

Pudge looked down at his torso as if considering the question for the first time. "Yeah, and you?"

"I'm okay. What just happened?"

"A miracle," Pudge said, "a miracle that we didn't get hit."

Belinda gathered herself as the cries of the child inside 5B gradually subsided. Then she shook her head. Pudge was wrong. You didn't need a miracle to explain their survival. In 1999, four cops assigned to the Street Crimes Unit had pegged forty-one rounds at an African immigrant named Amadou Diallo, missing their target from a distance of less than five feet more than half the time. Rakowski's inaccuracy came as no surprise, not when he'd yanked the door open, then fired wildly from a distance of twenty feet. The real question was if Rakowski had intended to kill, or if that was just his way of opening negotiations. One thing certain, though: Rakowski had been waiting for them to enter the hallway. More than likely, he'd spotted them earlier in the day or been warned.

"Rakowski knew we were coming," Belinda said. "He's had time to plan and he thinks he's in control."

"You're saying he's not?"

"I'm saying there's only two ways out of that apartment for old Finito, in cuffs or in a body bag. That pistol? I make it for a .22. It won't penetrate the door. That's why he had to open it, to expose himself. If we'd been a little more together, he'd be dead."

Pudge swiped at the beads of sweat on his forehead. "The barrel looked as big as a cannon," he admitted.

"Funny what adrenaline does to your judgment."

Behind them, a door opened, then slammed shut when Pudge shouted, "Police, get back inside." Belinda took the opportunity to regain her feet. "You need to go into the stairwell and call this in, Pudge. Tell the bosses we got a hostage situation here."

"Why me?"

"Because you have the phone."

Belinda waited until the door closed behind her partner, then dropped her weapon to her side and took a step forward. "Yo, Finito," she called, "you in there?"

"*La Negrita*, wha's up whi' chu?"

Belinda ignored the slur. "Ya know somethin', Finito," she said, "I was about to ask you that very same question."

• • •

Belinda's initial terror slowly gave way to an insistent and ulti-mately foolish confidence. She told herself that her one and only task at that moment was to keep Rakowski talking until the Hostage-Rescue Team arrived, that Rakowski could no more come out of that apartment than she could enter it. They were, the both of them, prisoners of the status quo.

"*Mira, La Negrita*, wha' happen? Did your *gordo* partner *caca* his panties?"

"Uh-uh, Finito. He went downstairs to hold off the Swat Team. The way it was supposed to work, they were gonna take the door off the hinges if a shot was fired, then kill you. They're just lookin' for an excuse anyway."

The ensuing silence came as no surprise to Belinda. Finito was thinking it over, perhaps reassessing whatever tactics he'd settled on. The bet here, Belinda's bet, was that the profiler was right. Unlike spree killers who wipe out whole families, then turn their weapons on themselves, sexually motivated killers want to live.

"You try to come in here, *chingada*," Finito said matter-of-factly, "I kill the *niña* first. I don't care how many cops you got."

At that, the child inside the apartment resumed her wailing, inspiring Finito to display his anger for the first time. "*Cono*, you don't shut up, I'll cut your fuckin' ears off your head and make you eat 'em."

Belinda's instinct was to calm Finito down, tell him that nobody was gonna come through the door, that as long as he didn't do anything stupid, a hostage negotiator would be calling him on the phone any minute. Instead, for reasons she would never understand, she stared directly into the peephole fifteen feet away and said, "Why don't you let the kid go? She's not doin' you any good."

Another silence, this one much longer, which Finito finally broke with a laugh. "I tell you what, *La Negrita*, I make you a deal, pronto, before your partner comes back. I make you a deal for the little bitch."

"And what do you want in return?"

"You, *La Negrita*. You for her. A little white bitch for a big black one."

When she heard the locks sliding back, Belinda raised her weapon and sighted down the barrel of her Glock. She wasn't surprised when a child's form appeared in the opening door, or by Finito Rakowski squatting behind the girl, or by the small automatic he held to her head. Rakowski's dark eyes were speckled by pinpoints of light, the left side of his mouth twisted to one side in a caricature of a smile. The girl was crying silently, an almost solid line of tears that ran down both sides of her nose, and she was quivering with fear.

"You put down the gun, come to me," Finito said, "I let the *niña* go home to her mommy."

"Finito, you hurt that child, I'll kill you myself."

"*Por favor, La Negrita*, I don' wanna hurt the kid. Whatta you think, I'm some kinda short-eyes freak? Jus' put down the gun, I let the *niña* go." Rakowski hesitated for a moment, his smile so unyielding that the corners of his lips might have been stapled to his cheek. "You don' wanna do the deal, I'll take the bitch and *vamanos* back inside, see what happens later."

Belinda kept her weapon right where it was, sighting on a narrow slice of Rakowski's head to the left of the child's. As she tried to frame a response, she became aware of an anomaly. Rakowski's heavily accented speech was a long way from that of the polished hustler who conned Maureen Owens in the Oriole Bar. He'd reverted now, to the feral mutt revealed by his rap sheet, and that meant he was a lot closer to breaking down than she'd thought. It also meant that she could not allow Rakowski to carry the child back into the apartment. Not anymore.

Belinda thought of her husband at that moment, how Ralph's

mustache curled around his lips when he frowned. She thought about never seeing him again, of never seeing her children again. She wanted to say something to them, take a time-out, make a phone call. Instead, she addressed Finito Rakowski, pleased to note that her voice was rock steady.

"Tell ya what I'll do, Finito. I'll just hold my weapon down like this." She let her hand fall to her side. The barrel of her Glock now pointed at the floor. "You let the kid go. When she gets halfway to me, I drop my gun and come to you. That's my best offer."

When the stairwell door pivoted on hinges badly in need of lubrication and Pudge Pedersson made an appearance, Finito's smile advanced a quarter of an inch as his eyes darted from Belinda to Pudge and back again. Belinda noted Finito's expression carefully and decided that some part of the man was still in control, still taking risks, still powerful. She would have to appeal to that man exclusively, ignoring the terrified and desperate child cowering just below the surface.

"Anybody wanna tell me what's goin' on here?" Pudge's voice was tight, as if he were trying to speak and hold his breath at the same time.

"We're makin' a deal," Belinda responded. "Me for her."

"Bull-*fucking*-shit."

The uncharacteristic profanity inspired a faint smile as Belinda dropped her Glock to the carpet and started forward, advancing to within a few feet of the child before she stopped. She was now in Pudge's line of fire, a shield, and she gave Rakowski several seconds to recognize the fact before she addressed his hostage.

"You run to that policeman back there," she said. "He'll take care of you." She placed her hand on the girl's shoulder and gave a little tug, setting her in motion. Then she watched the barrel of Finito's gun swing up until it found a mark in the center of her forehead.

"*Bueno*, he said as he scuttled backward into the apartment, as Belinda followed. Then he repeated the word several times: "*bueno, bueno, bueno.*"

Belinda closed the door without being asked, and without turning her back on Rakowski. As she assessed the apartment, fumbling with a pair of locks until the deadbolts snapped home, her eyes settled on a woman—Abigail Stoph, she assumed— seated on a couch in the living room. Stoph's mouth was gagged with duct tape and her hands, obviously bound, were hidden behind her back. Though the woman appeared to be unhurt, Belinda was thrown by the duct tape, remembering how many times Finito had used it to bind his victims. Binding them was the step he took after he used the gun to bring them under control.

Quickly, as Rakowski gained his feet, Belinda glanced around the apartment in search of a weapon she might use in a worst- case scenario. She was standing near a dining room table cov- ered by a brown tablecloth embroidered with leaves of red, gold and flaming orange. A cut-glass vase filled with dried flowers rested in the middle of the table. In her judgment, the vase was heavy enough to do significant damage should it come into con- tact with human flesh.

Getting to the vase was going to be a problem, though. Belinda was wearing a Grade I Kevlar vest, strong enough to stop a bullet from the small-caliber automatic in Rakowski's right hand. Unfortunately, at that moment, the small-caliber auto- matic was still pointed at her head.

"*La Negrita*," Finito said, sweeping his left hand from Belinda to Abigail, "meet *La Puerca.*"

Belinda nodded to the woman, hoping to reassure her, then stepped to the left, placing Rakowski directly between herself and Abby. Now he could not observe both of them at the same time.

"Why don't you let her go?" Belinda asked. "Then it'd just be the two of us."

"*¿La Puerca?*" Rakowski laughed. "Don' worry about *La Puerca*. She is *una mamao*. She don' even exist. She's like, you know, some kinda stuffed animal, a talkin' doll. But you, *La Negrita*, mos' definitely exist. I'm looking at you and I'm thinkin', If *La Negrita* gets a chance, she's gonna take me out. Poof, no more Finito."

"I'm here to help you," Belinda said, "not hurt you."

"Okay, tha's good. And I'm gonna believe you, too, right after I see you ain' carryin' no backup piece stuck in your fuckin' pussy. So why don' you jus' show me? Show me you don' have some little *pistola* pushed up your *chocha*."

Belinda dismissed the request with a wave of her hand. Step one, she knew, would lead inevitably to step two, the taping of her mouth and wrists. "As I already explained, Finito, I'm here to help. There's no sense in you gettin' all crazy. That's not gonna do you one bit of good."

Apparently so locked into his fantasy that he'd never anticipated any resistance, Finito's eyes widened in surprise. "*Tienes cojones,*" he finally admitted, "but you don' strip down, I'm gonna shoot you right in your face."

Again, Belinda simply shook her head. "Nobody kills a cop and lives to brag about it."

"Wha' chu think, *La Negrita*, I'm scared of dyin'?"

"Negative, Finito, I don't think you're scared. I really don't. But what's the point of dying *now*? See what I mean?"

"It don' matter. When your time comes, it—"

"Spare me the bullshit."

"You wanna call my bluff, *La Negrita?* That wha' chu wanna do?"

Behind Rakowski, Belinda saw Abigail Stoph lift her legs and begin to ease her hands down over her buttocks. It was a classic escape move for handcuffed prisoners and Belinda figured the woman had seen it on television. The idea was to work your wrists over the backs of your legs and the heels of your feet, to finish with your hands in front of you. Stoph's problem was that she was carrying an extra thirty pounds and her arms refused to pass over her hips.

Belinda wanted to tell Stoph there was a definite downside to inciting a sadistic rape-murderer. Instead, she calculated the distance between herself and Rakowski and the glass vase on the table, rehearsing the series of moves she would make: one step to the left, grab the vase, bring it back and up, step forward, drive the vase into Rakowski's head. Do not hesitate. Do not hold back.

"Finito, you're lookin' at this all wrong. You ever hear of a guy named Richard Ramirez? They called him the Night Stalker? This dude, Finito, he was sentenced to death in 1985 and they haven't iced him yet. That's eighteen years." Belinda intended to pursue a theme here, The Benefits of Surrender, and she would neither vary from it, nor allow her subject to change the topic. Call it Interrogation 101.

Out of the corner of one eye, Belinda saw Abigail finally yank her hands down over her butt. Now all she had to do was pull her wrists over her legs and . . . and exactly what? Did Stoph have a plan? Was she acting on instinct? There was no way for Belinda to know. Meanwhile, the woman had to be protected.

"*Pero,*" Finito countered, "eighteen years in a fuckin' cell. I'd rather be dead."

"See, there you go again with the negativity. The truth is, the Night Stalker lives large." She ticked the examples off on her fingers, vaguely recalling a documentary she'd watched on *Court TV.* "He has a fan club and he gets so many letters he can't answer them. Every other week some doctor or writer comes to interview him for a book. He even got married and he now has overnight conjugal visits with his beloved bride." Belinda leaned slightly forward on her toes in an effort to capture Rakowski's full attention. "Also, you might wanna remember that nobody's been executed in New York since 1963, and the way it's goin' in the courts, nobody's ever gonna be. Hell, you might be lookin' at another fifty years of life. You wanna throw that away?"

Belinda lapsed into silence, her best argument made. By this time, Rakowski had to know the gun threat wasn't going to work. He could retaliate by shooting her, of course, but that would hardly satisfy his sadistic inner child. Or he could attack her, maybe hit her with the gun, try to knock her out long enough to gag and bind her. Or he could nibble at the bait.

"How I know you ain't gonna kill me?"

"We could get a lawyer up here, if that'll make you feel safer." Belinda braced herself. Stoph had somehow hooked the heel of one shoe over the tape between her wrists but could not get any farther. Her face was red with the effort and she was sweating. "Hell, we'll get you Johnny Cochrane if that's what it takes. Believe me when I tell you this, Finito, because I'm talkin' to you from the bottom of my heart, the New York Police Department doesn't want anybody else to get hurt."

"*La Negrita*, you are some kinda woman. Rosaria was like you, not scared of nothin'. But it didn't help her none."

"That's because she was stoned out of her mind and you caught her by surprise."

"*¿Qué?*"

"I was there, Finito, at the scene. I know what you did and how you did it. I know that you hung around, took a shower, rolled her onto her face before you left. You were good, man, good enough to stay ahead of forty thousand New York City cops for months. But it's all over now. Now you gotta learn to live on your glory."

Finito's eyes closed briefly at that point, proof positive, as Belinda saw it, that he'd finally gotten the message. Both his anger and his fear were fading, replaced by a growing acceptance of the facts. This was the way successful interrogations commonly progressed. Given time, Rakowski would hand over the gun and surrender. Given time he wasn't about to get.

Abigail Stoph finally achieved her primary objective when she gave a last kick and her still-taped hands jerked over the sole of her shoe. The bad news was that in so doing she slid off the couch to land on the floor with a thud that could be felt as well as heard. Rakowski blinked twice, as if trying to shift course in the middle of a dream, then spun on his heel.

With no other viable option, Belinda took a step to her left, snatched the vase off the table and swung it in a great arc. Her eye was steady, her attention so narrowly focused she was unaware of the dried and dusty hydrangeas that cascaded onto her hair and shoulders. Nevertheless, she missed Rakowski's head by a fraction of an inch when he jerked away at the last second, the vase crashing into his right shoulder instead, a lucky shot that sent the .22 spinning across the wood floor.

The first lesson of the streets, learned by every rookie cop, is that when all the words have been spoken, when cop fighters choose to go the hard way, you must commit to winning. This was especially true for women. Your opponents almost always had a size and strength advantage, which you could only hope to overcome with speed and ferocity. A silent prayer didn't hurt, either.

This lesson was uppermost in Belinda's mind as she attacked Finito Rakowski. His right arm was dangling, and she took advantage, throwing a flurry of punches that drove him backward, away from the gun. When he finally managed to grab her with his left hand, she stepped forward, into his body, then jerked her head upward, slamming the top of her skull into his mouth.

As they grappled, a voice rang out from the corridor. It was Pudge Pedersson, demanding to know what was going on. Belinda responded immediately.

"Give it up, Finito," she shouted, "you've been disarmed."

Belinda's message was intended not only for Pudge, but for Abigail Stoph as well. The little .22 was lying out in the open. If Abigail were to pick it up while Belinda held Finito off, the good guys would have a clear advantage. But Abigail had other ideas. Leaving Belinda to fend for herself, she ripped the duct tape from her mouth, then turned her back and took what appeared to be a slender stick, maybe three feet long, off the wall.

Silently, Belinda cursed the woman. Finito's right arm had recovered sufficiently to grasp the lapel of her blazer, leaving her unable to duck the left he threw at her head. She staggered backward but did not let go, not until a second punch sent her reeling toward the door. For a long moment, her head spun in circles and she remained on her feet only through the force of her will, a small victory that had no effect on the outcome.

Finito had recovered the .22 and was turning to face her by the time Belinda shook off the cobwebs. Blood streamed from his lips and mouth, spilling over his chin, and he leaned to the right, favoring his injured arm.

"Slow it down, Finito." Belinda held her hands in front of her as she backed toward the door. "Detective Pedersson," she called over her shoulder, "take it easy out there. We're doin' fine. Everything's under control."

"You're bold, *La Negrita,* he said, "*el echao pa'lante,* like a man. But now the bullshit is over. I'm gonna cut your black ass into little pieces and—"

"Hey, don't be talkin' like that. You still have all the same choices to make. Nothing's changed."

But everything had changed, including the status of Abigail Stoph who was steadily advancing on Finito Rakowski. Belinda could now make out the object Stoph clutched in both hands. It was a pipe, an Indian peace pipe, with several white feathers attached to the stem just behind the bowl. What Stoph intended to do with the pipe Belinda couldn't imagine. Not until Stoph raised the pipe and the feathers swung away to reveal the head of a small stone hatchet.

As Abigail's arm started forward, the weight of the stone dragged the pipe stem backward until the hatchet dropped out of sight behind Stoph's back. Belinda was certain the stem would break, had no doubt whatever, was already planning what she'd do when it finally snapped. But the stem did not break. Instead, the hatchet rose from the small of Abigail's back, accelerated as it passed over her head, finally became no more than a gray blur as it crashed into the top of Finito Rakowski's skull.

With just an instant to think, Belinda made the right choice, leaping aside as Finito's body jerked in a final spasm and the little .22 went off. The bullet drove down into the floor within a foot of Belinda's toes, with Rakowski's inert body, the hatchet still buried in his head, following closely behind. That Rakowski would never get up was obvious at a glance. The man was as dead as it was possible to be. Nevertheless, Belinda pressed herself against the wall, knowing that if Pudge did something stupid, like empty his Sig-Sauer, the 9-millimeter rounds would punch through the door as if it were made of plastic wrap. Friendly fire is what they'd tell the media when they lowered her coffin. An unavoidable accident, so sorry.

"Pudge," she shouted, "don't shoot, for Christ's sake. Rakowski's down. I'm unlocking the door."

But it was already too late. Pudge Pedersson was in a place beyond hearing. Head lowered, shoulders hunched, he was charging down the corridor, a maddened bull heedless of any consequence. He never heard his partner call out, or the clack-clack of the deadbolts sliding into their housings, or the little squeak of the turning doorknob. No, Pudge hit the door expecting to take it off its hinges. When it flew open, he crossed the room in a series of mincing steps while his legs made a desperate attempt to catch up with his torso. He might have succeeded, too, even in clearing Rakowski's inconvenient body, if he hadn't caught the toe of a wing tip on the pipe stem protruding from Rakowski's skull. After that, Pudge was helpless, an unguided missile skidding across the wood floor, scattering a table and a lamp, until he finally met an immovable object, the cast-iron radiator beneath the window. Though it barely quivered, the radiator emitted a single reverberating bong just as an army of SWAT Team cops charged through the door.

THIRTY-ONE

"IT'S NOT FAIR that the entire world knows except for me," Pudge informed his partner after they ordered their dinners. "The whole business is driving me crazy."

"And what fool told you life was supposed to be fair? Sometimes you got no choice but to roll with the punches."

"That's easy for you to say. You're the hero. I'm the jerk."

Belinda waved the remark away. "That's too negative, Pudge, that's off the charts. If you recall, we're being decorated tomorrow morning. By the first deputy commissioner."

The conversation stopped momentarily as Ahmed Brown personally served their appetizers, gratin of tagliolini with shrimp. Ordinarily, the dish went for thirteen dollars, but Pudge and Belinda were eating on the cuff. They were Ahmed's guests, made especially welcome by the fact that Belinda was now a New York celebrity.

Recognized the minute she walked through the door, Belinda had first endured a sudden rise in the buzz of conversation, then the scrutiny of the many waiting patrons when she was led to the only empty table in the restaurant. Far from thrilled with her fame, Belinda yearned for anonymity. Her greatest regret was that she'd been unable to resist the job's relentless pressure and agreed to a series of television interviews.

Patient as ever, Pudge waited until Brown withdrew before responding to his partner's suggestion. "We might be gettin' decorated," he pointed out, "but we're not gettin' the same decoration."

"That's one of things I meant by unfair."

On the following morning, with Belinda's family and Annie MacDougald in attendance, Detective Frederick Pedersson would be awarded a Purple Shield, the job's equivalent of the Purple Heart, while Detective Belinda Moore would be handed a Medal of Valor, the job's equivalent of the Silver Star.

Unfortunately, Pudge's medal was richly deserved, at least in Belinda's opinion. Now that the bandages were off, the dent in his forehead (where a square inch of bone had been removed) was deep enough to be a third eye.

Belinda sipped at her wine, then said, "Why don't you look at the bright side? You're getting a medal instead of a disciplinary hearing. Plus you reclaimed the heart of the widow Mac-Dougald."

"I understand all that, but it's driving me crazy that I can't remember what happened." Pudge spun his fork through his tagliolini in a vain attempt to find the shrimp. "See, I recall taking the elevator to the fourth floor and walking to the fifth, but from there on it's a blank. When I try to think back, it's like I'm in a cave. I know something's there, but I can't find it in the dark." He tapped the edge of the table in frustration. "This is the kind of story that follows you forever. It follows you through your career, your retirement, and into the next world. I mean, when I knock on the Pearly Gates, the angels are gonna snicker."

"Pudge, if it was my decision to make, I would've covered your butt, only . . ."

Only there'd been a witness, Abigail Stoph, who'd told and retold her story to any media outlet willing to listen. She'd been

interviewed by magazine, newspaper, radio and television jour-
nalists, and she'd made the rounds of the talk shows, beginning
with a ten-minute appearance on *Oprah*. Redemption was a constant theme running through these interviews, a theme pursued
by Abby on the Web site trumpeting her forthcoming
memoir/self-help book.

"How about this," Belinda said after a moment. "Lieutenant
Jerry Malden's not gonna be at the two-five when we go back in
ten days. Don't tell me that doesn't cheer you up."

"C'mon, Belinda, we've been written off as untrustworthy, as
boss-haters. We'll be precinct detectives until we retire." Pudge
finished his appetizer, then put down his fork before changing
the subject. "You and Ralph making nice these days?" he asked.

"We're not fighting, but I think it'd be better if we were."
Belinda patted her mouth with a salmon-red napkin soft enough
to be lingerie. Something had changed in her marriage, a slip-
ping away too subtle to confront directly. Ralph didn't want her
to apologize, which she'd already done. He wanted her to say
she wouldn't reoffend, wouldn't go off half-cocked, wouldn't
put her life in danger. Thus far, she hadn't.

Belinda filled Pudge's wineglass before topping out her own.
They were drinking a white burgundy selected by the sommelier.
As she put the bottle down, Belinda's eyes trailed across the
room. Like most Greenwich Village restaurants, Orly's decor was
downscale. Pale orange paint hastily brushed across plaster
walls, red tile floors, a battered bar recovered from a tavern fire
in Provence. The look was bistro, not grand salon; the West Village, not the Upper East Side.

Meanwhile, dining at Orly's was an eighty-dollar culinary
experience, even if you begged off the dessert and the brandy.

Pudge and Belinda hadn't come to Orly's for the cuisine.
Reviewed favorably by the *New York Times* on its opening day, the
restaurant was currently booking reservations two weeks in

advance. Thus Ahmed Brown now had access to commercial financing and was paying off the loans taken from his family. Tonight it was the Ralph and Belinda Moore's turn to accept dinner and a check.

Unfortunately, Ralph had been victimized by a hiring freeze at the airline where he worked. What with the smaller workforce, the only way to get the job done was through mandatory overtime and his number had come up, no excuses accepted. Pudge was Ralph's last-second replacement.

The big moment came as Pudge and Belinda were working their way through slices of chocolate cake with burned almond crust in raspberry sauce, and snifters of aged cognac. Ahmed crossed the room and took a chair before presenting Belinda with an envelope bearing the restaurant's name and address.

"I'm so grateful to you and Uncle Ralph for having faith in me that I really don't know how to express it," he said.

"That's what families are all about, Ahmed," Belinda replied. "That's what families do. Me and Ralph, we always felt you had the talent to succeed."

Pudge covered the smile that jumped to his lips by shoveling a forkful of cake into his mouth. Though definitely amused, he wasn't inclined to judge his partner harshly. What others might condemn as hypocrisy, he understood as a healing ritual. Maybe his partner thought of her family as some sort of indivisible entity, but from where Pudge Pedersson sat, the Moore clan was mostly about shifting factions that fought for dominance with the tenacity of warlords.

"There's something I've been wanting to tell you," Pudge announced when Ahmed left to greet a pair of television actors. After several glasses of wine, the fumes from the cognac, when he raised his glass, were enough to make him reckless. "You were right, Belinda, and I was wrong. I'm talkin' about the case."

"C'mon, Pudge, gimme a—"

"No, I said the perp made mistakes in the past, fatal mistakes, but that isn't how it turned out. In fact, if you hadn't come up with the Rikers Island connection, good old Finito, he'd still be gettin' his rocks off by killin' women." Pudge extended his glass, then waited patiently until his partner accepted the toast. "Here's to detectives who detect. Here's to Belinda Moore, the best of the best."

For once unable to maintain her composure, Belinda's mouth opened into a smile that revealed teeth, gums and tongue. Being right didn't mean to her what it did to Pudge Pedersson. But it was definitely better than being wrong.

"Any more compliments?" she asked.

"Nope, and I intend to deny this conversation ever happened should you bring it up in the future." Pudge sipped at his brandy. "Anyway, I got news of my own. Good news and bad news."

"What's the good news?"

"Me and Annie, we're engaged."

"That means John Taggert is out of the picture for good."

"Annie thinks my injury makes me a hero."

"Uh-huh. So what's the bad news?"

Though he'd meant to deliver the punch line deadpan, Pudge couldn't repress a narrow grin. "The bad news is that now that we're gonna cohabit, Annie wants me to stop smoking. Next week I got appointments with her herbalist, her chiropractor, and a faith healer named Lefty."